The Ghosts
in the
Garden of Peace

The Purgatory of
John P. Sample

by

S. E. Stanley

Apogee Press LLC

Butler, PA

D1414125

S. E. Stanley/Apogee Press LLC
108A Charles Drive
Butler, PA 16001

Publisher's Note: This is a work of fiction. Names, characters, places, and incidents are a product of the author's imagination. Locales and public names are sometimes used for atmospheric purposes. Any resemblance to actual people, living or dead, or to businesses, companies, events, institutions, or locales is completely coincidental.

Book Layout © 2017 BookDesignTemplates.com

The Ghosts in the Garden of Peace/ S. E. Stanley. -- 1st ed.
ISBN: 978-1-7330428-0-2

For
Linda

John Sample didn't expect to die that day. True, at 5'11" and 224 lbs., he was overweight and almost never got any exercise. However, he felt good for a man of 69. Growing up, John had had big ideas and plans, though he rarely followed up on any of them. The effect of this was that John bounced from job-to-job and from place-to-place most of his life. Now, he lived in Monroeville, Pennsylvania, as he had for 27 years, and had recently retired from the Veterans Health Administration after working there for over 10 years.

John woke up at 5:30 a.m. without an alarm on that May morning just as he did every morning. He had fallen asleep at 11:30 p.m. the previous night, as he had every night while watching the local news before waking up and going to bed.

It was Sunday morning. He drank his coffee and ate his usual breakfast of Honey Bunches of Oats cereal. After watching his preferred news programs, he changed out of his pajamas and put on the pants and shirt he'd worn since the Sunday before. He went to the bathroom, shaved, brushed his teeth, and combed his thinning gray hair before going down to the garage and getting into his two-year-old Toyota Corolla. The car was like new since it was always garaged and only had 7,352 miles on the odometer. John's only travel since retirement was his weekly trip to the local grocery store and every three months to the psychiatrist's office where he received his standard checkup for bipolar disorder at the Veterans Administration in Pittsburgh. In addition, he saw his regular primary care physician at the VA every six months. She always chided him about his weight and lack of exercise. John's response to placate his doctor always was, "I'll try to do better."

Today, he was going to the grocery store. When he arrived, he picked out a buggy and started his routine. The store wasn't busy this morning. John put his usual items in the buggy; a box of cereal, a bag of pretzels, a bag of rippled potato chips, a frozen pizza, a half-gallon of 1% milk, and a dozen assorted frozen TV dinners. That was it. Next, it was off to the checkout. But just before he could get to the only cashier open, two very large women came out of nowhere and got in front of him with their two brimming buggies of food. John got in behind them and waited impatiently. They were taking their time putting their items onto the conveyor belt, and John could feel his blood pressure beginning to rise. Their choice of food seemed to be mostly junk. *No wonder they were fat,* he thought. Then he realized his own purchases weren't exactly haute cuisine either.

When the women finally emptied their buggies, the cashier began to bag the groceries. She was an elderly woman who seemed to be tired of doing her job, and the two women weren't trying to be of any help. Just when John thought the ordeal was over, one of the women pulled out a fistful of coupons and handed them over to the cashier. John could feel his face becoming flushed, and he was starting to sweat.

The cashier scanned the coupons, and it seemed as though every other one was rejected. Sometimes, the women argued over the legitimacy of a coupon, and the process seemed to take forever. Then the manager was called over to deal with the coupons.

John noticed a tingling in his left arm just before he felt the crushing pain in his chest. He slumped to the floor behind his buggy and was dead within seconds.

So, now John Sample was dead. He expected death to be a peaceful non-existence; however, he experienced instead something that was neither peaceful nor non-existent. John's spirit floated and watched the frantic scene from above as the cashier called 9-1-1 and the bag boy clumsily attempted CPR with chest compressions John never felt. It had been a painful but quick death. The EMTs arrived a few minutes later, and John watched while they strapped him down on the cart and loaded him into the back of the ambulance. He accompanied his body inside the vehicle while one of the EMTs worked on him.

When they got to the hospital, he was pronounced 'dead on arrival' in the ER.

"Time of death, 11:43 a.m.," he heard the doctor say. John tried to communicate with the people around him, but everyone ignored him. One of the nurses pulled John's wallet from his pants pocket and announced, "John P. Sample is the name on his driver's license. It looks like he's from Monroeville and not a donor." The nurse wrote his name on a tag and placed it on his big toe.

Two male nurse's aides arrived and transferred John's covered body onto a special cart that cranked his body down and hid his corpse from public view. One of the aides nonchalantly guided the cart through the hallways and down the elevator to the morgue as John floated alongside his body. When they arrived inside the morgue, the aide parked the gurney beside two other similar carts. After turning off the light, the aide left the room.

A man's voice spoke to him from beside another gurney.

"Where did you come from?" the odd voice asked.

"I came from the emergency room," John said. His own voice sounded odd as well.

"No, I mean where were you when you died?"

"I think I had a heart attack at the grocery store in the check-out lane."

The voice laughed. "So, you checked out in the check-out lane? That's priceless!"

John began to see where the voice was coming from as he gradually adjusted to his situation. A heavy-set, middle-aged balding man was hovering over another covered body just a few feet away, and there was a woman floating beside him. Both were casually dressed, and they had a shimmering glow about them. More than seeing them, John could now sense them in great detail.

"It may be ironic, Joe, but I don't see any humor in it," she scolded. She looked at John and said, "Our car was hit by a truck on Route 30 near Forest Hills late last night. We've been down here for a while now. Our daughter finally got here to identify us, so we should be going soon." The woman's mouth was smiling but her lips were not moving as she spoke.

"You don't look like you were in an accident," John said.

"Thank God," said the man. "I'd hate to be a bloody, mangled mess for the rest of eternity."

Just then, two men in suits entered the morgue. One had a cell phone with him and said, "Okay, Bill, we're looking for Joseph and Molly Russel." They lifted up the top of John's gurney and looked at the tag on his toe.

"This one says 'John P. Sample.' Must be the other two," the other said.

They lifted the tops from the other gurneys and identified the bodies. The two men replaced the tops and started to wheel them out of the room.

"I guess this is our ride, honey," said Joe. "Good luck to you, John."

"Thanks. You, too."

The Russel's floated alongside their bodies as the men pushed the gurneys outside the morgue, turned off the light, and closed the door. John had been a loner for a long time, but now he had a sense of loneliness he'd never experienced before.

It seemed like hours before someone came for John. Eventually, a gray-haired man in a black suit opened the morgue door and turned on the light. A second, younger man in a similar suit helped as they lifted the canopy off the gurney and checked his toe tag.

"John P. Sample," the gray-haired man announced.

"That's me," John said in reply.

Neither of the men reacted. They placed a sheet over his body, then replaced the cover onto the gurney and wheeled John's body outside the morgue before turning off the light and closing the door. There was no one in the hallway as they travelled the short distance to a set of doors that led to the outside rear of the hospital. There was a black Cadillac hearse waiting for them. The younger man opened the rear of the hearse before helping the gray-haired man move John's body into it. The gray-haired man took the gurney back inside the hospital, while the younger man strapped John's body down and moved it forward into the hearse.

John followed his body as the hearse made its way back to Monroeville to the Atkins Funeral Home. He'd been there before. It was where they had taken Brenda for her funeral after her massive stroke two years earlier, and the sad memories of those days came flooding back to him. John remembered sitting down with the funeral director and making all the arrangements with his daughter, Anita. There were so many questions and decisions to make, but they momentarily took his mind off his grief. He picked out her casket and made the plans for the funeral.

Before Brenda's funeral, John had had to buy a new suit because he had outgrown his old ones. Brenda had looked radiant in her casket. She wore the pale blue outfit he had bought her for one of their anniversaries. The funeral home had placed rouge on her cheeks, and she had appeared so life-like that he wanted to kiss her. But, he didn't.

There were several people who showed up for her funeral. His daughter, Anita, was there with her family and his son, John Jr., and his family. Anita had helped with the arrangements. Brenda's sister was there with one of her children, and several people from her church attended as well.

Brenda had attended the Monroeville Christian Church every Sunday without him. She had asked John to go with her on many occasions, but he'd always replied, "No thank you," to her requests. Brenda had never begged or cajoled, but he knew she was disappointed he never attended with her.

As per John's request, the service had been brief. Her minister gave the eulogy and had commented on her faith, stating he was confident she was in heaven with Jesus. John had hoped that this was true. If anyone deserved to be in heaven, Brenda did. She had been a wonderful lover in their youth and a steadfast companion until her death.

The trip to the cemetery had been difficult for John. He hadn't wanted to put her in the ground, but he knew it was something he had to do. It had been a beautiful, sunny day in May as John rode in the limo with his son and daughter and

Brenda's sister. When they arrived at the cemetery, John had forgotten how far out of town it was. The ornate iron sign above the entrance read, 'Garden of Peace'. A stately iron fence surrounded the cemetery and pink rose bushes bloomed along the fence rows. John and Brenda had purchased the plots years before, but he had hoped they wouldn't have needed them until they were both well into their 80s. It just didn't work out that way.

When the casket was set above the grave, John saw the flowers that had been placed all around. After everyone was quiet, the pastor said his final piece and added the words, "Ashes to ashes. Dust to dust," and the funeral was over. John waited near the casket and thanked the people as they left. Finally, he thanked the minister and the funeral director before turning once more to the casket, touching it, and saying his last goodbye to his wife.

Chapter 2

Now it was his turn, he thought. The Adkins funeral home was a simple, white brick, modern-looking building that appeared to have been built within the past 50 years. There was a large, drive-through carport to the side and parking in the rear. The hearse drove around and entered a garage in the back of the building. Once the garage door closed behind them, the driver and his assistant opened the back of the hearse and moved John's body onto a stainless-steel cart. From the garage, they pushed the cart into an elevator, and the gray-haired man pressed the button for the basement. When the doors opened, John could see the embalming room. Two metal tables stood in the room, and the two men moved him onto one of them.

John watched as the two men hung up their coats, put on masks, then put on aprons that covered them from their necks to their knees. They removed the sheet, and John floated above his own body for the first time since collapsing in the grocery store. He barely recognized himself. It wasn't at all like looking in a mirror; he looked heavier and certainly paler. His thinning hair was mussed, and his eyes were slightly open.

The two men removed John's clothes and placed him on a stainless-steel table, then washed and massaged his body. They kneaded his back, shoulders, arms, legs, hands and feet. The older man brought a tray over to the table and unwrapped a cloth that revealed several surgical instruments. He took the scalpel and made an incision near John's collar bone. There was little blood. John watched, engrossed in the process. There was no small-talk between the men as they connected tubes to the body, and a machine whirred quietly as it flushed the blood and replaced it with embalming fluid. The younger man closed John's eyes; he placed cups over them, then cemented the lips together. When the process was over, John watched the younger man replace the sheet over his body, remove the cups and glue his eyes shut. The older man stitched up the incisions. John was impressed with their efficient and professional manner.

They cleaned up their instruments before taking off their aprons and putting their suit coats back on. They left the body on the table, turned off the lights and left by way of the elevator.

John floated beside his body in the dark, thinking about how his wife had gone through the same process years before.

What seemed like many hours later, the lights came back on. The younger of the men came in carrying John's gray suit, white shirt, black belt and blue-and-white-striped tie, which he hung on a hook on the door, while the older man went to a cabinet and took out what turned out to be a makeup kit. He sat on a stool next to the table and began applying powders and other materials to John's face and neck, then combed and sprayed his hair. Carefully, the older man trimmed and cleaned John's fingernails. Next, the two men proceeded to dress him. The pants were too tight, so the older man turned the body on its side and used a pair of scissors to cut the back of the pants to allow them to go on easily. The shirt was also too tight at the neck so he used an extender to button the top button, then placed the tie around his neck and tied it in a half Windsor knot. It was obvious that the older man was extremely experienced in these procedures.

The younger man left, then came back with a grand-looking gray, metal casket which rode atop a rolling cart. Both of the casket lids were opened revealing an ornate, white interior. The two men transferred John's body to the casket with a body-lifting machine, and then the older man straightened the suit jacket and pants before adjusting the head on the pillow. He placed the hands one over the other, then smoothed the clothing one final time. Finally, the younger man took a yellow, sticky-note and wrote, "John P. Sample," on it and placed it on the side of the coffin before closing the lids.

The younger man pushed the casket off to the side, then went with the older man to the elevator. Then they were gone, and John was left waiting beside his coffin.

Later, the men brought down another body. This time, it was a young boy of 10 or so. His earthly body was emaciated and pale, and John felt sad for the family. The boy's spirit, on the other hand, was vibrant with brilliant blue eyes and short blond hair.

"Hello, young man," John said to the boy. "My name is John. What's yours?"

"Timmy," the boy replied. "But, I'm not supposed to talk to strangers."

"I don't think it'll hurt just this one time," said John.

"I'm scared, and I miss my mom and dad." The boy was not crying, but he was obviously distraught.

"Are your mom and dad still alive?"

"Yes. They were with me until the men brought me down here."

"Then, I wouldn't worry. You should see them again soon," John said reassuringly. "I'm sure they're waiting for you."

"I was sick with cancer in the hospital, but I don't feel sick anymore," Timmy said.

"I'm glad you feel better. I had a heart attack. I don't feel bad anymore either," said John.

"I guess I died, and that's me on the table."

"Yes. I'm sure that's what happened."

"I thought I was supposed to go to heaven. That's what my mom told me."

"You know what? I bet you will go to heaven, Timmy. I'm new to all this, too, so I don't really understand it myself," said John. "But, I think we'll understand more later."

The two of them continued to chat as the child's body underwent the embalming process.

Timmy didn't watch, and John thought that was a good thing.

When the men finished, they turned off the lights again and went into the elevator.

"I'm afraid of the dark," said Timmy.

"Don't worry," said John. "I'm right here with you. You can still see me, can't you?"

"Yes."

"Then we'll get through this together."

It was sometime later that the men came back and dressed Timmy. They dressed him in a little black suit and red tie. John and Timmy watched as they brought down the miniature white coffin. The men were very gentle with Timmy as they placed him in the coffin, then wheeled it next to John's. When the men were finished, they closed the coffin and placed a sticky note on it that read, 'Timothy Reynalds.' They went to the elevator and turned off the lights again.

"Are you still afraid of the dark?" John asked.

"Not so much now," Timmy replied. "It's good that I can see you, though."

"Good. You're a very brave young man," said John.

Hours later, the younger man came for Timmy's casket. *Thank goodness Timmy was going first*, John thought. *The boy wouldn't have to be left alone down here in the dark.*

"Well, I think you'll be seeing your mom and dad very soon, Timmy," John said.

"Good. I really miss them," said Timmy.

The man wheeled Timmy's coffin into the elevator.

"Goodbye," said Timmy as he left with his body. He waved to John.

"Goodbye," said John.

The elevator door closed, and John was alone once again. He worried about Timmy. He hoped his parents would be there to greet his body, and it pained him to think about the sadness the family would have to endure. Perhaps they knew Timmy was no longer suffering. Perhaps they'd be strong during the visitations and the funeral. Perhaps Timmy would be strong for them and somehow, convey a sense of peace to them. Perhaps.

John waited for what seemed like a long time. Finally, the young man came down and rolled John's coffin into the elevator. John didn't know what to expect. Would there be anyone there to greet his body? John certainly didn't expect much since he had been so reclusive since Brenda's passing.

When the elevator reached the garage, the young man rolled the coffin around a corner where he pressed a button that opened the double doors into a hallway. John's body was then rolled into a viewing room. John immediately recognized the place. It was the same visitation room Brenda had been in. And again, the memories flooded back to him.

There were already some flowers in the spacious room. The young man rolled the coffin into an alcove at the front of the room, then removed the sticky note. At the rear of the alcove were elegant pale green drapes, and beside the entrance to the room was a chrome-framed sign with a black background and white plastic letters that simply read, 'John P. Sample.'

John hovered above his casket and body as the young man lifted the coffin lid. Again, John barely recognized himself but felt they had done a good job of preparing him for visitations. He was grateful he didn't look so heavy in the casket.

Two men walked into the room. John recognized the older man as the person from the funeral home. The other was John's son. John P. Sample Jr. was 41 and a fine man in every respect. He wore a dark blue blazer, white shirt and no tie with charcoal gray pants. The two men approached the casket.

"He looks good," said John Jr. "You did a good job."

"Thank you, Mr. Sample," the older man said. "Would you like a few moments alone with your father?"

"Yes, I would. Thank you."

"Just come back to the office when you're finished. We still have a few details to go over."

"Thank you. I'll be there in a few minutes."

John Jr. stood there looking over his father's face and torso.

"Well, you look very nice, I must say, Dad," he said quietly.

John, Jr. looked nervous.

"Maybe you can't hear me, Dad, but I'm going to tell you anyway. I got the call late yesterday and took a flight out from Atlanta this morning. Mona and the boys will be here tomorrow. I guess they had difficulty locating me and Anita as your next of kin. Don't worry. Anita found your car at the grocery store. The funeral home had your keys to the car and house. Anita and I went through some files at your house to find your insurance. You let your life insurance lapse after Mom died, but I located your bank accounts and 401k information, and you have more than enough to pay for your funeral once the funds are released. Medicare and your VA benefits should take care of most of your ambulance and hospital bill. Anita is going to be your executor, so I'm sure she'll find out a lot more about your situation as she gets into the process. I notified Mom's sister, so she knows and will be here tonight. I also called your friend Eric. The funeral director put obituaries in the *Pittsburgh Post Gazette* and in the *Lafayette Journal and Courier*, so you might get some of your old friends here to see you tonight and tomorrow. You'll be buried beside Mom, of course. Other than that, I guess we'll learn what we need to know later. I'll be talking to Anita in a little while. I'm going to talk with the funeral director now. I guess I'll see you again tonight. I love you, Dad." John Jr. couldn't hold back the tears.

John appreciated the update. He tried to leave the room, but he still felt attached to his body. He wanted to listen in on the conversation between John Jr. and the funeral director. He also wanted to see how Timmy was getting along. But, he felt he couldn't leave the room.

John waited beside his body until that evening when people started to come into the viewing room. The young man from the funeral home brought in some chairs. The first people to arrive were some of John's former colleagues from the VA. They went up to the casket and looked at his body.

"They did a good job on him. He looks nice," said one of them. "I haven't seen him since he retired. It's a shame he died so soon after his retirement," said another.

Several other people arrived at the viewing, including some from his Service Merchandise jewelry department days.

Eric, John's best friend, arrived with his wife, Sharon. John had known Eric since Junior High School and had kept in touch over the years. Every time they saw each other or talked on the phone, it was as if they had just seen each other the day before. Eric came up to the casket and talked quietly.

"Hey, old man. You had a good run. Sorry to see you go so young. I'll miss you, buddy." Eric wiped his eyes, then went back to his seat next to Sharon.

Anita came with John's grandsons. She cried softly as her husband and boys tried to comfort her. Anita came up to the coffin and seemed like she wanted to talk to him. All she could get out was, "I love you, Daddy."

There was talk among the mourners about how John was a good man and what a shame it was that he died so young. After two hours, the remaining mourners left the funeral home. Then John was alone with his body again. *How strange it had been watching and listening to the living from his vantage point beside and above the casket,* he thought.

A little while later, the funeral director walked over, closed the casket, and turned out the lights. John remained with the casket until the next morning.

So, now it was Tuesday, the day of the funeral. *It was unusual not to have to sleep,* thought John. He could see through the windows as the sun came up, and it seemed like it would be warm and sunny for the funeral.

Later that morning, the funeral director came into the parlor carrying a podium, and after positioning it, he went over and opened the casket lid. The younger man brought in 40 folding chairs and set them up. They moved the other plush chairs to the front of the room.

John Jr. and his family, and Anita and her family, arrived a while later and went back up to the casket.

"I'm sure Dad will be glad to be with Mom again," said John Jr. John wondered when that would be. He really looked forward to seeing her.

"I'm just glad we have good weather today. And, if I remember right, it's a little bit of a drive out to the cemetery," said Anita.

John Jr. nodded.

They took their seats in the front row and John watched as people filed into the parlor. He was surprised to see that 25 people came to see him off.

The preacher eventually took to the podium with a piece of paper and began to speak.

"By all the accounts I've heard this morning, John Sample was a kind man and a loving husband and father. He worked at several different jobs over his lifetime and recently retired from the VA. Unfortunately, John only had a couple of years to enjoy his retirement.

John is survived by his son, John Jr. and his family, and his daughter, Anita, and her family. He has five grandsons.

As we have hope in a life everlasting, we also have hope that John will find rest and peace in the arms of his beloved wife and in the bosom of a loving God."

The preacher sat down and the funeral director took over the podium.

"The funeral will conclude at the Garden of Peace cemetery East of Murrysville where there will be a short ceremony. The procession will commence in approximately 15 minutes, so anyone going to the cemetery should follow the lead vehicles. We will have funeral flags placed on your vehicles if you wish to take part in the procession. If so, please turn your headlights on to let the attendant know you will be participating. Thank you."

The funeral was almost over. John could not find any fault with what had been said and felt t the service was as much as he deserved.

The group of mourners slowly made their way to their cars doing as they were instructed. After the people left, the funeral director closed and sealed the casket. John followed as the older man rolled the casket out through the back doors, and the younger man helped move it into the hearse. Ten cars were to follow the hearse. The younger man placed the flags on the vehicles and directed the cars in place.

As the motorcade left the funeral home, John suddenly noticed how bright everything was now—more so than when he had been alive. He noticed things he hadn't noticed in ages. The trees and grass were greener and the flowers in the yards more colorful. The sky was bluer, the clouds were whiter and fluffier, and the sun was far brighter.

John couldn't feel the wind in his face as the cars drove along Rt. 22 toward the cemetery as he floated above the hearse. When they arrived at the cemetery thirty minutes later, John noticed a cluster of beings like himself drifting toward the entrance. They were watching the funeral procession as it neared the gate, and one of them, a young man in an old military uniform, appeared to stand guard there.

"Welcome to the Garden of Peace!" said the saluting soldier as the hearse rolled through the entrance.

John didn't reply but saluted back as they passed by. The funeral procession made its way back to the section where Brenda was buried. John had hoped he would see her there. But when they arrived at the grave site, Brenda was nowhere to be seen. He could see many others like himself scattered across the cemetery and noticed they were more colorful than the living who were getting out of their cars. John Jr., Anita's husband, and two other men along with the funeral director and the younger man carried the casket the short distance from the hearse to the bier. A set of chairs were set up not far from the casket and the grave, and grass carpets on plywood had been placed around it.

John watched as his children and their families sat in the chairs and the others gathered near them. He smiled when he saw his grandchildren take their seats.

The funeral director then spoke, saying, "John Philip Sample was a good man who loved his wife, children and grandchildren. He will be missed. Now, he will be laid to rest beside his beloved wife, Brenda. Our hope is that he will find eternal peace with her in the life that follows this one. I encourage each of you to take a moment to say a silent prayer on behalf of John and his family before you leave."

With that, the funeral was over. *Short and sweet*, thought John. *What else was there to say?* Some went up to the casket and touched it, while others stood silently nearby with their eyes closed for a moment before leaving.

John Jr. and Anita hugged. Soon, everyone got into their cars and drove away. The funeral director waited until John Jr. had left the cemetery and followed behind him.

Two men in coveralls had been watching from beside a backhoe and pickup truck on the other side of the cemetery. John watched as one of them drove the pickup toward him while the other man started up the backhoe and drove it on the gravel road over to where John was waiting. Once they got to the grave site, the backhoe driver turned off the tractor and began helping the other man lower the casket into the ground using the automated pulley system. After retrieving the straps, pulleys, and other paraphernalia, they dismantled the tent that had been set up and placed the canvas, bier, plywood, chairs, poles, and ropes into the back of the pickup. The backhoe operator pulled the machine up close to the hole and began to fill the grave. The other man leaned against a shovel he had pulled from the backhoe. As the backhoe completed most of the filling process, the man with the shovel began to shovel the remaining dirt into the hole, which by now had formed a mound. John watched as the men gathered the various flower arrangements and placed them on the grave.

John noticed that his own gravestone had already been placed beside Brenda's. It reflected John's name and dates of birth and death, and the words, *"Beloved husband, father and grandfather."* The two men drove back to the white pole-barn and carried the items into the building. When the backhoe was parked inside, both men closed and locked the sliding door before getting into the pickup and leaving the cemetery.

Soon thereafter, a number of spirit beings began to gather around John. There appeared to be a couple dozens of them. John looked for Brenda but she was nowhere to be seen. Sadness swept over him the likes of which he had not experienced since Brenda's death.

Chapter 3

"John P. Sample. Welcome to the afterlife," said one of the male beings. He was a large man who looked to be in his late 60s, with white hair and blue eyes. "I guess this is all still pretty new to you."

"You're right. How do you know my name?" asked John.

"We can read the inscription on the tombstone. Besides, we listened in on your funeral."

"I'm looking for my wife, Brenda Sample. Have you seen her?"

"Sorry to have to tell you this, John, but Brenda left us shortly after she arrived. We're all happy for her because we're certain she's in a better place."

"You mean she's in heaven now?" John asked.

"We can't say for sure, but yes, that's our belief. So, I'd guess you'd call us the welcoming committee; that is, all of us. We're residents here."

"What do you call yourselves? I mean, are we spirits, ghosts or what?"

"We think of ourselves as souls, John. You're just like us now. Even though we're dead, we still have names and pretty much the same personalities we had when we were alive. By the way, I'm James. Because of my outgoing personality, I'm kind of the unofficial mayor of The Garden."

James reached out for John's hand and John felt a tingling sensation as they shook. Through that touch, he could sense James was a good man. John looked around at the crowd and began to feel a little better.

"I don't see any children?" John asked.

"They leave us very quickly. They go to heaven right away."

"How do they get there?"

"Well, we think there are special angels that come and guide them into the light, John. It seems like a very private experience. It's what we're all hoping for," said James.

"What about hell?"

"I don't know about hell. We think some have gone there, but one day the troubled soul is here, the next day they're not. We have a good idea where they went but we don't like to talk about it since we don't know for sure."

"Okay. What do you do around here? I mean, do you just stay here in the cemetery all the time?"

"That's about it," said James. "We're stuck here in a kind of purgatory. But, it's not so bad once you've had a chance to meet everyone and get used to the idea. There are quite a few of us still here. We keep each other company. And with the amount of time you'll have on your hands, you'll get to know almost everyone very well."

"What if you just want to be left alone?"

"You can always go off by yourself in one corner of the cemetery or another. But I don't recommend it. We find the souls who do that usually become solitary and sad. Let's just say it's not healthy. The best thing to do is introduce yourself and get to know everyone. You'll find that everyone here has a personality all their own. Most you will like and some you won't, but we all have one thing in common now—we're all dead."

"You say that like it's a good thing."

"I think it is a good thing. No more eating, sleeping, or worrying about bills."

"I guess there's that," laughed John.

"So, now it's my turn to ask a question. Who's the president now?" asked James.

"That would be Donald Trump."

"You've got to be kidding me. Really?"

"He lost the popular vote but won the Electoral College vote."

"Wow. I never expected that. The last person in here gave us an update on the election situation and she thought it would be Hillary Clinton in a landslide."

"Well, it didn't work out that way," said John. "Are you disappointed?"

"No. It doesn't really matter that much to me here. I was just curious. By the way, would you like a tour of the cemetery? It could be your home for quite a while," said James.

"Sure," said John. "That would be nice. How do you know how long someone will have to stay?"

"We think it depends on the condition of your soul. Some souls go on to heaven quickly. Some are here for a very long time, and we think some are taken to hell."

The two of them floated together over the cemetery. James pointed to a couple of mausoleums, a large obelisk, and several large headstones and told John who the inhabitants were.

The mausoleums were both constructed of light gray marble and were set relatively close to each other. The larger, older and more ornate one had two columns at the entrance and a dramatic metal door that featured a beautiful kneeling angel pointing the way to heaven. Above the door read the name, 'Garfield.' The other mausoleum was modern and plain with a black wrought-iron outer door and had no name on it.

"Are those people still here?" John asked as he pointed toward the mausoleums.

"One of them is. Peter Garfield is still among us. He's not too friendly, but he has started to come around. He's one of the oldest residents here. You'll meet him eventually, I'm sure. The others are gone. I guess everyone is curious about the rich ones."

"What about the obelisk?"

"That would be the Smiths; Donna and Charles. They're still here, and they're, well, rather interesting."

John looked around. The cemetery covered several acres and had a gentle roll to it. There were several large oak and maple trees dotting the landscape, and a large weeping willow tree leaned over a small pond near the center of the cemetery.

"Do live people ever visit here?"

"Yes, occasionally. They mostly come on birthdays and on Memorial Day. And, of course, they come to funerals like yours today."

John noticed there was an entourage of souls following them as they toured the area.

"So, what do you do the rest of the time, James?" John asked.

"Well, sometimes we wander around the cemetery during the day and reflect a lot at night, and we talk to each other the rest of the time."

"Sounds kind of boring," said John.

"It can be if you let it."

James and John continued to survey the rest of the Garden of Peace. There were brown and white ducks swimming on the pond and the reeds and cattails swayed along the edge. John continued to be amazed at how colorful and bright everything was. The cemetery was attractive, well-groomed, and had a wide array of tombstones and markers.

When they arrived back at his grave site, John asked, "Can't any of you get past the entrance?"

"No one has since I've been here, and that's been since 1992."

"Well, I'm going to try," said John.

"Be my guest," said James.

John floated near the entrance and tried to pass through the gates. He did not feel a barrier but rather, he felt a pulling sensation keeping him from passing through. He tried higher as he floated above the cemetery road but to no avail. He went back and joined James.

"That was odd," said John. "I felt like my body was pulling me back inside."

"Exactly."

"Why do I have such an attraction to my body," John asked.

"I don't know but I know it's real, and everyone here feels that same attraction," replied James. "Well, John, do you think you're ready to meet some of the folks here. They've been waiting to talk to you."

John looked back and noticed the other souls were gathered in a group not far from the entrance.

"Sure. I'm ready."

They went over to the group and James began the introductions.

"May I introduce you all to Mr. John P. Sample?"

An older-looking, heavy-set woman came up to him first. She was shorter than most of the other souls and had brown hair and hazel eyes.

"Hello, John. By the way, we usually just go by first names here. My name is Sally, and I've been here for a little over ten years. I was from Monroeville," the woman said.

"So was I! I guess we have something in common already." For some reason, John was feeling pleasantly warm and happy to converse. It was the most he'd talked to people since he'd left the VA.

"Wonderful! We're so happy to meet you, John. It's always exciting to have new souls in the Garden. It gives us all something new to talk about," she said.

The man in the WWI Army campaign hat and uniform was next. He appeared to be in his early twenties with a slight build, blond hair, and blue eyes.

"How do you do? I'm Rex. I've been here the longest. I died in 1918. I was killed by a German bayonet in France in the war to end all wars."

"I remember seeing you when I first came into the cemetery. It's nice to meet you, Rex," said John. "I served in the Army in the Vietnam War in 1970."

"It's nice to see a fellow veteran, John. Why didn't you have a military funeral?"

"I don't know. Probably no one thought about it when they were making the arrangements."

"We'll have to tell our war stories to each other one of these days."

"I look forward to it, Rex."

Next came a middle-aged woman with wild red hair and green eyes.

"I'm Alice. I don't usually talk too much. Most conversations around here are boring and irritate me," she said.

"I'll try to keep that in mind."

One by one, the souls greeted John. He hoped he'd be able to keep track of all of their names. *Perhaps he would be there long enough to get to know each and every one of them*, he thought.

After he'd met most of the souls, John noticed there were still several other souls floating around the cemetery by themselves. He went up to one young man and introduced himself.

"Hi! My name's John. I'm the new guy," said John in his friendliest manner.

"I'm Al," the young man said without looking up.

There was something different about this soul. He was almost gray as if he were in some kind of fog and not nearly so bright in color as the others.

"Are you okay?" John asked.

"Yeah. I guess so. I'm just not in the mood for small talk at the moment," he said. "Maybe someday I'll feel like chatting." With that, the young man moved away.

John went back to James.

"What's up with Al?" John asked.

"Al's a hard case. Sad really. He was a suicide."

"He looks so young."

"Al was only a teenager when he did it," said James. "His parents used to come here fairly often, but they're older now and have only come to visit on his birthdays the past several years."

"That's sad," said John. "What about the others that didn't come to greet me?"

"Well, some are just very shy. Some pine away for loved ones while others are angry with God, and some are very sad that they're dead and miss the things they had in life," replied James. "Several of them have been that way for years. We try to reach out sometimes but after a while, you just kind of give up on them. Maybe you'll have better luck."

"Maybe I'll try after I've had a while to adjust to things around here myself."

"Sounds like a plan."

John went back to the congregation of souls who were still milling about and chatting with each other. It was starting to get dark. *Where had the time gone?* he wondered.

Sally approached him again.

"You wouldn't know this, John, but we all go back to our grave sites after dark. I don't know why, but that's just the way it is. I just didn't want you to think we were abandoning you."

"Far be it for me to change the rules."

Sally laughed.

"You're going to get along just fine here, John. By the way, if you want to get to know someone better, hold hands with them."

She waved goodbye, and John saw the other souls heading back toward their respective headstones and markers. He went to his fresh grave site and floated near his headstone.

What a day, he thought. It was odd how well he felt he fit in with the other souls in the garden so quickly. He also felt strangely comfortable with his new environment.

Chapter 4

As night covered the Garden of Peace, John thought about what James had told him with regards to a time of reflection, and he guessed this was it. He thought about Brenda and how much he missed her. That was the one thing he had hoped for when he died—to be with Brenda again in the afterlife, if there was one. But he was happy for her that she'd gone to heaven. *If anyone deserved heaven, it was Brenda,* he thought. She was so kind and generous to everyone, especially to her husband. Brenda had not worked outside the home for several years but she made up for it as a homemaker. She cooked, she cleaned, and she went to church every Sunday.

John decided to start at the beginning; at least the beginning he could remember. His first memory was from when he was about three years old. They were living in Lafayette, Indiana on 10th Street near the Hippensteel Funeral Home. He walked out the back door and started down a narrow concrete walk. That's when he saw the neighbor boy aiming a B-B gun at him. John heard the '*pfft*' sound of the rifle, then felt the B-B hit him in the left nipple. He screamed and ran into the house where his mother extracted the round B-B from his skin. There was no blood, but she was furious. She took John's hand and walked with him down the alley behind the house until they came to the perpetrator's door. John didn't understand much of what was said, but he heard the boy getting a spanking.

Another memory from that house was when John threw a stick and hit a car from the back yard. The car's tires screeched and the driver stopped in the middle of the street. John's mother immediately ran outside and heard from the driver what had been done. She put John over her knee and gave him several hard swats on the butt. The driver witnessed the spanking, then drove off.

From the 10th Street apartment, the family moved to the small community of Battleground, which was the historic site of William Henry Harrison's battle with the Indians commanded by Tecumseh and his brother, the Prophet. The memories of that place were of a picnic near the battlefield monument and of outdoor movies projected onto a plywood screen behind the Battleground grade school. John started kindergarten at that grade school but then they moved back to Lafayette where they lived in one half of an old duplex next door to John's aunt and uncle.

John remembered his first bike and how he'd learned to ride it. It was a girl's bike and seemed like a red tank and was very heavy with fat tires. And, at only five years old, he remembered riding the bike around the community with no supervision.

They had two goldfish there. One day, when they came back from swimming at the park, they found one of the fish dead on the floor and the other floating upside-down in the fish bowl. Before anyone could say anything, John's mother flushed one of the fish down the toilet. After much begging, John convinced his mother to let them bury the other goldfish in the back yard, so she helped to form two Popsicle sticks into a makeshift cross. John and his younger brother, Paul, got a serving spoon and the Popsicle sticks and took the goldfish out to bury it. They dug a shallow grave, placed the fish in it, covered it with dirt and placed the cross above the buried fish before saying a prayer over it. Two days later, John was curious to know what had happened to the fish, so he tried to dig it up. However, the goldfish was nowhere to be found. John never figured out what had happened to the fish. He figured it must have gone to heaven.

It was about this time John began to wet the bed. John recollected that when he was asleep, he would dream he had to pee and would get up, go down the hall, and stand in front of the toilet. It was only after he started to pee he realized he was wetting the bed. This happened several times over the years, even up until he was a teenager. His mother would change the sheets and wash them without making too much of a fuss over the incidents.

John went to Vinton School while living at that house and remembered taking naps on the classroom floor on colorful woven mats. He also remembered getting ice cream treats in little round paper containers and eating the ice cream with little wooden spoons.

From there, the family moved to Oxford Street in the Edgelea neighborhood on Lafayette's South side. This was a newer house that was one of hundreds of pre-fabricated homes in the area. John started the second half of the first grade at Edgelea grade school. He remembered walking to school by himself and later, playing in the construction site behind the school. There were little pools of water that were home to frogs, toads and thousands of tadpoles.

John's mother believed in his aptitude so much that she signed him up for piano lessons starting at the age of five. They did not own a piano but John remembered playing the piano at his teacher's home once a week.

John also remembered playing baseball next to the school. While playing third base once, a batter hit a line drive that bounced in the dirt in front of him and hit him squarely in the forehead, knocking him out. When he woke up, there were people and players standing over him. He remembered feeling fine but he had a knot on his forehead for a day as a result.

The most difficult memory John had was when he was in the third grade. The family was at home when a three-year-old girl was struck and killed by a car right in front of their house. She and her family had been visiting from out of town. After he heard screams, John's dad went out to see what he could do but she had died instantly. The child had apparently darted out from between parked cars in front of the house across the street. The driver of the car said he never saw her and had purposely slowed down because he was watching other children playing close to the street. This all unfolded directly across the street from the picture window of John's house. John was so distraught that he told his mother that if he ever killed a child like that, he would hang himself. John's mother consoled him and told him it was an accident and couldn't be helped, and that suicide was not permitted by God. She also said the little girl would be in heaven that very day. John remembered watching the fire department hosing down the blood off the street. This tragedy haunted him for many years.

When John was nine, he became religiously preoccupied. By this time, his uncle, Brad, had become the minister of his church and took over many of the duties of John's grandfather. One day, John asked his uncle if he could be baptized. His uncle told him that if John could tell him the five steps to baptism he would baptize him. The next Sunday, John went to his uncle and recited the five steps: hear, believe, repent, confess, and be baptized. John's small church did not have a baptismal, so they scheduled it at the nearby Elmwood Church of Christ. Several church and family members were in attendance that day as John emerged from the changing room in a white frock for the baptism. The water was cold as he stepped down into the baptismal to meet his Uncle Brad who was already in the water wearing chest high waders. John could see the people watching him from their seats as his uncle proceeded to tell the assembly the importance of baptism and how this young man had decided of his own free will to take this important step.

"John, do you believe that Jesus is the Christ, the son of the living God?"

"Yes."

"Then I baptize you in the name of the Father, the Son, and the Holy Ghost."

John's uncle placed a folded white handkerchief over John's nose and mouth and pushed him down into the water. When he came back up, John didn't feel any different, but he could hear the congregation singing the hymn, *Are You Washed in the Blood?*

John's uncle guided him back up the steps, and John found his way back to the changing room. *All his sins were forgiven*, he thought. *Now he was guaranteed to go to heaven when he died.*

John's family moved again, this time to a house on the corner of 13th and Greenbush Streets on the north side of Lafayette. It was a very old house that had a treasure trove of relics in it. John overheard someone say the house had once belonged to a sheriff. There was a trunk in the basement that contained many old and rare objects, such as campaign buttons and ribbons from as early as the McKinley election. There was a pair of antique iron handcuffs and a pair of swords in the basement from some bygone era.

The basement was scary enough to a 10-year-old but the furnace was the stuff of nightmares. It was a giant, coal-fired octopus-looking beast. One of John's chores was to go down into the basement in the winter time, turn on the lights, and build a fire in the furnace with newspaper and kindling, then shovel coal from the coal bin into the furnace. The lights were clear, hanging bulbs that were turned on and off by pull-strings that were nearly impossible to find in the dark. There was no light switch at the top of the stairs, so John had to go down into the darkness and feel around for the string and pull it before there was any light at all, and before Frankenstein's monster could grab him.

Not long after moving into the Greenbush house and starting school at Linnwood School, John became very ill. He was between semesters in the 4th grade and began having pain in his belly and his skin and eyes were yellowing. He felt like he had a bad case of the flu. John's mother had him pee in a Mason jar to take to the doctor. The urine was bright orange. As soon as the doctor saw it and did a physical exam, John was sent to St. Elizabeth Hospital with a diagnosis of "infectious hepatitis."

The hospital room was large, and the staff and family had to wear masks and gowns when they entered the room. John received flowers from the church and a stack of old comic books from an uncle which really helped pass the time. A few days later, John's brother, Paul, joined him in the hospital room as a patient with the same illness. John received "get well" cards from his classmates and teacher at Edgelea. This gesture was particularly gratifying to John, and he read them several times.

One day, a Catholic priest came to visit him. The priest was very kind and spent several minutes talking with John about how he was feeling and how he liked school. John was appreciative of the visit but was sorry to know this kind man was going to hell—at least, that was the opinion of John's preacher grandfather who believed that the pope was the closest thing to the devil on earth. One reason the Catholics would not go to heaven was that they only sprinkled babies into the church. According to his grandfather, that kind of baptism didn't count because the bible called for total immersion. John was pleasant to the priest and didn't tell him he was going to hell.

Once he got back home, it was still a couple of weeks before he could go back to school. He was anxious to go back to school at Linnwood Elementary, which was just a block from his house. It was a very old two-story brick and stone building with high ceilings and no gymnasium. His classroom was on the second floor. This was a far cry from the new one-story schools he had attended at Vinton and Edgelea. They had a playground across the street from the school. The ground at the playground was covered with gravel and they used to play kickball there during gym class and recess. There were also two basketball hoops with metal chain nets.

John began violin lessons while in the 4th grade. Mr. Snyder was his teacher and he was very patient with John and the three others in the class. Mr. Snyder taught several students from most of the grade schools in the area, as well as the junior high school and high school orchestras.

When he was in the 5th grade, John became a patrol boy. His job was to wear a patrol boy's belt and use a yellow flag to stop traffic at the corners opposite the school to let children cross the street. He took this job very seriously except for one time when his friend chased him up the street while he held the yellow flag with the aluminum pole in it. John chased his friend and the flag got caught in a crack in the sidewalk and the pole hit him in the mouth, knocking out one of his front teeth. The friend immediately went and retrieved John's mother for help. The tooth was nowhere to be found but there was a lot of blood. When his parents took John to the dentist, the dentist had to make a tooth connected to a plastic partial plate that fit the roof of his mouth.

John had his first date while he was in the 6th grade. He asked Vickie, a girl from his class, to go bowling with him on a Saturday and she accepted. That weekend, John walked to her house and they walked together to the nearby Star Lanes bowling alley. John had a coupon from a calendar for a free game, and they had a good time bowling together before walking back to her house.

That summer, John's parents took him and Paul to Southern Indiana where they visited with their great uncle Bret and great aunt Gladys. Uncle Bret was a tall, stout man in his 50s, with thinning blond hair. Aunt Gladys was tall for a woman and seemed more sophisticated than her husband.

John was to stay and attend church camp there the following week. The camp was sponsored by the Women's Christian Temperance Union, an organization John's grandmother belonged to that believed smoking and drinking were sins. Uncle Bret was quite a character, and his property included a camp and a large, beautiful cave called Porter's Cave. John and Paul were given permission to go to the cave, so they followed the wide trail down a steep hill. To the right of the trail were three gravestones that marked the bodies of dogs Uncle Bret had owned. Each headstone had an epitaph. One said, *"Here Lies Trey - Ate Too Much Bacon."* The second one said, *"Shep - Faithful Friend."* The third read, *"Beauty - She Was the Best."*

At the bottom of the hill, the trail came to a 'T.' The entrance to the cave was to the right and appeared to be about 40 or 50 feet above the creek below. The mouth of the cave was about 10 feet high and 30 feet wide, and water flowed over the lip forming a beautiful waterfall. The cave was cool inside and narrowed quickly with the stream of water in the center of it as it went back inside. The cave was said to be about a quarter of a mile in length but without flashlights or lanterns, the boys did not venture far inside. They went back outside and followed the rocky trail down along the cliff above the creek. When they got down near the creek, they found a round wishing well that had been made out of an old wringer washing machine but was now encapsulated with small, round rocks and had a ladle hanging from the rafter of the small roof above it. The boys used the ladle to take a drink. The water in the well came from a small side stream. It was cold, tasty and crystal clear and there were coins resting on the bottom of it.

Farther down the trail, they found the large white structure that was the main building of the camp. The boys went inside and to the left, saw a large dining room on the main floor. In the center of one wall stood a rubble stone fireplace. Through double doors on the right was the commercial-sized stainless-steel kitchen. Once back outside, the boys found a ramp in the rear that led up to the upper part of the building. Above the dining hall were two large rooms which made up the dormitories. Each side was a mirror image of the other, with windows all along the sides and bunk beds throughout. Back outside, they found a bath house and restroom area. Beyond the bath house was a beautiful, natural swimming pool made from the dammed-up creek. There was a curved sidewalk that followed along one side to the concrete dam. In the center of the pool was a statue fountain of a young boy riding a fish. Out of the fish's mouth was a spout of water that reached nearly 15' beyond the fountain and splashed onto the pool.

The boys went past the pool and down a trail which led to a wire cage that housed a large black bear. On the side of the cage was a wooden sign that read, "*Smokey.*" The boys stayed well back from the cage as they watched the bear pace back and forth. Farther down the trail was a small softball field with a backstop, home base and canvas base bags. Beyond the ball field was nothing but high weeds, so the boys headed back to Uncle Bret's house. Their great aunt Gladys met them at the chicken coop as she had just finished feeding the chickens and gathering the eggs. John and Paul got to carry the eggs back to the house.

John remembered his camp week as having been fun but serious due to the teachings of the prohibitions of smoking and drinking. There were classes devoted entirely to the ills of those sins and one day, the boys and girls were each required to create posters with those themes. There was also swimming and softball. John met a girl named Lonnie during camp, and they explored the trails on the other side of the creek, all the while holding hands.

After camp was over but before John's parents came to pick him up, John met his Uncle Bret down near the main camp building. The two of them sat next to each other on wicker chairs. Uncle Bret lit a cigar and leaned back in his chair, then blew smoke into the air.

"I don't drink, but I do love a good ceegar," he said. "I know those old biddies mean well, but I'm too old to change now. I think they're against just about everything I'm for."

John smiled.

Uncle Bret looked over at John and said, "Did I ever tell you how I shot the deer that I have mounted on the wall in the den?"

"No," John said.

"Well, sir, I was hunting along the creek down here below the swimming pool. After a while, I spotted this big buck. I aimed my rifle at him and just as I pulled the trigger, he turned and jumped away from me. I thought I'd missed him but when I got to the spot where he jumped, I found a small blood trail. I tracked him for about a hundred yards and there he was, lying dead as a doornail. When I checked him over, I couldn't find where I'd shot him and thought maybe I'd scared him to death. So, anyway, I hung him up from a tree limb with a rope I brought with me. When I started to dress him, I saw that the guts were all shot up. Sure enough, I'd shot the bastard directly in his asshole."

John chuckled but was too embarrassed to laugh out loud at such a dirty story.

Uncle Bret took a deep draw from his cigar and blew a perfect smoke ring above his head.

"Now, if I were you, I wouldn't repeat that story to your folks. They might not think it's so funny."

John nodded in agreement. The two of them walked up the trail back to the house. Along the way, Uncle Bret would occasionally stop and thrash the weeds with his walking stick.

"Damned Copperheads!" he'd say.

By the time they got back to the house, John's parents were there and after some small talk between John's mom and Aunt

Gladys, John waved goodbye to Uncle Bret. He was sorry to have to leave. Uncle Bret smiled and raised his hand as the car pulled away.

John's parents moved again, this time to a corner duplex on 18th and Columbia Streets. John was now in the 7th grade at Sunnyside Jr. High School. His parents had a falling out with their church and began attending the Elmwood Church of Christ. The first time he attended the church, John was awestruck by the beautiful sound of the congregation singing hymns acapella. There was no piano or organ. The Church of Christ did not believe in using musical instruments in the church. They also did not believe in dancing. It was a beautiful church with padded pews and gorgeous blonde wood throughout the structure. John immediately felt comfortable at the church and met three boys his own age; Eric, Larry and Jessie. Eric went to Sunnyside Jr. High, while Larry went to Tecumseh and Jessie went to West Lafayette. They immediately became friends and were always together at church functions. John's Sunday school teacher called them the "four horsemen of the apocalypse."

John remembered the times the Sunday school class went to the Veterans Administration home for widows of veterans. They went there after church and stopped for lunch at the new McDonald's. He bought a hamburger, fries and a chocolate shake all for less than a dollar. Upon arrival at the home, the students would form a choir, sing hymns, and say a prayer. One time, Larry was asked to give the prayer. He did fine right up until he said, "And bless these old ladies until they die." John, Eric and Jessie thought this was hilarious and couldn't stop snickering.

At school, John was having trouble with wood shop class. His teacher's name was Mr. Spevack and he was quite tough. Inside the shop classroom, there were work tables and stools that the students sat on during class. There were dowel holes in the tables about 4" deep, and Mr. Spevack gave strict instructions for the students to avoid putting pencils in the holes. One time, John had to hold up his hand to be excused to go to the restroom. When he came back to class, everyone was looking at him and some were even laughing. Mr. Spevack was holding his long wooden pointer and tapping it on his palm. Finally, the student seated next to John pointed at the dowel hole in front of him. Inside the hole was half a pencil. It was obvious that the teacher had whacked the pencil while he was gone. John took the broken pencil out and placed it on the table. This was the only class John got an 'F' in throughout junior high school.

It was in this year that John's parents decided to move again. This time, they moved into a new house just outside of Lafayette on Poplar Lane close to the Aca Y Ala roller rink. It was a yellow aluminum-sided ranch with three bedrooms and 1 ½ baths. The house was one among many in a new small subdivision. John rode the bus to his junior high school, and that's how he met the girl his age that lived across the street. Her name was Lydia, and John immediately developed an unrequited crush on her that lasted for years.

Chapter 5

John noticed the sun coming up and floated back to the assembly.

"How was your first night, John?" Sally asked.

"Actually, it was quite nice. James said I would have time to reflect, so that's what I did."

"I'm glad it was pleasant for you. Many souls have so many regrets that they dwell on what could have been and fall into a kind of depression. Sounds as if you are going to get along just fine here," said Sally.

"I hope so. I reflected on my life last night. What do I reflect on tonight?" asked John.

Sally laughed.

"Well, that depends on you. You probably figured out that you have an excellent memory now, so you can go back and relive your entire life minute-by-minute if you want to. Or, you can just dwell on the important parts. It's really up to you."

"I don't know if my own life was interesting enough to relive my 69 years all over again."

She laughed again.

"You're funny, John. Most of the people here are not so self-deprecating. You'd be surprised at how many of us take ourselves seriously to a fault. Maybe that's why we're all still here."

"So, Sally, why don't you tell me about yourself?"

"Okay, John. Let's go down to the pond."

They drifted down to the pond together and watched a flock of ducks swim near some cattails.

"Please don't think that I'm being too forward, John, but let's hold hands while I tell you about my life. It will make all the difference," said Sally.

"I haven't held a woman's hand since my wife died but I'll make an exception for you."

"You're very sweet," Sally said and smiled at him.

When they held hands, John felt a similar tingling sensation that he'd felt before when James shook hands with him. Then, as Sally began to talk to him, he could actually experience her history.

"I was born in 1943 and was an only child, so, of course, I was very spoiled. My parents were well-to-do and had me when they were in their late 30's. I don't have many memories about the war, but my parents followed it very closely. My father tried to join the Marines, but by that time, he was already over 40 and had bad feet, so none of the branches would take him. I think he was ashamed of the fact he couldn't serve. I was still a small child, so I didn't understand it at the time.

My mother, Clarise, was a nurse who worked at Mercy Hospital in Pittsburgh. She worked with the mentally ill there until her death in 1965 from an aggressive brain tumor. My father's name was Mark, and he was an attorney who worked in downtown Pittsburgh. He passed away three years after he retired in 1969. Growing up, I had a nanny who raised me. Her name was Greta."

John could see and feel everything Sally was feeling as she told her story. He saw her petite mother in her white nurse's cap and dress. He also saw her father, a portly man with a moustache, a 3-piece suit, and gold watch-chain looping down from his vest pocket. John saw the nanny and felt the attachment between her and Sally.

"I grew up in Monroeville and went to St. Joseph Catholic grade school there. I started piano lessons when I was five and continued until I was in Gateway High School. My parents were always home for dinner, and we had wonderful conversations at the dinner table where we often talked politics, the law, and mental illness. Father could be stern at times, but he always had a soft spot for me. Mother was always concerned about my studies at school. I got good grades, but maybe that was because she pushed me so hard. I went to college at Duquesne University and received my degree in education. I taught high school

English, got married to a handsome young man named Rick, and had two children; Amy and Reed.

Rick and I were very happy. We lived in a nice house in Monroeville and had a nice life."

"Do your children and husband come to see you here?" asked John.

"My husband still comes here on Memorial Day. He brings flowers and talks to me a little bit. But he's elderly now and doesn't stay long. The children have both moved away. I miss them terribly and think about them every day."

John could feel the deep longing and sorrow she felt when she talked about her family.

"How and when did you die?" John asked.

"I died five years ago from diabetes. I never kept my diet under control. You wouldn't know it now, but I went blind two years before I died. That was a difficult time. Thankfully, I can see perfectly now."

"It sounds as if you had a pretty good life, Sally," John said.

"I guess I did, didn't I? So, John," she said, "Tell me about you."

John proceeded to tell Sally a shortened version of his life. She was very attentive and expressed sympathy when John talked about Brenda.

When he was finished, John said, "So, that's all there is, Sally. Not too interesting, huh?"

"Don't talk like that, John. You lived a very interesting life. You were very fortunate to find your soul-mate, and you had a wonderful life together."

"You're right. Brenda did make my life interesting."

"No, John. You made your life interesting. Brenda was just part of your life. She was an important part, for sure. But your life is so much more than just your relationship with her. Remember that."

Sally patted John's hand.

"You have other souls to meet, John. Thank you for sharing your life with me. Don't think you're through with me, though. I will want more details the next time we get together."

"Likewise, Sally. Thank you. By the way, why do you think you're still here?"

"I wish I knew. Maybe I have a purpose here. I don't know. It's not a bad existence, and I enjoy being with most of the souls here."

"Well, it sounds to me like you deserve to go to heaven."

"Thank you, John. I guess I wish you were the one deciding the issue."

Sally laughed again, then she was off to be with the others.

John followed Sally to the congregation of souls that clustered near the center of the cemetery. Sally picked out one of the men and brought him to John.

"John, I'd like you to meet Ben. Ben, this is John. You're both very fine gentlemen, so I think you'd appreciate getting to know each other."

"How do you do, John? It's nice to meet you," said Ben.

"Likewise, Ben. What brings you here?"

"You're too funny, John. Let's go over to my tombstone and we can talk."

They floated over to a large, granite tombstone with two names on it.

"Benjamin and Rachel Weiss," John read, and he noticed the Star of David in the center of the headstone. "So, you're Jewish. I haven't known many Jews. I'll be very interested in hearing about your life."

"I used to be Jewish," he said. "That doesn't really matter much here."

"Wow! That had to be a shocker for you after you died," said John.

"More than you know. I was really an atheist in life," said Ben. "I didn't believe in an afterlife. I thought everything was over when you died. When your heart and brain stopped functioning, that was it. To say the least, I was very surprised when I ended up like this."

"Do you mind if I shake your hand and hold it while we talk, Ben?"

"Not at all. I appreciate your interest in my life."

The two men shook hands and hovered near the tombstone.

"So, where to begin . . ."

"Why not begin at the beginning? Where were you born, Ben?"

"I was born in New York City in 1929, the year of the historic stock market crash. My father, Abraham, was a diamond merchant there. My mother, Sarah, worked with him in the shop until I was born. My father did very well during the depression because people were selling their gold jewelry and diamonds for pennies on the dollar just to get money to eat and have a roof over their heads. Some people resented him for taking advantage of the situation, but he always said it was just business."

John could tell Ben was conflicted about this and asked, "How do you feel about it now?"

"I kind of understand why he did it, but I do think he could have been more generous in his dealings during the Depression. He essentially got very rich off the poor and desperate. I think that might have cost him dearly in the afterlife, but I don't really know what happened to him."

"Tell me about your mother."

"My mother was a very intelligent woman and a wonderful musician. She played the piano as well as anyone I ever heard. She could play Chopin, Liszt, and Rachmaninoff with the best of them. She was amazing. My two sisters followed her into music and became professional musicians on their own. One became a concert pianist and the other became a well-known violinist."

"What did you end up doing?" John asked.

"I decided to follow a different path. I became a surgeon."

"Your parents must have been very proud of you."

"Yes, I'm sure they were."

"What was it like growing up Jewish?"

"My parents were reformed Jews, so even though we went to synagogue and celebrated Jewish holidays, we did not hold to all the Jewish traditions in our household. As for me, I did not attend synagogue after I graduated from high school. I spent all my free time studying to become a doctor.

I met my wife, Rachel, while I was doing my residency in Pittsburgh. She was a nurse and was a few years younger than I was. We got married a year after I accepted a position at Allegheny General Hospital in general surgery.

I was always working or on call, so we didn't get to see much of each other. She worked as a nurse on an orthopedic floor at the University of Pittsburgh Medical Center until our first child, Michael, was born. From then on, Rachel worked as a mother and wife, and she was wonderful at both. We had two other children; David and Sandra."

"Is Rachel still here?" John asked.

"No. She went on shortly after I got here. Now, I believe there is a heaven, and believe she is there. I'm certain of it. I miss her very much," said Ben.

"Okay," said Ben. "Now it's your turn, John."

"My life was not as noteworthy as yours, Ben," said John. "It was kind of boring."

"Nonsense!" exclaimed Ben. "Everyone has a story to tell."

John told his story as Ben listened intently.

"You led a good life, John. You were an honorable man, and you loved your wife intensely. You were a lucky man to have had such a wonderful woman in your life."

"You're right, of course. I didn't realize how much I had to be thankful for at the time."

"You and me both," said Ben.

"How did you and your wife die?" asked John.

"Rachel died from pancreatic cancer. It was horrible to see her deteriorate like she did. For six months, she was in a lot of pain, but she never complained. She was a very brave woman.

Me, on the other hand, I died of complications from a hip surgery. I got an infection. Kind of ironic for a surgeon to go like that, huh?"

"Well," said John, "you had a very good life, too, I think. Do you see your children very often?"

"No," replied Ben. "They never came back after the funeral. I guess they thought that was the end, so there was no reason to visit. I don't blame them, really. I used to feel the same way.

Michael is an architect. He's married with two children, and they live in Denver. David is divorced and still lives in Pittsburgh. He's an attorney. Sandra is married with one child and lives with her husband in Baltimore."

"The main thing is that you got to enjoy them while you were alive. And they got to enjoy you, too. That's something to hold on to."

"You're right, John. Thank you for reminding me of that. It's been so good talking with you."

"Thank you for talking with me, Ben."

After their conversation, the two of them went back to the gathering and prepared for the evening.

Time went by quickly that night as John reflected on his life. His memory was clear now, and he'd enjoyed the time thinking about his youth. When he was 16, John got his first official job that summer. He'd had to get his social security card to get the job. He worked for the DeKalb Company in the seed-corn fields near Lafayette. They picked him up from a parking lot near downtown Monday through Saturday mornings at 6:30a.m., starting in late June. His mother dropped him off and picked him up at the pickup point each day. His first job was to walk down the rows of the low corn and cut out the rogue and volunteer corn with a long, hooked knife. The rogue corn was taller and had larger exposed roots at its base. The volunteer corn looked like a clump of thick-leafed grass that sprang up between the rows.

A few weeks later, the corn was getting ready to come to tassel, so he joined another crew that did the detasseling. This was much harder work as each corn stalk had to have its top removed by pulling it out of the stalk. Each person took care of the stalks to their left and right down the rows. The fields were often several hundred acres each, and breaks were only taken at the end of each row. It was hot, sweaty work. John quickly learned to wear light, long-sleeved shirts to work to keep the sun off his arms and to keep the corn leaves from cutting him. He also wore a wide brimmed straw hat to keep from getting too much sun. There were several days he thought about quitting but he was getting paid $1.00 per hour, plus time-and-a-half for overtime past 5 days per week.

One Saturday, John got sick and couldn't go in to work. He felt quite a bit better by Monday morning, so he went to the pickup point only to find that no one else was there from his crew. In fact, there was only one crew left across the street from where he was usually picked up. John walked over to the crew and asked where everyone was.

"They laid everybody else off on Saturday," one of them said.

"Do you think you could use another hand on your crew?" John asked.

"If one of our guys doesn't show up, they might take you on. This is a machine crew, so there's supposed to be 5 of us, including the supervisor. If he doesn't get here by the time the supervisor shows up, then you're probably hired."

As luck would have it, the other fellow didn't show up, so John joined the machine crew even though he didn't know what a machine crew did. When they arrived at the field, John saw the big, orange-pipe machine with the small tractor tires located at each corner of the machine.

"Our job is to clean up red fields," said the supervisor. "Those are fields that didn't pass inspection from the first time they were detasseled. The crew rides up on those metal stands, leans over the rail, and picks out the tassels as we go by. If you miss one, you need to run back, pull it out, and run back to the machine. This is pretty easy work compared to what you've been used to."

The supervisor climbed aboard, sat in the centered tractor seat and started the engine, while everyone else climbed onto their stands. John soon found out that the stands were placed just so he could reach over his railing and pull out the tassels. The supervisor was right. It was easy work, and John was glad to have it. After a couple more weeks of this, the season was over, and he was let go.

John didn't stay unemployed long. He heard that a local farmer was hiring boys to put up hay. John was the youngest and smallest worker there and probably the weakest. It was very hard work. He followed beside the bailing machine that was pulled by the tractor and threw the 60 lb. bails up onto a flatbed trailer. The guy on the flatbed would stack the bails as high as he could. When the trailer was full, it was towed back to the barn and situated so that the bails could be thrown down onto a conveyer that transported the bails up from the ground to the hay mow. There were three jobs at that point. One person threw the bails off the trailer onto the conveyer. One person in the hay mow would catch the bails as they came off the conveyer and would throw them back to where one or two boys would carry the bails back into the barn and stack them. The hay mow was hot and humid, and the air was thick with hay dust. The sweat rolled down John's face when he worked the hay mow.

But, lunchtime was a treat. The farmer went to McDonald's and bought them all lunch, including chocolate milkshakes. The boys sat on the grass in the shade and ate their lunches. After lunch, they went back to the fields and started the process again. By the end of the day, John was extremely tired but exhilarated by the fact that he was paid $2.50 per hour. That was more than double he had ever made before.

John bailed hay for a few days until the fields were done. He was called back for one more cutting that summer. It had been a productive summer, and John had some money to show for it.

Chapter 6

The sun was coming up over the willow tree, and it looked stunningly beautiful with its rays flickering between the thin green leaves. The other souls were milling about, so John decided to learn more about his new neighbors.

John went back to the group and immediately noticed that something was different about the gathering. There were many sad countenances among them, and some even seemed to be crying.

"What's wrong?" John asked Ben.

"It's Al. He's gone. And, unfortunately, we have a strong suspicion as to where he went."

"Oh, no. He was such a sad young man."

"Yes, he was. We don't know exactly why or how it happens," said Ben. "One day they're here and the next day they're gone. It seems to happen to the saddest among us or the ones who are angry with God. They don't adjust to things around here, and they're focused on their own grief more than they are on the feelings and history of others. Al was like that."

"I'm so sorry to hear that. I tried to speak with him the other day, but he told me he didn't feel like talking."

"That was Al. Don't worry. It wasn't anything you said or did, John."

John and Ben moved away from the crowd.

"Tell me about him, Ben."

"Well, we never learned too much about him. All I know is that he was a teenager from the Plum area who overdosed on sleeping pills. He killed himself because he was rejected by a girl with whom he was infatuated. She never even came to his funeral. His parents were devastated at the time of his death. But, as time wore on and they got old, they came to the cemetery less and less often. Eventually, they only showed up here on his birthday, which was yesterday, and they didn't come."

"That's so very sad," said John.

"Yes. It is."

"I'm not trying to be callous, but how long will everyone be in mourning?"

"It varies with the soul. A few will be sad for some time, but most will be ready to communicate with you soon."

Ben pointed toward the souls who were not with the congregation.

"You see them, John?"

"Yes, I do. Those are the ones who really need the most help, I'd guess."

"You'd guess correctly. They are the angry and sad ones. Today might be a good day to try to make an acquaintance with one or more of them. It couldn't hurt, and it might do you some good, too, John."

"Thanks for the advice, Ben. That's what I'll do."

John floated quietly past the pond, the ducks, and the willow tree to the far north corner of the cemetery. There he found a young woman by herself. She was floating next to a small marker that was nearly flush with the dewy grass. The marker had raised bronze letters that spelled out the name, "*Wanda Charles.*"

"Hello, there. Are you Wanda?" he asked.

"Yes. I'm Wanda. What do you want?" she asked curtly. She was a pretty blonde young woman with blue eyes that glared at him when she spoke. Wanda had that same foggy look to her that Al had.

"My name is John. I'm kind of new here, and I just thought you might like to talk a little, so we could get to know each other."

"You look like you could be a dirty old man. Why would I want to talk to you?" she spit back.

John looked away for a moment, then turned back and said, "You look like you could be someone who could help me forget."

"Forget what?" she asked.

"Forget that I miss my wife so very much."

"I knew it! You ARE a dirty old man. If nobody's told you yet, there is no sex here, John. So, why don't you go and "forget" with someone else?"

"I didn't mean it like that, Wanda. I assure you. I just wanted the pleasure of talking with you."

She looked back at him.

"Oh," she said. "I'm sorry for snapping at you."

"Not a problem. Would you like me to tell you about myself or would you like to start?" asked John.

"Why don't you start, John? Tell me about your wife."

"Should I hold your hand as we talk?"

"I guess so. But, don't try anything funny," she said smiling. Her gray cast seemed to lessen, and John was happy to see she had a sense of humor.

"I promise."

John reached out and held her hand. He felt a pain in his mind that he had felt once before. There was something dark and dangerous about her life.

"Brenda was the love of my life," he said.

John proceeded to talk about Brenda and the life they had together. He also talked about his two children and five grandchildren.

"I was adopted," Wanda blurted.

"No kidding?" said John gently.

"My real mom and dad died in a car accident when I was eight. They were very good parents, but I never forgave them for leaving me. I was in foster care for three years before I was adopted. It was a terrible time being packed off from one set of foster parents to the next. Some of them were cruel and were just in it for the money from the state. There were nice ones, but I still resented them because I felt they didn't want me since they wouldn't adopt me.

Finally, I got my adoptive parents. At first, I was happy. Then I realized how strict and stern they were. Maybe I needed that kind of structure, I don't know. But at the time, I felt it was too much to deal with, so I never bonded with them. By the time

I was 13, I was already getting into trouble. I got caught shoplifting and I smoked weed. I also started having sex. My adoptive parents tried to control me, but I was uncontrollable.

I ran away when I was 16, but the police found me and brought me back home. From then on, my parents practically had me under lock and key. So, at 17, I ran away again, this time with my boyfriend who was 21 at the time, and we got married out-of-state. His name was Zack. He used to smack me around because I would always mouth off to him. Then he'd bring me flowers and we'd make up and start the process all over again."

"Why didn't you leave him, Wanda?" John asked.

"I didn't leave him for years because I thought I loved him, and I thought he loved me. He would always apologize after hitting me. He would even cry and beg for my forgiveness."

"I see," said John.

"Eventually, I got tired of getting beat up. When he put me in the hospital, I decided to get a divorce."

"Good for you," said John.

"I had to get a restraining order against him because he kept trying to get me to go back with him. I'm just glad we didn't have any kids.

By that time, I was 22 and felt like I was 50. I began hanging around in bars and would go home with just about any guy who showed interest in me. There were some nice guys among them, but most were more like Zack.

I worked as a waitress at a diner for several years, then got married again to a nice guy. His name was Tom. He was a welder and the first person who ever treated me nice."

"So, you lived happily ever after?"

"No. We didn't. I eventually went back to hanging out at the bar, then cheated on Tom with a man I'd never met before."

"Why in the world did you do that?" John asked. "You said your husband treated you well."

"I don't know exactly why I did it. I guess I was still lonely. I don't really know."

"Did he find out?"

"Yeah, he did. The man I cheated with showed up at our house and wanted me to go away with him. He told my husband everything," replied Wanda.

"What did your husband do?"

"Tom threw me out of the house and told me never to come back. I begged him for forgiveness and told him it was just a mistake; that I'd never cheat on him again. But, he wouldn't listen. I had nowhere to go, so I went with the man I cheated with.

As it turned out, this guy was bad—worse than my first husband. He took me to his apartment where he immediately tried to rape me. I was so upset I didn't want anything to do with him and tried to fight him off. He was so enraged I wouldn't have sex with him that he choked me to death."

"My God! I'm so sorry you had such a horrible experience," said John.

"It was a terrible way to go, that's for sure. It was all my fault, too."

"No, Wanda," John said shaking his head. "It was not all your fault. What he did to you was not your fault. You may have made mistakes but you did not deserve to get murdered. You have to forgive yourself."

"Thank you, John. That was the first time I told anyone what happened to me. Now, I'm here in the Garden. I felt so ashamed I didn't want to be around the other souls."

John felt her spirit lift after she had told her story. She hugged him and the grayness left her.

"You look wonderful now, Wanda. Your cloud has lifted. Your eyes are sparkling and you're smiling at me."

"It's all your doing, John," she said.

"But you met me halfway, Wanda. I think that means you're ready to start healing now. Why don't you come with me? I think there are some souls you're going to want to meet."

Somewhat reluctantly, Wanda followed John to the group. When they arrived, John held Wanda's hand as the congregation of souls looked on in amazement.

"Group, this is Wanda. Wanda, this is the group." There was joy in all their voices as they greeted and welcomed her. Her smile was all he needed to be happy that day.

Ben went over to John while the others gathered around Wendy.

"You, my friend, have a gift. John, you can't imagine how important this step is for her."

John hung out in the background while the congregation of souls welcomed Wanda into their inner circle. Wanda's story had somehow weakened him but at the same time, he felt a sense of achievement.

That night, John floated back to his gravestone to contemplate his experiences. He thought about his own teen years and felt fortunate to have had caring parents. They didn't push but they encouraged him in his studies during his years at Jefferson High School. His grades were barely above average and he was considered, by many, to be an underachiever.

John got a dishwashing job at the Lucky Steer Steak House restaurant while living at home, so he had a little spending money. John's father helped him buy a green and white, six-cylinder, 4-door '57 Chevy to drive back and forth to school and work. It was in fairly good shape and proved to be dependable transportation, though it certainly wasn't anything fancy.

John started smoking when he got a job at a nearby grocery store. The first time he bought a pack of cigarettes of his own, he put them on the seat of his car and went to pick up Paul at a dance. Though smoking was strictly forbidden by his mother and father, John was smoking when Paul and his girlfriend got into the car.

"You shouldn't be smoking," said Paul.

"Just don't say anything about it to Mom and Dad."

John drove Paul's girlfriend to her house and then they went home. When they got home, Paul went inside while John hid his cigarette pack behind a cardboard section under the dash on the passenger's side of his car. When John went into the house, his mother was waiting for him.

"Have you been smoking, John? You smell like cigarette smoke," she asked.

"No, Mom. I was just around guys who were smoking at work."

"Okay. Goodnight."

"Goodnight, Mom."

The next morning, John woke up to find his father sitting on the edge of his bed.

"Good morning, John."

"Good morning, Dad."

"Last night, your mother thought you had been smoking but you told her you hadn't. So, this morning at 3 a.m., we went out and searched your car. Guess what we found?" John's father produced a pack of cigarettes from his shirt pocket.

"Are these your cigarettes?"

"No, Dad," John said. "Those are my friend's cigarettes. He was riding in the car with me and must have forgotten them in the car. I didn't want to leave them sitting on the seat, so I hid them."

John's dad stared at him.

"All right, I'll believe you this time. But if I ever find out you've lied to me . . ."

It was at about this time that John's mother yelled, "Luther, get in here!"

Paul began yelling, "I didn't mean to tell! I didn't mean to tell!"

John was crestfallen. The jig was up and he knew it.

"John, get in the kitchen!" John's dad yelled. "Louise, you and Paul get in there, too!"

Once they were all in the kitchen and dining area, John's dad took off his belt.

"I can stand a lot of things but I will not tolerate a liar!" By now, John's dad was nearly frothing at the mouth with rage. "Now, pull your pants down and turn around."

John obeyed. He knew he was in for a beating but vowed to himself he would not scream or yell when he got hit. He wouldn't give his dad the satisfaction. John pulled down his pajamas and leaned against the dining room chair.

"Pull down your underpants, too."

John turned around and looked at his dad in disbelief.

"Do it!"

John pulled his underpants down and resumed his position leaning against the chair. He was furious that his father would have him standing naked in front of his mother and brother.

Whack! Whack! Whack!

John knew his father was putting his full strength into the belting and though he quivered and shook with each strike, he refused to cry out.

Whack! Whack! Whack!

"Don't . . . you . . . ever . . . lie . . . to . . . me . . . again!" he said between strokes to John's butt and legs. Even though the strokes still hurt, John could tell his father was tiring.

Whack! Whack! Whack!

"Now, pull up your pants! And don't ever lie to me again. Do you understand me?"

"Yes, sir," said John as he pulled up his pants.

John remembered this incident vividly. He never fully forgave his father or his mother for it. He knew he had lied and deserved punishment but to have him standing naked at 17 years old in front of his younger brother, Paul, and his mother during the beating seemed unforgivable. *Perhaps now was the time to forgive*, he thought.

John remembered another time he was awakened by one of his parents. It was a Saturday morning and his mother sat on the bed next to him.

"I'm afraid I have some bad news for you, John." She hesitated for a moment, then continued.

"Your friend Larry was killed in a car accident last night."

John couldn't believe what she was saying.

"Oh, my gosh! I just saw him at church on Thursday night. Are you sure it's him?"

"I'm afraid so, John. He apparently rolled his VW Beetle after going off the side of the road. He was only a few blocks from home when it happened. It took them quite a while to identify him because he had several fake ID's in his wallet. He also had alcohol in the car with him at the time."

John knew Larry drank a lot. He used to hide bottles of vodka under bushes in other people's yards. He also wore a lot of cologne to mask his alcohol use.

When John went to the viewing, he and Eric were there to comfort Larry's mother and father. His mother did not bear up well under the pain and cried while they were there. When John and Eric went up to look at Larry's body, they barely recognized him. The undertaker did not do a good job of making him look like himself, despite all the makeup.

John couldn't escape feeling that Larry was there, behind the casket by the draperies, looking down at his two friends. *If he was there*, he thought, *he was probably laughing at us.*

The next day at the funeral, the funeral home was filled to standing room as there were hundreds of students from high school in attendance. John and Eric were standing in the back, making it impossible to hear the service. After the service, John and Eric rode with Jessie in his red Corvair Spider to the cemetery. On the way, they talked about their adventures at church camp and some of the funny things the four of them did. It seemed odd to be laughing when one of their best friends was dead.

They also talked about Larry being a great swimmer on the high school team and how he and his brother swam in a race down the Mississippi river the year before. The issue of Larry's drinking also came up. Eric and Jessie said they knew Larry was an alcoholic like his dad before him. His father had given up drinking years before and attended church regularly. After the service at the cemetery, the three friends were quiet on their way back. They knew they would miss their friend and that things wouldn't be the same without him.

After graduation from high school, John did not know what he wanted to do. A friend from church was attending Abilene Christian College in Abilene, Texas and suggested John apply. It sounded like a good idea at the time, so John took the ACT exam and received the score necessary to get into the college. John's parents were thrilled he was going to attend a Christian college, so they helped to foot the bill for the first semester. His church also gave him a scholarship of $35 per month to help with expenses.

John took a Greyhound bus to Abilene. It was quite a long trip from Lafayette, Indiana. It cost $36 and took 36 hours. The bus seemed to stop at every Podunk town, dropping off and picking up passengers along the way. Once he arrived, John got squared away in his dorm room. His roommate was a Texan named Tom who was from College Station. They immediately struck up a friendship and got along great throughout the year.

Money was very tight while he was at ACC, so John took on a couple of part-time jobs. One job was handling dry cleaning for his dorm. The other job was working in the cafeteria basement in what was referred to as "the snake pit." It was a large dishwashing room that handled all the cafeteria trays after the students had eaten. The trays would go down a conveyor belt where the first person in the assembly line would remove the paper and silverware from the trays. At the next station, two people placed glasses into overhead bins and scraped the leftover food into a trough where running water flushed the food down into a commercial disposal. The last station was the dishwasher. He gathered up the glasses, silverware, plates and trays and fed them into a giant conveyor-style dishwashing machine.

When everything was working well, it was a very efficient operation. In down times, the workers used to kid around and sometimes had food fights using the leftover food from the trays as they came down the assembly line. In busy times, the line would stall because there was just too much to handle. John worked at each of the stations at one time or another. It was hot, dirty, greasy work, and John went back to his dorm every night smelling of grease.

John could not get into studying. When he tried to read, he would fall asleep. He spent many of his waking free hours playing tennis, handball, shooting pool or bowling.

He attended his classes but often missed the required morning chapel. At one point, he had missed several weeks in a row which generated a letter from the administration stating he was being given a warning. If he missed again, he would be given a second warning and a reprimand. If he missed a third time, he would be kicked out of school. It wasn't long before he got his second warning, so John began going to chapel every day.

John only went to church once during his time at ACC. He just wasn't into it. He was required to take religious courses each semester and felt that was enough. John had some good friends who were genuine Christians but also knew some real hypocrites. One guy he knew talked about being the son of a preacher in Kansas City and he planned on becoming a preacher, too. He said the money was good if you could lead a larger church. The benefits included a free place to live and a new car every three years. This guy also bragged about beating up "queers" in downtown Kansas City for fun. He said he went to jail once for breaking a "queer's" jaw. In church, you'd never suspect he was a real jerk.

A contrarian as far as religion was concerned, John considered himself to be an agnostic, so he questioned everything about religion. He also smoked cigarettes in his dorm room, which was allowed as long as his roommate didn't object. However, smoking was forbidden everywhere else on campus. John never drank except once when he rode with two other ACC students back to Lafayette for Christmas vacation. They stopped at a restaurant and had a beer with their meal. Of course, John was under age but they never checked his ID.

He started dating a girl from Ft. Worth named Pamela. She was a beautiful 18-year-old blonde he'd been fixed-up with one weekend. They immediately hit it off and John made the trip to Ft. Worth twice—once by hitch-hiking and the other by way of a ride in a 1963 Corvette with a friend who was headed for Dallas. The Corvette ride was exciting as the driver drove over 110 mph at one point.

John barely got through his first semester with a "C" average. Later, in the second semester, John got a letter from one of the elders of his home church in Lafayette stating he'd been accused of drinking while on campus and buying alcohol in the town of Impact, Texas. If these accusations proved to be true, the church would cut off his $35-per-month scholarship. Abilene was in a dry county, while Impact, which was just across the county line, had several liquor stores that sold alcohol to students. John was not one of those students. He wrote back to the elder and told him that not only had he not had a drink at school, he had never been to the town of Impact and wouldn't even know how to get there. The elder wrote back saying the church would continue to support him. He finished his first year but felt it was a waste of time.

Pamela and John continued to write to each other while he was attending ACC but once he got home, he felt a long-distance relationship would be fruitless and quit writing.

John received correspondence from his friend, Eric, who had enlisted in the Army earlier that year. Eric went through basic, then trained as a Communications Center Specialist and was assigned to a unit in Germany. He said he enjoyed the Army and recommended it to John.

Chapter 7

The next morning, it was raining in the Garden of Peace. John never felt the rain, but he noticed the wet leaves on the trees and the grass, and watched as the droplets hit the water on the pond. The granite tombstones glistened.

John went to the gathering and noticed Wanda there. She appeared to be happy and talking with the others in the group. John caught her eye and she smiled at him.

"Thank you, John," she said and then turned to continue her conversation with the others.

John nodded and waved.

Rex was off to one side, so John decided to talk to the young man in uniform.

"Good morning, Rex," John said.

"That was a good thing you did for Wanda," he said. "She's much happier now."

"All I did was listen to her story. That's what she needed."

"Whatever you did, you helped her, sir."

"Don't call me sir," said John in mock anger. "I worked for a living."

Rex laughed. "I haven't heard that one for a long time, John."

"Why don't we shake hands and you can tell me about yourself, Rex?"

John shook his hand and held onto it as they moved toward the cemetery entrance.

"Where do you want me to start?"

"To start with, when were you born?"

"I was born June 1st, 1899 and grew up in Greensburg, Pennsylvania. My parents were Martha and Edmond Brooks, and I was the youngest of nine children. My father was an engineer for the railroad."

"Interesting. Did your father ever take you for a ride on the train?" asked John.

"Yes, he did, and he even let me blow the whistle once when I was 10."

"That must have been fun."

"It was very exciting. I never forgot it."

"What was it like growing up in a house full of kids?"

"It was kind of fun, actually. We had a big house and I had five brothers and three sisters. My brothers used to tease me relentlessly but they also protected me because I was the runt of the litter. I eventually got bigger but I was very slight of build until I was 15.

Mostly, I helped my mother. She was a wonderful cook and I helped her in the kitchen just about every day after school. She taught me how to make pierogis, meat pies, cookies, pies, and cakes. I was never embarrassed to help her. In fact, it made me want to become a cook."

"It sounds as if you had a very nice childhood, Rex," said John.

"I guess I did."

"Tell me about your time in the military. Were you drafted?"

"No. Not long after war was declared, I decided I wanted to be a Marine, so I joined in 1917. I went by train to Philadelphia where I did my training. It was tough training but I learned quickly and got along well. I was part of the 3rd Battalion 5th Marine Regiment when we took a troop ship to France. When we got there, we were certain we would be able to end the war with our fighting ability. I mostly fought in the trenches until June 6th, 1918. Several of my friends were killed by machine gun fire as we attacked the Germans at Belleau Wood. I almost made it to the German lines but encountered a young German soldier that afternoon. We had already fixed bayonets on our rifles and we stood there facing each other—both of us out of ammunition. I tried to remember my training days and managed to fend off his first thrust with a parry. But I slipped in the mud and lost my balance. He thrust once more and stabbed me in the belly. I remember lying on the ground and moaning in tremendous pain for what seemed like many hours. Then I went unconscious.

I vaguely remember being transported to a hospital aid station in the rear where they tried to patch me up. I thought I was going to make it. They put me on a ship back to the U.S., and I spent some time in a hospital in Washington, D.C. All I remember afterwards is that I got an infection and had a bad fever.

My parents came to visit me in the hospital just a day before I died. They decided to take my body back to Pennsylvania, and that's how I ended up here."

"Wow," John said. "That's quite an experience."

"That's true. I have the Purple Heart along with my other medals to prove it."

"Do you regret having served?" asked John.

"No regrets at all. I became a Marine and died a Marine's death. I do wish I hadn't died, of course. I missed a lot."

"Why are you still here do you think?"

"I wish I knew. Maybe it's because I feel such an attachment to the Garden here. As I'm sure you've noticed, I guard the gates when new souls arrive."

"I remember. Perhaps that's a noble cause."

"I have to say, I am getting tired these days. Maybe I'll start thinking of moving on soon. I've been here for nearly 100 years now. It seems like a long time."

"That is a long time."

"How rude of me, John. I've been doing all the talking. Why don't you tell me about your own military service?"

"Okay. Well, since I didn't go back to college after my first year, I was designated 1A for the draft. My draft number turned out to be 35, so I knew I would be drafted if I didn't enlist. I didn't want to let the military dictate what branch of service I would go to, and I didn't want to end up in the infantry. So, I decided to enlist in the Army and tried to get the same job that my friend had—the Signal Corps. I was inducted into the Army at the Indianapolis in-processing station in September of 1969."

John then went on to recall the day he left for basic training.

"My mother cried and hugged me while I prepared to get on the bus. My father shook my hand and said, 'Be careful, son, and don't be a hero. Just do your job, and you'll be fine.'

I boarded the bus and waved to my parents as the bus left. I admit I got a little misty-eyed, but I didn't cry.

When I got to the in-processing station, I followed other young men into a waiting area and sat on a long, wooden bench with the others. I didn't have to wait long. All of us were hustled into a large room that had yellow shoeprints painted on the floor.

'Stand on a set of footprints, drop your pants, and take off your shirts and undershirts,' said a middle-aged slender man with a clip-board. He sported a black flat-top haircut and barked his orders as if he did this all day every day. 'Keep your underwear on until you're told to drop them.'

A doctor in a lab coat soon came by with a stethoscope and put it to the chest of each of us and listened, no doubt, for irregular sounds of the heart. Next, the doctor went behind us and listened to our lungs as we were directed to take deep breaths.

'Drop your underwear,' said the flat-top when the doctor had finished listening to our lungs.

'Now, bend over and spread your cheeks,' he said with enthusiasm. The doctor used a small flashlight and inspected each man's rear end.

'Okay, let go of your cheeks and stand up straight. Keep your shorts down. When the doctor gets in front of you, turn your head and cough.'

Each of us coughed in turn as the doctor, with a gloved-hand, pressed his fingers under our scrotums. I felt more like a nameless piece of meat than a human being after suffering these indignities. But at least I wasn't alone. I'm sure each man felt the same way.

When the doctor had finished, Flat-top said, 'Now, pull up your pants, put your shirts on, and go back to the waiting area. Sit on the bench until your name is called.'

We all did as instructed and waited on the bench. It seemed like a long time, but, eventually, Flat-top reappeared with a clipboard in hand.

'When I call out your name, sound off 'Here!' then get in line behind me. Arnett, Bigelow, Donaldson, Fisher . . .' I knew I would be among the last to be called. 'Moore, Parsons, Randall . . . Randall, is that your last name or your first name?'

A weak voice spoke up. 'My last name.'

'That's 'Last name, sir!' he barked. 'And speak up like you have a pair. I know you do because the doctor just checked.'

'Randall is my last name, SIR!' yelled the young man.

'Sample.'

'Here, sir!' I yelled.

'Taylor and Williams.'

The others and I formed a loose line behind Flat-top.

'Follow me,' he said.

The line of men followed Flat-top down a hallway, then entered another large room that had a flag on a pole in the corner and a large picture of President Lyndon Johnson on the wall.

'Stand on a set of footprints,' growled Flat-top.

Each of us found a set of yellow shoe-prints to stand on.

'Now, when I start, you will each take the oath as I recite it to you. And when I say, 'State your name,' you are to say your name at that time. You don't say, 'State your name.' Do you understand me?'

'Yes, sir!' we sang out in chorus.

We all followed the instructions:

'I, John Sample, do solemnly swear that I will support and defend the Constitution of the United States against all enemies, foreign and domestic; that I will bear true faith and allegiance to the same; and that I will obey the orders of the President of the United States and the orders of the officers appointed over me, according to regulations and the Uniform Code of Military Justice. So, help me God.'

I was now in the U.S. Army but had no idea of what was in store for me."

"Yes, I remember going through all that, too. How was your basic training, John?"

"It was pretty tough. Shortly after we were sworn in, we all boarded a Greyhound bus to Ft. Knox, Kentucky. The drill sergeants there were all Vietnam vets, and since Vietnam was very active at the time, I think they felt a special mission to harden us enough to go over there.

When they picked us up at the reception station, they looked very intimidating in their drill instructor round and brown campaign hats that were kind of like yours. They all seemed like they were angry at us. By this time, we had all received our fatigue uniforms and boots and stuffed them in a duffel bag. The duffel bag was heavy, and the drill instructors made us hoist the bags onto our shoulders and double-timed us for over a mile to our basic training unit. Some of the men couldn't keep up, and the DI's were merciless on them. I'd never heard so much swearing in all my life. It was if they had turned cussing into an art form. When we finally got up the hill to our unit, they made us drop the duffel bags in front of us in the company street and immediately started making us do push-ups. I remember at least one trainee throwing up.

While we were still in the push-up position, the Senior Drill Instructor—a tall, trim, dark black man—stood up and began to yell a speech at us about how their mission was to prepare us for combat and that 'every swinging dick' was going to be ready to kill 'gooks' in Vietnam by the end of our 8-week training."

Rex laughed. "That sounds a lot like the beginning of my basic training in the Marines."

John continued. "He then got us to our feet, had us lift our duffel bags to our shoulders again, and marched us in front of several barracks. The Senior DI had a clipboard and began reading names off, assigning us to one of five barracks. I was assigned to the last barracks which they called 5th platoon. He informed us that our unit was called Echo-19-5, which meant, E Company, 19th Battalion, 5th Training Brigade.

Once we were all separated into our platoons, we got into a rough formation in front of the barracks that would be our home for 8 weeks. The barracks was a long, two-story, yellowish-beige wooden building that sat atop concrete blocks about 2 ½ to 3 feet above the ground. There were windows along each side and a short set of stairs leading up to the building near the front. A yard of sorts separated each barracks on one side and what I learned later was a 'low-crawl pit' on the other.

When we met our platoon's drill instructor, he turned out to be a stocky, black man by the name of Staff Sergeant Walters. He was of average height and looked like a heavy-weight boxer. He didn't yell at us. Instead, he spoke with a low, gravelly voice that was at times difficult to hear, which was sometimes worse than yelling because we couldn't hear what he was ordering us to do.

'I will be your mother and father for the next 8 weeks,' he'd said. 'You will do what I say, when I say it. There will be no back-talk.'

With him were two assistants—both thin, one white, one black, and both wore three stripes on their sleeves and painted helmet liners we called 'hard-hats' on their heads. They smirked each time the DI swore at us or called us names.

When we were told to, we scurried into our barracks and lined up in front of the bunks. Our DI came into the barracks and told us how we were to keep the barracks spotless and keep the 'butt cans' properly filled with water and cleaned each day, even though we were not allowed to smoke in the barracks.

The first thing they did was to get bunks, lockers and footlockers assigned to us. We were shown how to tie our laundry bags to the end of our bunks, how we were to display our shoes and boots under the bottom bunk, how to hang our dress uniforms in the lockers, and how to make our beds. Later that day, we were marched to the local Post Exchange, or PX, to purchase black shoe polish, a razor, shaving cream, deodorant, a toothbrush, toothpaste, and a can of Brasso for polishing our brass. The sergeants marched us back to the barracks, and spent the rest of the day teaching us the fundamentals of drill and ceremony. We were taught how to come to the position of attention, right-face, left-face, about-face, at-ease, parade rest, dress-right-dress, and hand salute. The sergeants barked at us if we didn't do as we were told. Some who repeated mistakes were put down for push-ups. Sometimes, they made us do push-ups for no apparent reason.

I had a top bunk, and when we finally turned in for the night at 9 p.m., I was physically and mentally exhausted. The sound of *Taps* was heard over the loud speaker. It was the loneliest sound I'd ever heard. I immediately fell asleep and slept soundly until 4:30 a.m. when they woke us up with the clamor of trash cans being banged with their lids and the sergeants' yelling. We all sprang from our beds and stood by our bunks in our skivvies.

'When I say go,' the drill sergeant said, 'you will get in the latrine, do your 3 s's, that's shit, shower and shave, then get your fatigues and boots on and be in the company street in 30 minutes. Do you understand me?'

The platoon answered with a variety of faint replies such as, 'yes, sergeant, yes, drill sergeant, and yes, sir.'

Sergeant Walters had a disgusted look on his face.

'Don't look at me, you pussies! Keep your eyes straight ahead and stand at the position of attention when I talk to you. When I tell you to do something, you say, 'yes, drill sergeant!' And you will say it like you've got a pair. Do you understand?'

'Yes, Drill Sergeant!' we yelled.

'Go!' he shouted.

All of us immediately went for the doorway of the latrine. It looked like a scene from a *Three-Stooges* movie as we all tried to go through the doorway at the same time.

I was among the closest to the door and got right into the shower. I soaped myself down, rinsed, and got out quickly. Even though there were eight sinks, I had to wait for a sink to shave in. I shaved quickly and nicked myself more than once with the double-edged razor. As my hair had been buzz-cut while in the reception station, there was no hair to comb. I went back to my bunk, got dressed with the same fatigues I had worn the day before and made my bunk before going out to the company street. Some of the men were already there milling around and having a smoke. By the time I got out there, the sergeants were already barking orders.

'Get in formation!' one of the hard-hats yelled.

We tried to remember how to line up and dress-right-dress, but our formation wasn't very uniform.

'We've got a bunch of morons!' he said. 'These trainees can't even remember how to get in formation. We only taught you that yesterday. Dress-right-dress! Don't look at me, you idiots. You should be looking straight ahead.'

Sergeant Walters got in front of the assembled formation and began giving lessons on drill-and-ceremony and how to march properly. Several of the trainees stumbled or made missteps while we marched. The hard-hats took them out of formation and had them do push-ups while the rest of us continued our lessons.

Finally, we got back into formation at parade-rest in front of our barracks and awaited our next command. A voice in the distance yelled, 'Company!' Sergeant Walters and the other drill sergeants then said, 'Platoon!' The voice in the distance commanded, 'Atten-tion!' We all snapped to the position of attention. The next thing we heard was the sound of *Reveille* being sounded over a loud speaker."

"I remember those things, too," said Rex. "I guess we have a lot in common."

"I'm sure all members of the military have to go through a lot of the same things. Do you want me to go on?"

"Absolutely," said Rex. "You're bringing back some great memories."

"Okay. Well, after *Reveille*, we were marched to the mess hall. We were the last in line, so the sergeants had us doing physical training while we waited. We did push-ups, jumping jacks, and other exercises. We also did our turns on the horizontal ladder, which was set up right beside the mess hall.

When we finally got inside the mess hall, even the cooks yelled at us to hurry up. The Senior Drill Instructor announced we only had 10 minutes to eat. When we sat down, we gobbled up the bacon, eggs, and toast like we hadn't eaten in days. It tasted good but I was in such a hurry I barely chewed my food."

Rex laughed. "I remember that, too."

"After breakfast, it felt like we were going to get into a routine. We marched back to the barracks and did more physical training and drill-and-ceremony. When we got back into the barracks, we found most of the bunks had been stripped.

The hard-hats were waiting for us inside.

'We taught you how to make your bunks but most of them looked like shit. Now, make them over again, and this time do it right. If you can't remember how to do it, get someone to teach you,' the white one said.

Fortunately, I had made mine correctly, so I helped others.

'I should be able to bounce a quarter off your bunk when I come by to inspect it,' the black one said.

When Sergeant Walters came into the barracks, the hard-hats called us to attention. He told us we had to learn the chain-of-command. There were pictures with names hanging on the wall of the officers and generals who made up the chain-of-command. The president of the United States was pictured there as Commander-in-Chief. There was also a poster on the wall of the ranks of the Army, which we also had to learn. Finally, there was a poster that explained the general orders and the Code of Conduct. We had to learn those, too.

The drill sergeant explained that each squad was responsible for standing fire guard at night, which just meant we had to take turns walking the hall with a flashlight for two hours while everyone else slept. After this training, we went outside for more PT until they got us back into formation in the street.

From there, they marched us as a company to a concrete block building that sat next to a large, flat, gravel field. We took a break, and the hard-hats told us to, 'Smoke 'em if you've got 'em.' Almost immediately, a large cloud of smoke went up. I had smoked some when I was in high school and college, so I bummed a cigarette off one of the other guys standing next to me. The skinny white hard-hat got in front of us and instructed us on the process of field-stripping a cigarette. We were then told to put the cigarette butt in our pants pocket until we came across a butt can or trash can.

After our break, we were marched into the building and took our seats. A drill sergeant got up to a podium and began teaching a class on military history.

From then on, it was practicing our drill-and-ceremony, PT, and classes for about a week. The next exciting thing that happened was when they issued our weapons. We lined up at the armory building, and we were each issued an M-14 rifle with a serial number we were to memorize. Once we were issued our weapons, we were taught how to break them down, clean them, and put them back together."

"I was issued a Springfield," said Rex. "Got to be a pretty good shot, too."

"We did a lot of rifle training, didn't we?"

"I think that was the most fun we had," replied Rex.

John agreed.

"So, we trained and fired our weapons. We fired from the prone position, the kneeling position, the standing position, and the foxhole position. And then we trained, shot, and trained and shot some more. Eventually, we started training for our PT test.

The Physical Training test was comprised of the horizontal ladders, the low-crawl, the grenade-throw, the run-dodge-and-jump, the 150-yard man-carry, sit-ups, and the one-mile run."

"You were lucky, John. We had to run 3 miles in the Marines."

"Wow. I had trouble running just one mile, Rex.

Because of my high scores on the initial testing, they had me try out for Officer's Candidate School. But after my interview, they told me their quota was filled and I should try again in 6 months. I immediately decided that I didn't want to become an officer because that would have meant an additional year of service. Plus, I'd heard 2nd lieutenants didn't have a very long life-span in Vietnam. Some of them were even getting 'fragged' by their own men. I decided, 'no thanks' to becoming an officer."

"Officers seemed to have it pretty good, though, didn't they John?"

"Yeah, they did. But I didn't get to know any officers until I got back from Vietnam.

In the 3rd week, there was one trainee, Private Langston, who was always screwing up and causing us to have extra PT. One night, my squad leader said we were going to have a blanket party for him. I had heard about it and was hopeful I'd never get one. Five of us from our squad, plus the fireguard that night, were all in on it. We snuck upstairs to Langston's top bunk, then three of us got on each side with the fireguard at the head of the bunk. Two men grabbed the blanket and pulled it over Langston's head, and the fireguard held it down so he couldn't move. The rest of us began punching Langston for about five seconds.

'Keep the blanket over your head, and don't say anything, Langston, or you'll get another one even worse. Now, stop screwing up,' the squad leader whispered next to Langston's head.

We all went back downstairs and got into bed. I was ashamed of what I'd done and had trouble falling back asleep. The next day, Sergeant Walters asked Langston why he was all bruised up.

'I fell down the stairs, Drill Sergeant,' Langston replied. No more was ever spoken about the incident.

So, anyway, we got to the 4th week. By then, we thought we had become accustomed to military life and were on the downhill slide. That's when our drill sergeant and the hard-hats had a different idea. When we got back from training one day, we went into the barracks and it looked like a tornado had hit it. We found our bed covers thrown around, and the contents of our footlockers and wall lockers were in disarray. We were in shock. Then the drill sergeant and hard-hats came in. They looked angry and disgusted. We came to attention and feared what would happen next.

'You pathetic pieces of shit haven't learned a thing. You forgot how to make your bunks, and your lockers and footlockers look like crap. Now, you've got 15 minutes to put it all in order the way it's supposed to be. When you're finished, fall out into the company street. Do you understand me?'

'Yes, Drill Sergeant!' we all yelled.

Fortunately, my things weren't that badly messed up. I generally kept my stuff squared away. So, I got my things taken care of in about 5 minutes and ran out to the company street. As soon as everyone was outside, we formed up the platoon and stood at parade rest until the drill instructor came back.

'Now, you're going to do a little PT, and then we'll visit the low-crawl pit,' the drill sergeant grunted.

We did push-ups, squat-thrusts, and jumping jacks until we were exhausted. Then he marched us to the sawdust-filled low-crawl pit and by squads, we got into the low-crawl position in the pit and raced the other squads to the other end of the pit and back again. I could barely move afterwards. My clothes and body were covered with red sawdust and sweat. The low-crawl pit was not just exercise in preparation for the PT test, it was punishment.

After two trips through the pit, we were formed back into a platoon in the street. We were still panting from exhaustion, when the drill sergeant spoke again.

'You thought you knew what was going on around here and started getting lax on me. From now on, until the end of your 8 weeks, you will keep your shit straight and follow orders. Do you understand me?' he said with authority.

'Yes, Drill Sergeant!' we shouted.

'Now, hit the showers, change into clean fatigues, and get ready for chow,' he said, then added, 'Private Sample!'

'Yes, Drill Sergeant!' I replied, suddenly afraid of what was coming next.

'Come see me after you get cleaned up.'

'Yes, Drill Sergeant!'

As I showered and changed, I couldn't help but worry what Sergeant Walters wanted with me. When I was ready, I went to his room and knocked vigorously on his door.

'Enter!' a voice grunted from inside the room.

When I entered the room, the drill sergeant was sitting on his bunk and leaning against the wall, while the hard-hats and the platoon guide from New York stood in the room.

'Private Sample reporting as ordered, Drill Sergeant!' I said firmly.

'Private Sample. I heard you were a dumb son-of-a-bitch,' said Sergeant Walters.

I'm sure my face reddened, but without missing a beat, I looked at him and said, 'I may be dumb, Drill Sergeant, but I'm no son-of-a-bitch.'

Sergeant Walters laughed, then the others followed suit.

'Private Sample,' he said. 'I'm promoting you to squad leader.'

'Thank you, Drill Sergeant,' I said in shock.

'I just fired the last squad leader. So, if you can't keep your shit together and keep your squad in line, I'll fire your ass, too. Do you understand me?'

'Yes, Drill Sergeant.'

'That's all. Congratulations,' he added with a smile, then threw the arm-sleeve corporal stripes at me.

I left the room, and went out to the company street where I took my new position as squad leader. I was glad I got the promotion but worried I wouldn't live up to Sergeant Walters' expectations. The other squad leaders shook my hand and congratulated me.

All in all, it had been a very strange day," John said.

Chapter 8

"On my first day as squad leader, I met with the other squad leaders and the platoon guide. We met in the platoon guide's room, which was just like the drill sergeant's room. I couldn't believe my eyes when I went in there. They were sharing a marijuana cigarette and asked me if I wanted a hit. I declined, and they all laughed.

I had no idea the squad leaders had special privileges. I got special passes to go to the PX, and I got to go bowling one Saturday night. We drank 'near beer' that was only 3.2% alcohol, but I still got a little tipsy.

From then on, we trained like men on a mission. We just wanted to graduate from basic training and move onto the next phase of our military lives. Our training in the previous two weeks involved more weapons training, including the M-60 machine gun, grenade training, and the M-16 rifle. We did more hand-to-hand combat and bayonet training, and went through night-fire training.

They had us use B-B rifles twice. Once was in preparation for what was called 'quick-kill', which was to help us get used to a technique of making quick, accurate shots with a rifle. The other time we fought other squads in the woods at night. We wore face shields during the fight, but the B-Bs still stung when we got hit.

We had exercises where we negotiated barbed-wire hazards by lying on our backs with our rifles balanced on our bellies, and low-crawling backwards through the obstacle. We also low-crawled our way through a live-fire exercise where we had to crawl beneath live, machine-gun fire at night. With orange tracers being fired over our heads, we low-crawled past explosions going off in sand-bagged bunkers. It really gave us a sense of what it must have been like in WWII battles, except that no one was killed or injured."

"I remember similar training when I went through it 50 years earlier," said Rex. "It really got your blood pumping, didn't it?"

"You bet," said John.

"One of the last things we did was to go on bivouac for a couple of days. While on bivouac, we trained on the obstacle course and went through gas training. The gas training was done in two phases. First, we took classes about the different kinds of gas attacks, including CS gas, mustard gas, and nerve agents. We were taught to yell, 'GAS! GAS! GAS!' then put on our masks if we noticed the signs of a gas attack. We were shown how to put on the M-17 protective mask and how to clear it. Finally, we were sent to the 'gas chamber.'

The instructors lined us up outside of a plain block building and gave us last minute instructions on how to deal with a gas attack. The instructors popped CS gas canisters and yelled, 'GAS! GAS! GAS!' I removed my helmet, placed it between my knees, put on my mask, cleared it, and then replaced my helmet. From then on, we kept our masks on until we got to the gas chamber. When we got into the gas chamber in teams of two, we could see through the masks quite well. The room was manned by three instructors, each of whom had their mask on. Two were seated at a small table, while one stood near the entrance. One of them was heating the CS gas pellets with a Bunsen burner causing a thick cloud of white smoke to fill the room.

'When I tell you to, you will remove your helmet, place it between your knees, take off your mask, replace your helmet, take two deep breaths, say your name and your service number, then walk slowly to the door at the rear of the building. Do NOT run. Do you understand?'

'Yes, Sergeant,' we said.

'If you screw up, you'll go back and do it again until you get it right.'

We did as we were instructed. I could feel the burn in my throat by the time I started reciting my name and service number. I was fine and thought it wasn't so bad until I opened the rear door. As soon as I hit the cool, fresh air, my eyes swelled shut and tears streamed down my cheeks. This was a wooded area, so I was afraid I was going to walk into a tree. Just then, another trainee took my arm and guided me to the formation. It took a few minutes, but my eyes eventually cleared up. Some of the men threw up, while others fanned each other's eyes with their ponchos. Several of them were still coughing when the instructors called the men to attention.

'Now, you know how well the protective mask works. This is serious business, men, so don't ever take your mask for granted,' the instructor said. It was a good lesson.

We were still on bivouac when we marched to a weapons area where we practiced firing our rifles while wearing the M-17 protective mask. It was very awkward, and I could barely see the targets. But, I passed.

Later, we went through another live-fire exercise. This time, in teams of two and with live ammunition, we went through a course where one of us would cover, while the other moved to a log or a makeshift wall. The drill sergeants were close behind us during this drill until we had shot our last targets and cleared our weapons.

We also camped overnight twice using our tent-halves. It was only September, but it was cold the first night. We ate in the field between exercises, then marched up two long and steep hills which were aptly named '*Agony*' and '*Misery.*' Just as they did whenever we marched long distances, the drill sergeants called cadence in songs, which we mimicked to help the time go by quicker.

My favorite song was this one:

'*The prettiest girl I ever saw, was sipping bourbon through a straw. I put my hand upon her toe, she said young man, you're mighty low. I put my hand upon her knee, she said young man, quit teasing me. I put my hand upon her breast, it felt so good, we did the rest. And now I've got a mother-in-law, and 14 kids who call me 'Pa.' The moral of, the story's clear, instead of bourbon, stick to beer.*'

In each section, we would repeat the phrase and then call off the ending. It made marching tolerable.

By the time we got back to our barracks, we were totally exhausted. We turned in our weapons and reformed the platoon in front of our barracks.

'Platoon, atten-tion!' the drill sergeant shouted. 'Now, you're going to put away your shit, take a shower, change into clean fatigues, and get ready for chow.' Then he said, 'Fall-out.'

We did as we were told. The hot shower felt good, and I wanted to stay in there forever. But I was also hungry, so I didn't linger. Chow was delicious that evening. We had meatloaf, mashed potatoes and gravy, corn and bread. I didn't know food could taste that good. Even though we still couldn't dawdle, I savored every bite. And, that night, I slept without dreaming. I was beat.

We were almost through. We took the final PT test, which I almost aced except for being 20 seconds off a perfect time on the mile run.

At the rifle range, I scored a respectable 'Sharp Shooter' score, one down from 'Expert.'

One of our final classes was on Explosive Ordinance Disposal (EOD) or bomb disposal. They talked about the different kinds of explosives we were likely to encounter in the field, like the Claymore mine, the 'Bouncing Betty' and unexploded artillery shells. At the end of the class, the instructor asked if anyone was interested in taking up EOD as a Military Occupational Specialty (MOS) for extra pay. No one from our group volunteered. It certainly sounded too dangerous to me.

Finally, we were down to one day before graduation. We looked back on our time in basic and realized how much we had endured and how much we had learned about the military. We were proud of ourselves.

That night, when we were about to go to our bunks, a fight broke out in the latrine between two guys in a different squad and a guy name Engels, who had once been a squad leader and a bully. The two trainees were the aggressors and they began to beat the other guy mercilessly. Everyone stood around and just watched. I was in the back of the crowd and couldn't see much but what I did see was very ugly and made my stomach turn. Eventually, they stopped after the bloodied and bruised victim could no longer stand. We all went back to our bunks. I was a squad leader and should have stopped the fight when it began but didn't. And again, I was ashamed.

The next morning, one of the hard-hats came into the platoon and called everyone to attention.

'I hope you pathetic pieces of shit are satisfied with yourselves. Private Engels is in the hospital and won't be able to graduate today. You're all a bunch of cowards and you disgust me.' And, with that, he left.

I didn't think I could feel worse about the incident, but I did. He was right. We were a bunch of cowards."

Rex spoke up. "You had no way of knowing how badly he was beaten."

"True, but it was still cowardly of us to watch and do nothing while it was happening."

"Go on, and try not to dwell on your mistakes, John. That doesn't help here."

"Well," said John, "we prepared to go to the graduation ceremony. It was the first time I'd ever worn my dress green uniform. The hard-hat sergeants came into the barracks and showed us how to display our brass, tie our ties and wear our dress caps. We checked ourselves in the latrine mirrors. It was the first time I felt like a real soldier.

The ceremony was impressive. First, we were all marched into a large building that accommodated the entire battalion. There was a stage where the top trainees got certificates of achievement and where the battalion commander gave a stirring speech congratulating us for graduating from our rigorous basic training.

After the ceremony, we were full of pride as we marched back to the company street."

"Yowzah, John! Your words brought back so many great memories. I remember when I graduated from basic training in the Marines. There is nothing like it in the world."

"I still had a lot more training to do before I went to Vietnam. I went on to Ft. Gordon, Georgia. But now I've been doing all the talking. Tell me more about your life, Rex. Did you have a girlfriend back home when you left for Europe?"

"As a matter of fact, I did have a sweetheart. Her name was Mildred, and she was a beauty. She had bobbed dark brown hair and dark eyes that melted my heart. Mildred worked at the library in Greensburg. We went to the same school and got to know each other a year before graduation. We weren't officially engaged but we had planned to marry when I got back from the war. Life just didn't turn out that way.

Mildred came to my funeral and visited my grave for a while. She used to talk to me even though she didn't know I was there. She told me how sad everyone was that I had been killed in the war.

The last time she came to visit, she told me she had met a young man who would make a good husband. She cried and said she missed me and wished we had gotten married before I left. I tried to let her know it was all right to move on and that I just wanted her to be happy. I hope she was happy."

"Thank you for sharing that, Rex. I feel bad that your life was cut so short. You seem like a very good man."

"I appreciate that, John. I think you're a good man, too. Well, I'd better get back to the gate. It looks as if we are going to have another resident, and I want to be there to greet them."

Chapter 9

John went back to the congregation and watched as the pickup truck came through the gate and drove back down the lane to the shed. The two men got out, talked a while, then looked at a paper before opening the shed door. They went into the shed and soon, the backhoe emerged with its large tires bouncing as it went along the lane. The other man walked behind it with a shovel riding on his shoulder.

The backhoe was set up at a distance from the group not far from a maple tree and the men began to dig.

John felt a hand on his shoulder. It was Alice. She was a medium built attractive woman who appeared to be in her 40s, with light brown hair and brown eyes.

"It looks as if you won't be the new guy around here for much longer," she said. "I saw you've gotten to know Rex. What do you think of him?"

"He seems like a great guy. It's a shame he died so young. I wonder why he's still here after all these years."

"Yeah. It makes you wonder what he's hiding."

"You think he's hiding something?"

"In my experience, all men are hiding something, honey," said Alice with a smirk.

"I'm kind of tired of talking about myself," said John. "Why don't we talk about you and your life, Alice?"

"Mister, that's the best proposition I've had in years. Come with me."

Alice grabbed John's hand and pulled him over to the bench by the willow tree. They floated by the bench while Alice held John's hand in both of hers.

"So, what do you want to know about me, honey? Did you want to know about my being a hooker?"

"For real?"

"Don't tell me you've never been with a prostitute, John. A handsome man like you surely had to mess around once or twice."

"No. I never did mess around. I was very happily married to the same woman for over 43 years."

"You're a rare one, John. Well then, let me tell you a little about myself. I was born in Pittsburgh in 1947, a year after my father got out of the Navy. My father went to work at the steel mill, and my mother was a hairdresser. My sister, Joanie, was born three years later. We lived in Millvale near Pittsburgh."

"I know exactly where that is," said John.

"Good for you, John. Anyway, my mom seemed to become an alcoholic sometime while I was in grade school. She quit her hairdresser job—or was fired—so all she did after that was lie around the house and drink beer. My dad would come home from work and find her passed out on the couch with beer bottles lined up on the coffee table. When she came to, they would fight, and my father would beat her. He fixed our suppers most of the time. Sometimes, he would leave after the fight and my sister and I would have to fend for ourselves. Mom used to take her frustrations out on us by slapping us around. This went on for several years until Mom disappeared. One morning, we woke up and she was gone. I didn't know where she went but I was glad she was gone."

"That's terrible," said John. "No child should have to grow up that way."

"You don't know the half of it yet. After Mom left, my father began to drink more, too. And when I was 13, he began to, how shall I say this, well, take a special interest in me."

"You mean he raped you?"

"Yeah. I mean he raped me. He told me if I didn't 'participate' he would do the same to my sister. So, I learned how to satisfy his urges. I hated him. Then, one night when I was 16, he stopped coming to my bedroom. I was so relieved that it didn't occur to me what was going on."

"What was going on?"

"The pig started raping my sister. That's why he was leaving me alone. When I found out, I threatened to go to the police. He put his hands around my throat and told me he would kill me if I even tried to get the police involved. He said t he had killed before and wouldn't think twice about doing it again."

"So, did you go to the police?"

"No. I was terrified of him. I knew he wasn't kidding."

"What did you do?"

"When I was 17, I quit school and ran away from home. I stayed with a boy who was 20 and had his own apartment in Homewood. It was a filthy place and he treated me badly but at least I was away from my dad. I felt bad for Joanie, but I was still afraid of what Dad would do to me or Joanie if I went to the cops.

Then, the boy I was staying with went into the military and I was left on my own without a place to live or any money to live on. I was out on the street with nowhere to go. That's when I met Lincoln.

He drove a new white Cadillac with gold chrome all over it. On day, he saw me standing on the corner by myself. He asked if I was hungry and offered to buy me lunch. I was starving, so I took him up on it. We talked and he said I could stay with him until I found a place of my own. He took me to a salon and paid for a manicure and to fix my hair. He also bought me new clothes. I never had anyone treat me so well.

I didn't know he was a pimp when I first met him. In fact, I don't think I even knew what a pimp was at the time. But it wasn't long before Lincoln said I would have to earn my keep and that he owned me. He said I could earn a lot of money doing what I did with my dad, and he was right. I did earn a lot of money, but I had to pay him half of what I made. I met his other girls, and we would hang out together during the day.

It wasn't long before I started smoking grass, doing coke, and using heroin. By the time I was 20, I looked like I was 30, and Lincoln started beating me because I wasn't earning as much, and I was high all the time. That's when he sold me to

Andrew—another pimp. Andrew sent me to rehab and got me clean. I was still hooking, but I gave up the drugs.

I was with Andrew for 5 years until he got into a fight in a bar and was stabbed to death. From that moment on, I decided to work for myself. I moved to Murrysville and became a madam with my own girls. We were higher class, did all our business by referral, and we made a LOT of money. I lived the good life for about 20 years. Unfortunately, I also started using again. One night, I was doing heroin and overdosed. So, here I am."

"Wow, you led a very interesting life, Alice. Thank you for sharing with me. You really went through a lot. You seem to have a tough exterior but I think you're a real softie inside. I'm sure that had to be difficult for you to talk about."

"Surprisingly, it was not that tough. I've long since gotten over the trauma of my childhood. Thank you for listening to an old hooker, John. Now, let's get back to the group. We have a new member coming this way soon."

John and Alice went back to the congregation which by this time had moved to the new grave site. The grave diggers had already prepared the grave and were back at the shed sitting in the pickup. It wasn't long before the hearse and other cars were seen on the road. Rex took his place by the gate and welcomed the female stranger as the hearse drove by.

"Welcome to the Garden of Peace," said Rex.

There was a long line of vehicles following the hearse, far more than at John's own funeral. When the hearse got closer, John realized the new soul was a slender young woman in her 20s with long, straight blonde hair. To John, it seemed tragic for people to have died so young.

The funeral was very sad and lasted for some time. A middle-aged couple, who appeared to be the mother and father of the young woman, were inconsolable. A young man sat next to them. He held a small boy of four or five on his lap and was obviously grieving. The young woman's spirit stayed close to them until the family and the procession left the cemetery.

"Why can't I go with them?" she cried at Rex when she was stopped at the gate.

"I'm sorry, Miss. You just can't. The best thing to do is to go over and meet the group. It's best not to linger here at the gate for too long," Rex said compassionately.

She went back to her grave and watched as the two men filled in the dirt, arranged the flowers, and cleaned the grave site. John was filled with compassion for the young woman and decided to approach her.

"Young lady? My name is John. Welcome to the Garden of Peace."

He reached his hand out to her, but she ignored him.

"I'm fairly new here, too. There are some good souls over there in the group, and I'm sure they are hoping to help you through your grief. Would you like to go over and meet them?"

"Not now. I want to know why I can't be with my family. They need me so much," she said as she looked down the road to where the procession had now disappeared from view.

"I don't know the answer to your question. We're all stuck here near our earthly bodies. And, I don't know how long we'll be here. The word among the congregation is that we will all eventually be moving on to another place, but no one knows when that will be."

She looked at Rex, and he nodded.

"He's right, Ma'am. John is a good man. You should go with him," Rex said.

"My name is Judith but everyone calls me Judy," she said.

"Hi, Judy. I'm sorry we had to meet under such difficult circumstances. Let's go over to the group and I can introduce you to some souls who know exactly what you're going through," said John reaching out to her again.

"Okay."

Judy took John's hand this time, and the three of them floated over to the group which was now gathered near Judy's grave. He felt her agony through her small hand.

"Group, this is Judy. Judy, this is the group," said John.

Several of the souls reached out and touched Judy on the arms and back. John knew this was an opportunity for the congregation to express empathy toward their newest member.

"How did you die, Judy?" asked Sally.

"Ovarian cancer. It seemed like it took a long time to die, but I wanted to stay with my husband and little boy so badly. I did my best to stay with them. Now they're alone, and I'm sure they miss me like I miss them."

"I'm certain they do," said Sally. "But I also have no doubt that time will heal them."

"What am I doing here?" asked Judy.

John spoke up. "As one of the group explained to me recently, it appears to be a kind of purgatory where we stay until it's time to move on. We don't know what's beyond this place. But since we're here, we try to make the best of it by leaning on each other. As we console each other, it appears that we heal ourselves."

"Thank you, John," Judy said.

John left Judy with the congregation and decided to wander around the cemetery. As he neared the Garfield mausoleum, he noticed Peter just coming out of it, so he approached him. Peter was a thin old man in a black suit and gray tie. His gray hair was slicked back and his gray-blue eyes seemed cold and vacant.

"Hi, Peter? My name is John. I'm kind of new here, so I thought I'd come over and introduce myself."

"What do you want? I don't have any money for you."

"I'm not looking for money. It seems that money doesn't mean much anymore," said John.

"Money always means something. If you don't have it, you want it. If you've got it, you want to keep it and get more of it," said Peter.

"Well, I can assure you I don't want your money. I just thought I'd come over to talk to you. Were you just in there visiting your remains?"

"I was visiting my wife. Her name was Betty."

"How long has Betty been gone?" John asked.

"She died 15 years before I did, so I had this mausoleum built for her."

"Why don't you tell me about Betty? I'd like to hear her story."

"All right. Let me introduce you to her," Peter said. He grabbed John's hand and led him through the ornate closed door.

Peter's hand felt cool to the touch unlike the others but he continued to hold on as they went into the mausoleum and hovered near one of the two ornate metal caskets.

"John, this is Betty. Betty, this is John."

"Is Betty still here someplace?" John asked.

"She's right there in the casket, stupid! Where do you think she is?"

"I was referring to her spirit, Peter. Is her spirit still here at the cemetery?"

"No. She was gone before I got here, and I've been here for years."

"Why don't you tell me about her, Peter?"

"Betty was a wonderful woman and a perfect wife."

"When was she born?"

"She was born on September 30th, 1920. When I met her in 1944, she was dancing on Broadway in New York City. Betty was very beautiful and graceful as a butterfly. I worked on Wall Street as an investment banker at the time. I was several years older than she but when I introduced myself to her after one of her shows, she was so charming I knew I would marry her someday. For me, it was love at first sight."

"I know that feeling," said John.

"Try not to interrupt me when I'm talking, John. Anyway, I wooed her over the next two years before she finally agreed to marry me. Betty was originally from Pittsburgh, so we agreed to move there when she fell and broke her leg. That ended her dancing career. I didn't want to move since I was already doing very well in New York but she was so sweet, and she missed her family so much that she convinced me. I bought a large house in Squirrel Hill with the expectation of children, but we never had any.

With the money I'd made in New York, I decided to become a venture capitalist in Pittsburgh. I invested in start-ups and small companies. There were plenty of opportunities at that time in Pittsburgh, and I made the most of them. Betty started a dance school and over time, she developed a well-to-do clientele of children of wealthy parents.

We were very happy together until we found out she couldn't have children. Betty wanted to adopt but I didn't. After that, she was kind of sad all the time. I took her on trips around the world to try to cheer her up, but she was never quite the same person I married. I think our big house was a reminder of the fact we would never have children to fill it up.

Despite her sadness, our marriage lasted 22 years until she was hit by a drunk driver and killed. I was devastated by her death and began drinking heavily. I had this mausoleum built for her with room for me to take up residence later.

It was then I realized I was very rich but had nothing of value to me. With a housekeeper, cook, and a man-servant, I didn't need to go out, so I became a reclusive drunk and never left the house. My business suffered because it was no longer of interest to me, so I retired.

A year later, I committed suicide by shooting myself in the head. And now, I'm here. I had hoped to be with Betty but I never saw her soul here. She was already gone when I arrived."

"My goodness," John said. "That's very sad. But I'm sure Betty is in heaven waiting for you."

"I don't need your pity, John. And, of course, she's in heaven. The real question is whether I will ever see her again because of what I did to myself."

"Are you sorry you did it?"

"I can't say I wouldn't have done it again under the same circumstances. I had no reason to continue living. But if I had known I might never see Betty again because of it, I probably wouldn't have done it."

"I guess that's a start. Why don't you spend some time with the group? It might do you some good."

"I don't need them. I'm fine by myself, thank you very much," he said sarcastically.

"Well, thank you for telling me your story, Peter. I hope you'll find Betty someday. And if you ever feel like talking with someone, I'm always ready to listen."

"I don't think there's much chance of that. I think there are other souls over there who need you more than I do. So, goodbye then."

Peter let go of John's hand.

"Goodbye, Peter."

John left the mausoleum. As he emerged on the outside, John felt a great weight had been lifted off him. He felt pity for Peter and hoped he would eventually find peace.

John went back to the congregation, which was just about to adjourn for the night. He approached Sally and asked about Judy.

"She's starting to do better," said Sally.

"Glad to hear it. Maybe I'll talk to her tomorrow."

"I think you're doing so well here, John. I saw you talking with Peter. Some of us have never been able to talk to him. He just stays at his mausoleum and ignores the rest of us."

"Thank you, Sally. Peter has some issues but I think I'll keep them confidential for now. What I will tell you, though, is that he misses his wife. I don't think he'd mind me saying that."

"Anyway, it's good that he talked to you. Maybe he'll open up a little more to the group now."

"Perhaps," said John.

"I guess I will see you tomorrow, John."

"Bye."

John and Sally went their separate ways back to their graves, and night crept over the Garden of Peace once more.

Chapter 10

That night, John reflected again upon his time in the military after he'd left basic training. He remembered taking a bus to Ft. Gordon, Georgia and finding his new barracks very similar to the one he'd just left at Ft. Knox. He got to know a few of the men there, and they were all in some kind of signal MOS. John was a 72 Bravo or Communications Center Specialist. He was learning to type all over again because as a 72B, he was supposed to become a teletype operator. Eventually, he got to 45 words per minute but that was kind of slow.

They had two different types of electric teletype machines that looked like old typewriters. One machine was set at 60 words per minute, while the other was set at 100 words per minute. When the operator was typing, two things happened; the machine typed a message on a paper page and simultaneously, a paper tape was created with perforations on it like an old stock exchange ticker-tape. The tape could then be sent back through a machine to send that message.

He also attended classes five days a week, learning how to send and receive messages in a communications center. After four weeks of this, he was sent to a new classroom called "the cage." It was aptly named because it was a series of small barracks-type buildings that were surrounded by a high, barbed-wire fence with guards patrolling the perimeter. This was the security portion of the training, and he had received a top-secret clearance to train there. In those classrooms, John learned what was known as "crypto" or cryptographic equipment and procedures. It was all very boring, but he passed his tests.

It was after this training that John was given his orders for Vietnam. He had expected these orders but they were still a punch to the gut when he got them. His friend Eric had gone through the same training six months earlier and had been assigned to Germany. *It was just a matter of luck,* John thought, or bad luck as his case had been.

Following the receipt of his orders for Vietnam, John had to undergo more training. This training was called "RVN" or Republic of Vietnam training.

First, he and several busloads of soldiers were sent to a movie theater on base. He and the other men were lined up with their fatigue blouses off as they received overseas inoculations in both arms as they all filed in front of the medics who were giving the injections. John received five injections that afternoon.

After he put his fatigue blouse back on, he went and sat in the theater with the other men. After a while, three soldiers walked across the stage. One of them was a Green Beret who was walking with a terrible limp and using a cane. A captain took the microphone and introduced himself and the other two soldiers.

"We are going to oversee your training for the next two weeks. But what you are about to watch now is a movie called *Why, Vietnam?* narrated by President Johnson. In this movie, you will see actual film footage that was captured from the North Vietnamese. It shows the killing of American troops. If you do not wish to be IN one of these movies, I recommend you listen to your trainers and do exactly what they tell you. Even if you think your MOS is expected to put you in a rear area, I'm here to tell you that in Vietnam, there is no such thing as a rear area. Even if you're a cook or a clerk, you could still find yourself using a rifle to defend yourself and your buddies from the North Vietnamese or the Viet Cong. It's that simple. Do you understand?"

"Yes, SIR!" we all yelled.

The men then walked off the stage and took seats in the front. A moment later, a black and white movie began. President Johnson was reading a speech. It began with the words, 'Why, Vietnam?' For the next 20 minutes, the president made his case for why the United States was in the Vietnam conflict. He said it was to stop the spread of communism and to protect South Vietnam from an invading North Vietnam. He said three presidents from Eisenhower to Kennedy to himself had made a pledge to South Vietnam to protect it, and it was our solemn duty to keep that promise.

Then there were the film clips of dead and dying American soldiers being dragged through the jungle by North Vietnamese and Viet Cong. It was devastating, and John felt sick to his stomach afterward.

After the film, the Green Beret got up on stage again.

"Now you know a little more about what war is like. Do your training with that film in mind, and it might save your life."

He talked more but John didn't pay attention. He was in a daze after the film.

When they were dismissed, all the men filed out and loaded onto the buses. There were more men than could fit on the seats, so the center aisle was filled with men who stood holding onto the ceiling railing. John sat on an aisle seat and stared straight ahead. A few moments later, John looked around. Every man in the window seat was staring out the window. Every man in the aisle seat was staring at the back of the head of the man in front of him, likewise with the men who stood. No one said a word. It was positively eerie.

When John got back to his barracks, he went to his bunk, lay down, and stared at the bunk above him, all the while thinking about what he had seen and heard at the theater. He thought about home, and he thought about his mom and dad. He wrote a letter home which he had not done in a while. He left out the part about the movie but told them he was headed for Vietnam.

The Vietnam training at Ft. Gordon was depressing. One day, they were at the rifle range qualifying on the M-16, while the next they were in the field on deuce-and-a-half trucks going into a planned ambush. They had their M-16s but without any ammo. As soon as the firing of blanks started from the tree line, the trucks stopped and a lieutenant ordered the men out of the trucks. He stood in the road and had the men lay in a prone position alongside the road, point their weapons at the tree line and yell, "bang-bang" at the attackers. Next, the lieutenant set off white smoke canisters nearby and someone yelled, "GAS! GAS! GAS!" John put on his mask and went back to pretend-firing at the tree line. A loud "pop" was heard nearby.

"You guys are dead. That was a grenade, and you're all dead," said the lieutenant.

No one could survive that situation, John thought. It was too depressing to think about. Once the exercise was over, John took off his mask, put it back in its case, and loaded back onto the truck completely frustrated by the experience.

From there, the men were taken to an outdoor classroom in a wooded area. John sat up high on the bleachers and soon, a sergeant stood in front of the group. He was holding a rifle but not one John had seen before. The sergeant then fired the rifle on automatic into the air causing the men in the class to recoil in surprise.

"That was the sound of an AK-47," he said. "Remember that sound. It's very distinctive, and it is your enemy's weapon of choice. This one has a wooden stock, so you know it's made by the Chinese. The same weapon is made by the Russians but has a metal stock. This weapon is as good as the M-16—maybe better. They can use our ammo but we can't use theirs."

All of this was said very matter-of-factly.

"Next, I'm going to teach you about the M-18 Claymore mine," he said holding one up for us to see. "It is one of our most lethal weapons when used properly in ambush and perimeter protection situations. As you can see, it is curved. It is designed to be used with the front toward the enemy. For the stupid among you, it even has a sign right on it that says, *'Front Toward Enemy.'*

The Claymore mine has two layers. The first layer is composed of C-4 explosive material. The second layer is composed of ball bearings. When the Claymore is set, wired, and detonated using a 'clacker', the mine explodes and sends the ball bearings out in front of it to approximately 100 meters, killing anyone in its path. One must also be careful not to get too close to the Claymore even from the rear because it has an explosive force that can kill even 50 meters behind it. I have set up a half-charge Claymore among the trees in front of you to give you some idea of the explosive nature of this weapon. I will now detonate it. 3-2-1..." and then the device exploded with a tremendous 'bang.'

"Never stick your head up to see what you might have hit, especially in perimeter protection situations. The enemy is very, very clever. They have been known to sneak up and turn a Claymore around so that when the mine is detonated, it fires back toward our troops. When such things were done, we learned to put a grenade under the Claymore so the enemy is blown up when they try to turn it around. The bottom line is, be very careful."

After the lecture, they marched over to a mock-up of a Vietnamese village and were given another short lecture as they sat on the ground near the entrance. The gist of the lecture was that they were going to be involved in a clearing operation. They were told to watch out for booby-traps, such as trip-wires, venomous snakes, and punji sticks set up in the village. They had their M-16s but still without ammo.

A hard-hat staff sergeant got them up and had them start in single file. John was near the middle of the formation, so he thought he might have a better chance of survival in this exercise. Unfortunately, John was wrong again. Even though the leaders in the group found most of the trip wires and fake snakes in the hooch's, John was surprised by an "enemy" soldier who was hiding in a pig pen. He jumped up and shouted, "Bang! You're dead" before John had a chance to react. John just stood there with his weapon pointed at the ground until the exercise was over. Afterwards, they were told to sit on the ground outside of the village again, and the staff sergeant began to speak once more.

"Men, you'll have to be more alert if you want to survive in Vietnam. As many of you learned today, the enemy and his weapons are very dangerous. The best thing you can all do is to listen to your non-coms and officers and learn from them when you get over there. Does anyone have any questions?"

No one did.

That was the last training John would receive at Ft. Gordon. He was given his orders to report to Ft. Lewis, Washington and was given 14 days' leave. John caught a flight to Indianapolis two days later. He was wearing his dress green uniform and newly-received Private First-Class stripes for finishing in the top 10% of his class when he boarded his flight. John was proud of his uniform, which sported his red, white, blue and yellow National Defense Ribbon, also known as the "fireguard" ribbon, because he received it just for being in the military.

John had planned to meet his father at the airport in Indianapolis. When they met, John dropped his duffel bag and they hugged.

"It's good to see you, John."

"It's good to be back home again in Indiana, Dad."

John put his duffel bag in the trunk and got into a green Mercury he had never seen before.

"Is this a new car?"

"It's new to me. She's two years old but only has a little over 30,000 miles on her."

"It's nice. How is everyone?" John asked.

"Pretty good. Your mom is worried about your going to Vietnam. She watches the news reports every day on TV, so she knows how bad it is over there."

"Well, she shouldn't worry. With my job, I will probably just be typing in an office somewhere in a rear area."

"That's good to hear."

John and his dad talked about how things were going with the family, and John talked about his training. John's father was a Navy veteran of WWII, but he didn't talk about it much.

When they got home, his mother was waiting in the living room. They hugged and she kissed him on the cheek.

"It's good to have you back home, John," she said. Tears of joy were running down her cheeks.

"It's good to be home, Mom," John said.

"How long are you going to be home?" she asked.

"About two weeks."

"You look so nice in your uniform. Your dad was already out of the service when we met, so I never got to see him in his uniform. You look very handsome. Have you gained weight?"

"I gained about 25 lbs. during basic training, but it's all muscle," John said and laughed.

"I believe it. You look really fit."

"Are you hungry?" his mom asked.

"I can always eat."

"How about if I fix you some bacon and eggs?"

"That sounds great, Mom."

John ate the late breakfast and talked about his training, though he avoided his weapons and Vietnam training. His mother was very religious, so she caught John up on the latest goings on in the church. She and John's father were members of the local Assembly of God church now. His mom's father had been a protestant minister, so John grew up going to church three times a week. His mom and dad met at the Cincinnati Bible Seminary and were married by her father. John's parents now believed in the speaking-of-tongues, slaying in the Spirit, and the baptism of the Holy Spirit. After much reflection about church, John had rejected the strict interpretations of the bible and only attended church on special occasions as a favor to his mother after leaving Abilene Christian.

John thanked his mother for the meal, and went into the living room where his dad was sitting.

"How's Paul?" John asked his dad as he sat on the couch.

"Paul is doing very well. He's attending a church retreat this weekend and will be home Sunday night. Have you been going to church while you've been in the Army, John?"

"I went once in the first week of basic training. They marched us all to the church, and we listened to a short sermon from the military chaplain. I haven't gone since then, though."

"Well, you should try to find a service to go to when you get over there. I'm sure they will have chaplains over there, too."

"You're probably right. I'll try to go." It was a hollow statement since John had no intention of going.

John was surprised at how long the two-week leave seemed to last. After the first couple of days at home and after seeing

Paul, there was not much else to do. John went to church with his parents and felt very uncomfortable with everyone glad-handing him just because he was in uniform. He didn't care much for the raising of hands and the attempts at speaking in tongues but he tried not to be too obvious about it.

He tried to look up old friends but only found one on the phone one day, and he had to go to work. His other friends were either away at college or in the service. John had no girlfriend at the time, and Paul was away at school during the day, so John stayed at home watching TV with his mother most of the time while his dad worked.

When the day finally came to leave, John got up, got into his dress uniform, grabbed his duffel bag, and went downstairs. His mother was sitting in the chair by the fireplace reading the bible.

"I need to talk to you," she said looking up at him.

"Okay, Mom."

"I've given this a lot of thought, John, and I'm worried about your soul."

"I'll try to go to church there. I promise."

"It's more than that, John. As much as I'm worried about your safety, I want to be sure you will get into heaven with your dad and me. So, if you're ever in a situation where it is kill-or-be-killed, I want you to let them kill you. Do you understand? I don't ever want you to kill anyone."

John felt like he'd been kicked in the gut.

With his eyes welling up, John said, "I'm sorry to disappoint you, Mom, but if that situation ever arises, I will do my very best to kill that enemy, so I can survive and come back home alive. I'll worry about heaven later."

With that said, John went into the kitchen and fixed himself a bowl of cereal. John's father came downstairs and joined him at the table. After breakfast, John grabbed his duffel bag and headed for the door. His dad got his keys and went out to start the car. His mother came over and kissed John goodbye.

"Goodbye, Mom," John said.

"Goodbye, John. I love you."

"I love you, too, Mom."

John threw his duffel bag into the back seat, then got into the front seat with his dad.

John and his dad talked on the way to the airport.

"Did I ever tell you about the time I had a monkey when I was in the Navy?"

"You had a monkey?" John laughed.

"Yeah. When I was on the island in the Pacific doing my postal job, I lived in a Quonset hut. There was a guy who left to go home and he couldn't take his monkey with him, so he gave him to me. The monkey's name was Mike, and he was a real character.

There was one guy in our hut who wore a beard. I don't know if Mike hated the guy or just his beard, but every time the guy came into the hut, Mike would scream, jump off my bunk, jump onto the guy's face, and take a crap right on his shoulder. The guy complained to the commanding officer, so I had to put Mike on a leash."

John and his dad laughed. This was the most John had ever heard his father talk about the service.

"Did you ever see any fighting when you were in the Navy?" John asked.

"The Japanese made a few bombing runs and strafed our island a couple of times while I was there, but no one ever got hurt. All they managed to do was to blow up our chow hall once. We had good protection with our anti-aircraft guns.

I hope you have as good of luck as I had while I was in the service."

"I hope so, too," John said.

The rest of the trip was small talk about John's training. When they got to the airport, the two of them hugged. Afterward, John hoisted his duffel bag onto his shoulder.

"Be careful over there, son."

"I will, Dad."

John had not mentioned his conversation with his mother, but he would dwell on it for the next five days until he landed in Vietnam.

Chapter 11

The next morning seemed to come quickly. John went to gather with the assembly.

"I don't think we've met yet," said a voice from behind him. When John turned around, he saw that the voice belonged to a tall, older, black man with very distinguished features, deep-set eyes, and a dark complexion.

"You are correct, sir," said John smiling and extending his hand. They shook hands.

"My name is Gerald but everyone calls me Jerry."

"It's nice to meet you, Jerry. I'm John. How long have you been here?"

"I've been here nigh unto 50 years now," said Jerry looking up as he calculated. "I don't always come to the group these days. I just thought I would come over and take a look at the new faces."

"Well, I'm glad you did. Where is your grave, if you don't mind my asking?"

"I've got a nice little spot over in the southeast corner of the Garden. It's underneath a big oak tree, and it's usually shady there except in the winter time, of course. It was a little oak tree when I got here. I saw you when you moved in. You've got a nice spot, too."

"Not too bad. My wife and I picked it out several years back. She was gone before I got here. I miss her. She died over two years ago but I thought I would see her when it was my turn."

"Sorry to hear that, John. My wife died in childbirth with our third child. That was over 75 years ago."

"Where are you from, Jerry?"

"Wilkinsburg. We had a fine house there. I was a real estate attorney and had an office in town there. Mostly, I did title work and closings for the banks in our neighborhood."

"How in the world did you get laid to rest way out here?" John said laughing.

"Oh, Penelope and I were out driving in my '33 Buick one Sunday afternoon and we found this quaint little cemetery with the pretty sign that said, *'Garden of Peace.'* She told me that's where she wanted to be buried."

"Tell me a little about your life, Jerry. Do you mind if I hold your hand while you talk?"

"Don't mind at all. I was born in the Pittsburgh community of East Liberty back in 1905. I went to school there, then went to college and graduated from the University of Pittsburgh. I graduated Magna Cum Laude and went to law school at Duquesne University. I met Penelope at Pitt when she was still a nursing student. She went into emergency room nursing at Allegheny General Hospital, and we were married right after I passed the bar exam in 1930. She rode the trolley to work six days a week until our first child was born in 1935. As I said, we had three children. The oldest was Evan, then Sarah and finally, Rebecca.

Penelope was a fine, strong, beautiful woman, and we had a wonderful life together. She died of a hemorrhage while she was giving birth to Rebecca.

I was devastated by her death, and I never remarried. I had three small children that I tried my best to tend to, and then I hired a nanny from the neighborhood. Edna was wonderful. She was almost like a wife and took wonderful care of the children. She cooked and cleaned and took the children to the park to play. Fortunately, I was home most evenings by 5 p.m., so I got to spend a lot of time with them. I also got to see them grow up and become wonderful people. I died of a stroke in 1966, and, well, that's how I got here."

"It sounds as if you had a wonderful life except for your wife's death. Was she still here when you arrived?"

"No. She had moved on to heaven before I got here."

"That's my situation as well, Jerry," John said. "How do you pass the time?"

"That's the hard part. I relive the time I spent with Penelope and the children. I just try to remember the good times we had."

"I hope this isn't too sensitive a question for you, but did you experience much in the way of racism while you were alive?"

"Yes, of course. I especially experienced it while I was growing up in East Liberty. There were just a few of us Negroes living in that community at the time, and we were often called names by the older white kids. It hurt but it was just the way life was at the time. My parents were both very supportive, so I still had a great deal of confidence as a child growing up. I was fortunate to see many changes over the years for Negroes. I got to see Martin Luther King march and speak on TV."

"I was in college when he was assassinated. What a terrible waste."

"Yes, it was. I had been here in the Garden a few years before I found out from one of the residents. Martin was a good man, and I'm sure he could have done a lot more if he hadn't been killed so early in life."

"Do you have any idea why you're still here after all these years, Jerry?"

"I wish I knew. Maybe it's because I'm still so attached to my body. I do stay close by it and always have."

"That seems to be the natural order of things around here," said John. "I understand that's why we can't escape from the cemetery."

"That appears to be the case, John. I think everyone tries to leave but they all get pulled back just like a gum band."

"Do you think there's anything we can do to get to heaven?"

"I don't know, John. I've seen many a soul pass on since I've been here but I could never make rhyme nor reason of it. One day they'd be here, the next day they'd be gone. I guess we're kind of on God's time schedule around here. When He wants us, He'll come get us."

"That sounds like sound reasoning, Jerry."

"Now, it's your turn, John. You'll have to tell me about yourself."

John was happy to oblige and gave Jerry the synopsis of his life. Jerry seemed genuinely interested, especially when John talked about his experiences in the military.

"Thank you for the wonderful conversation, Jerry."

"Likewise, John."

After their conversation, John and Jerry went back and talked with the group until nightfall.

That night, John thought more about his military experience. He remembered flying to Ft. Lewis, Washington and staying for three days then being on Flying Tiger airlines for a 22-hour flight from Tacoma Air Force Base to Vietnam. They stopped off in Anchorage, Alaska for a short lay-over. John went into the gift shop with others on his flight. There were stuffed toys that looked like seals and walruses, walrus tusks with scrimshaw drawings, and Eskimo dolls. John didn't buy anything because he had very little money but it was fun to look at everything.

Once back on the plane, John thought about what his mother had said to him. *How cruel*, he thought, *to have one's own mother say such a thing just before leaving for such a dangerous place.* But the longer he thought about it, the more at peace he became. He knew his mother was concerned for his immortal soul more than she was worried about his mortal body. It was her way of showing love, and he was sorry he hadn't just said, "Okay, Mom," kissed her goodbye and been on his way. *Funny*, he thought, *how his mother's words had turned into guilt on his part.*

The flight was long and uncomfortable. He spoke with the guy sitting next to him who was a sergeant on his way back to Vietnam for a second tour. His name was William Hartford, and he was in the infantry. He said he liked the adventure of the war and had been in several firefights. John noticed the combat infantryman's badge on his uniform. Bill, as he wanted to be called, was part of the 101st Airborne unit attached to an artillery unit in Da Nang.

To say the least, Bill was 'gung ho.' He enjoyed going out into the jungle and staying out there on long range patrols. He liked setting up ambushes for the North Vietnamese Army and said he'd killed several of them during his first tour. Bill described a comradery among his platoon he wanted to experience again. He said there was nothing back home for him and that his family didn't understand why he wanted to go back.

Bill told John he'd stopped by to see his girlfriend who was away at college at Berkley, California. He wore his uniform proudly with the blue braid, Screaming Eagle patch of the 101st Airborne Division, and bloused boots all indicative of his being part of one of the toughest and most elite fighting units in the U.S. military. When he was out with his girlfriend one night, a female friend of hers went up to him, called him a baby killer, and spit on him. After that incident, he didn't wear his uniform in public until he was ready to leave again for Vietnam.

John sympathized but hadn't experienced anything like that in Lafayette, though he had heard of such things in the news.

Bill didn't do much to allay John's fears about Vietnam. John thought about what it would be like when he landed and pictured mortars and rockets raining down on him the moment he stepped off the plane.

John's plane stopped for fuel at Yakota Air Force Base in Japan but they did not disembark until they landed in Cam Ranh Bay in the Republic of Vietnam on February 7th, 1970. When he got to the door of the plane, the heat and bright sun were overwhelming. All he saw was a sea of concrete and a few buildings off in the distance. He carried his duffel bag down the flight of stairs and lined up to get on the buses that were waiting. John felt exposed as he waited to get on the bus. He had no weapon and was just waiting for bullets to fly in his direction. The buses were painted olive-drab green and had wire mesh covers over the windows, presumably to prevent grenades from being tossed into them.

The bus ride to the processing station was a quick one. Once there, they got off the bus and headed for a supply Quonset hut. They exchanged their old fatigues and boots for Vietnam fatigues and jungle boots and a set of dress khakis. They also gave him a pair of flip-flops. From there, they were marched to the Quonset hut barracks. The sergeant in charge stated they would all be there for a few days before getting specific orders for their new duty station. He told them to get comfortable because there was nothing to do but wait. He showed them where the mess hall was and where the latrine and shower building were located.

There was sand everywhere, but there were paths made of corrugated steel sheets with holes in them that made it easier to walk over the sand. John noticed a water tank trailer near the mess hall marked 'Potable Water.' He picked out a bunk in his designated Quonset hut, unrolled the mattress, and placed his duffel bag beside the bunk. John lay down on the bunk and promptly fell asleep. When he woke up, he was sweating and hungry, so he went to the mess hall to see if they were serving. They were, and it was good to get some hot food inside of him. It was already close to 6 p.m. when he left the mess hall, so John decided to take a shower. He went back to his bunk and pulled out a towel, a fresh set of green skivvies, and his flip-flops from his duffel bag.

When he walked into the shower room, he was shocked to see two Vietnamese women squatting in the middle of the room. They were wearing white blouses with black pants that looked like pajamas and had the traditional conical straw hats slung over their backs. They paid no attention to him as they tended to their laundry duties on the concrete floor near the drain. Another GI came into the shower room and began to shower in front of them. Neither the soldier nor the women seemed to notice one another, so John hung up his pants with his wallet, his skivvies, and towel and began to shower. The shower room was about 20' x 20' and had shower nozzles spaced about every 4 feet.

The shower was lukewarm, but it felt good. John finished his shower about the same time the women finished their laundry. He toweled himself dry, then put on his skivvies, pants, and flip-flops before going back to his bunk. After getting dressed, John sat on his bunk and read Mark Lane's book, 'Rush to Judgement' about the Kennedy assassination.

So, for two more days, John followed a routine: showering, shaving, eating breakfast, reading, eating lunch, reading, napping, eating supper, and reading before going to sleep. He was bored silly and was ready to go anywhere by the time a sergeant handed him his orders to go to Nha Trang. He was to fly out by helicopter at noon that day. When the time came, John put his duffel bag in the back of a Jeep and rode with two other guys to the helicopter pad. He and the other soldiers got into the helicopter with their duffel bags, and the door gunner told the men to roll down their sleeves during the flight. Once he figured out how the seat belt worked, John buckled it and waited for the take-off. The pilot, co-pilot, and door gunner wore helmets and microphones, and when they started the engine, it was very noisy and the side doors were left open. The door gunner was right behind John. When they lifted off the helipad, John could see the ground in front of the pilots as the helicopter rose and moved forward. It was an eerie feeling. When they were well off the ground, it felt as if the body of the helicopter was suspended by a large rubber band. The helicopter made zig-zag movements as it followed the ocean coastline north toward Nha Trang.

After a relatively short flight, the pilots landed on a helipad on a sandy hilltop. A Jeep was waiting for them. As soon as John and the others cleared the area, the helicopter rose again and headed back South. John and the men got into the Jeep with their gear and took a ride down the hill toward the ocean where the driver picked up a road going inland. Along the way, John saw wooden towers spaced about 100 yards apart. They were fortified with sandbags and each was manned by a single soldier. They eventually reached a wide gate which appeared to be the only entrance to the populated area. After talking to the gate guard, the driver continued driving until they got onto a dusty dirt road that led to a plywood building with a metal roof and open doors on the sides.

"This is the place," the driver said. "That's the Personnel building. When you go in there, show them your orders, and they'll get you squared away."

John and the men grabbed their duffel bags and thanked the driver for the ride. When the men entered the building, they saw several soldiers sitting at desks near file cabinets. Small oscillating fans dotted the room. The room was open to the metal roof with wooden rafters spanning the area.

"Come over here and sit down," one of the soldiers said to John. "I'll get you processed in."

The soldier, a specialist 4th class in a faded uniform, asked John his name.

"Private First-Class John Sample," he replied.

"Sample, Sample . . . Okay, I've found your file. Give me your orders."

John obeyed.

"Says here you're a 72 Bravo and you're supposed to go to Pleiku. As it happens, there are just too many 72Bs in this battalion. I just checked your GT scores, and they're good. How's your typing?"

"I type about 45 words a minute," John replied. "What's a GT score?"

"General Testing. When you first got in the Army, you took tests in English and Math. You got a combined score of 135, which is well above average, and 45 words a minute is good enough. Just so you know, a GT score of 90 – 100 is supposed to be average, and it takes a score of 110 to get into Officer Candidate School. How would you like to work here in Personnel?"

"I don't know anything about Personnel."

"Don't worry. It's not that hard, and we'll teach you everything you need to know. If you decide against it, you'll probably be burning shit up in Ban Me Thuot."

"Personnel it is then," John said with a smile.

"Good decision, Sample. I'll finish up your paperwork, then I'll take you to your barracks."

"Sounds good to me."

The Spec 4 asked several questions, then typed up John's new orders.

"Okay. As soon as I get a signature on this, you will be the newest member of Headquarters, Headquarters Company of the 459th Signal Battalion. Welcome aboard, Sample."

Soon, the Spec 4 returned and attached the paper to a brown file folder.

"This is your 201 File. It has your entire military life in it. Let me file that away. Are you ready to see your new quarters?"

"Absolutely."

John grabbed his duffel bag and followed the soldier a short distance down the dusty road to a two-story wooden barracks building with a metal roof and wood and sandbag walls built up around the first floor. There were screens all along the hallway and a screen door at both ends.

"I'm going to put you in with Sgt. Franks for now." He pointed to the first room on the left of the first floor with plywood walls and a screened window on one side. "This is your bunk and footlocker. You're wall locker is over there. And, by the way, my name is Stewart Butler."

The two men shook hands.

"We're lucky. The mess hall is right behind our barracks, and it's one of the best mess halls in Vietnam. Generals like to come here to eat when they're in the area."

"Sounds good."

"Stow your gear on the bed and I'll show you around the place."

John did as instructed and followed Stewart down the hall and through the rear exit. There were wooden staircases at each end of the barracks.

Upon exiting, Stewart pointed to an open 55-gallon drum set into the sandy soil at an angle, surrounded on three sides by 4 ft. sections of plywood.

"That's the piss tube for when you have to go."

They got on a concrete walkway and walked a short distance.

"That's our bunker," Stewart said pointing at what appeared to be a large mound of olive drab sandbags with two entrances to the underground bunker. "That's where we go during mortar and rocket attacks."

They walked a little farther over to a rectangular, screened building.

"That's the latrine. They put half drums under the thrones. Someone brings the drums out every day, pours kerosene in them, sets them on fire, and stirs them up. Don't worry. If you keep out of trouble, you probably won't pull shit-burning duty."

A few steps further was another wooden building with screens on the side windows.

"Finally, this is the shower and sink area."

There were two long metal troughs with water spigots placed every few feet on both sides of each of them. Above each spigot were a soap dish and a mirror. The shower room looked the same as the one he'd used in Cam Ranh Bay.

Stewart then pointed to a small metal building with a heavy wire mesh over the door.

"That's the armory. Let's get you a weapon, a steel pot, a gas mask, and a flak jacket."

The sergeant inside the building issued John an M-14 rifle but no ammo.

"You only get ammo when you go on guard duty or if there's an attack. And, here's your flak jacket. You grab that when there's an attack. Go ahead and put it on. It's easier to wear it than to carry it."

The flak jacket was heavy. John put it on and carried the rifle like he'd been taught.

"Well, that's the tour, John. You can have the rest of the day off to get your stuff put away. You can put your M-14 and mask in your wall locker and your steel pot and flak jacket on your foot locker."

"Thanks," John said.

"You're welcome. I'll probably see you at chow. Then you need to be at the office at 7 a.m. tomorrow. You okay?"

"I'm okay. Thanks again."

John spent the rest of the afternoon unpacking his duffel bag and putting his clothes away. There were a few wire hangers in the wall locker, so he hung up his khakis and shirts in there along with his new fatigues. John hadn't thought to ask about laundry and how that was to be done, so he just tied his laundry bag to the end of his bunk just like he'd been taught in basic training and put his dirty underwear in it.

He rolled his socks into balls, rolled his skivvies, folded his undershirts, and then placed them all neatly into the wooden foot locker. He placed the extra pair of boots and dress shoes under his bunk and his shaving kit went on the shelf in the wall locker.

"Don't put your boots and shoes under your bunk," a voice said from the doorway.

John looked to see who it was. It was a tall, thin sergeant who leaned against the doorway.

"Where should I put them, Sergeant?"

"You can put your dress shoes in the wall locker. The boots can go in your foot locker or at the end of your bunk. You just don't want anything in your way when you have to roll under your bunk."

"Roll under my bunk?"

"Yeah, like when the mortars start coming down, you want to get under your bunk in a hurry. By the way, my name's not 'Sergeant.' It's Dan. Dan Franks. I work in the motor pool. I guess you're my new roommate for the next couple of weeks." He went over and sat on his bunk.

"My name is John Sample. What happens in a couple of weeks?"

"I'm going HOME! That's what happens in ten days and a wakeup."

"Wow. Congratulations, Dan."

"So, how short are you, John? It must be like 360 some days left for you. Man, I can't even remember back that far."

Stewart stuck his head in and knocked on the door.

"Don't rub it in, Dan."

Dan grinned. "Just gloating."

"You ready to go to chow, John?"

"I'm ready. See you later, Dan."

"It's the same old shit, Stewart. Roast beef again, or water buffalo, or whatever the hell it is."

"It could be worse, Dan. We could be eating out of cans in the boonies," Stewart said.

"You got that right."

"Did you get everything put away all right?" Stewart asked.

"Yeah, I think so. I'm just glad I don't have to lug that duffel bag around anymore."

The two men walked around to the entrance of the mess hall that was just behind the barracks. There was a palm tree near the entrance to the plywood building. They went through the screen door and down a narrow hall to the left. There was a shoulder-high wall separating the hall from the table area.

"Oh. This is Thursday, so it's malaria pill day," said Stewart. There was a tall black cook handing out a large orange pill to every soldier as he came up to the food area.

"Make sure you take your pill, newbie," he said handing the pill to John. "Malaria is some nasty shit, and you don't want it. Trust me."

John looked over at Stewart who was nodding his head.

John was hungry. The roast beef and gravy with mashed potatoes and green beans looked good. He also got a piece of thick-sliced white bread on the side with a pat of butter. He had water to drink in a brown melamine cup.

The two men sat at a table with two other men. "John, this is Ralph and Mark."

John shook hands with the two men.

"John's new here," said Stewart. The three men laughed.

"His bright green fatigues were a dead give-a-way," said Ralph.

"Don't worry, John. After your mama san washes your clothes in a mud puddle a few times, your fatigues will start looking like ours," said Mark. The three men laughed again.

John didn't understand too much except that he had learned that 'mama san' referred to an older Vietnamese woman who often did cleaning chores for the men.

"How do I start the laundry process?" John asked between bites.

"I'll fix you up with my mama san. She's always looking for more work," said Stewart.

"How much does she charge?"

"I pay her 500 Piasters a month to wash my clothes, shine my boots, and sweep the floor. That's about $2.50. She comes in once a week. Don't pay her in MPC."

"What's MPC?"

"Military Payment Certificates. That's how we get paid over here instead of green backs. You don't need much money over here unless you buy stereos, cameras and stuff to send home. You'll get a ration card for cigarettes, beer and soda, too. The rest of your money should be put in the bank if you're smart."

"You have a bank here?"

"Yeah. The Bank of America is not too far from here. You can go with me when we get paid at the end of the month."

"Seems like there's a lot to learn around here," said John as he finished up his meal.

"Don't worry, John. You'll get the hang of it sooner than you think. By the way, you might want to hold your bread up to the light before you eat it," said Stewart.

John held his bread slice up toward the light.

"There are some little black specks in it."

"Those are bugs," said Stewart. "I just wanted you to know before you ate it."

"So, what's a little extra protein going to hurt?" John spread the butter and finished his bread.

The four men left the mess hall together out the back door. There were trash cans marked for paper and garbage and a small table where the trays and cups were stacked. John noticed that several dogs had gathered near the trash cans.

"You'll know you've been in-country for some time when you know all the dogs' names," said Mark. "Come here, Bullshit! Come on!" he said.

A hearty-looking, black-and-white short-haired mutt came forward as Mark threw him some leftover roast beef and the rest of his bread.

John laughed.

"Sorry guys. I already ate everything. I'll try to remember next time," John said to the dogs.

When they got back to the barracks, John stopped at his door.

"See you tomorrow at 6:30 for breakfast if you want any, John. We've got coffee at the office if that's all you want," said Stewart.

"Thanks. I'll see you then."

The three other men left to go to their rooms.

John stayed in his room and finished his book on Kennedy, then got into bed. He was tired, so he turned off the light and went to sleep.

John woke up to someone shaking his arm. It was still dark.

"John? John? Are you okay?" came a voice from beside him.

"I'm fine. Why are you on the floor? What's going on?"

"You didn't hear that?" asked Dan incredulously.

"Hear what?" John said as he sat on the side of the bed. Dan had low-crawled over to John's bed.

"For Christ's sake, we just had a mortar attack! Get your war shit on, pick up some ammo and get down to the bunker. Stay low."

Now, John was scared and he could hear the wail of a loud siren. He put on his pants and boots and didn't bother tying them. His flak jacket went over his undershirt and he put his steel pot on. John got his M-14 and mask out of his locker and went to the door. Crouching, he looked to his left and right down the hall. No one was in sight. He ran down the hall, bent over, to stay below the screens and went out the door.

He ran past the bunker over to the ammo shed where there was still a line of men waiting for ammo. The line went quickly. In the distance, John could hear the sound of canons.

"Here!" the sergeant growled as he handed John a magazine of ammo. "Try not to shoot yourself or any of us."

John took the magazine, inserted it into the rifle, then ran back to the bunker. As he got to the stairs, he saw two men set up with an M-60 machine gun on top of the bunker. John was among the last to arrive. Everyone else was sitting quietly on both sides on wooden benches. He sat on the end of the bench, and the man beside him scooted slightly to allow him some room.

Some of the men began talking in low tones.

"How long do we stay down here?" John asked the man next to him.

"Until we hear the all-clear signal or until you hear shooting. If you hear shooting, that means the gooks have breached the wire and we'll all have to get out there and protect each other."

From then on until the all-clear signal, John stayed quiet. Other men began talking more loudly and some were even laughing. When the all-clear sounded, everyone began filing out of the bunker. It was light outside now, and John's watch said it was 7:05 a.m.

"Welcome to Vietnam, John," said Stewart as he came up to him on their way back to the armory. "That was pretty close."

"What scares me is that I slept through the whole thing. Dan had to wake me up. I didn't hear a thing."

"You're kidding me! That's unbelievable."

They stood in line to hand in their ammo, then went back to the barracks.

"Put your gear away, wash up and shave, and I'll see you at the mess hall. Everybody's going to be late for work today."

John went back to his room, took off his gear and put it away. He tied his boots, got his shaving kit and went to the shaving area. After shaving and brushing his teeth, John went back to his room and got the rest of his uniform on before heading to the mess hall. There was already a line, and everyone was talking about the attack.

After going through the chow line, John saw Stewart and Ralph at one of the tables, so he sat with them.

"So, Stewart tells me you're a deep sleeper," said Ralph laughing.

"I guess so," John said sheepishly.

They all finished their bacon, eggs and toast, and the three of them went out and stacked their trays and cups. When they got to the office, the W3 warrant officer was already there doing paperwork. He was a short, thin older man likely in his late 40s, with graying hair.

"Good morning, Sir," Stewart and Mark said. Then John added the same greeting.

"Good morning," he replied. "Quite a bit of excitement out there this morning, huh? Anyone hurt?"

"I don't think so, Sir," said Stewart.

"That's good. I don't think we've met, Private," he said to John.

John walked up to the warrant officer's desk, saluted and said, "Private First-Class John Sample reporting for duty, Sir!"

The warrant officer smiled, gave a half-hearted salute and said, "You don't have to salute me, Private. I'm William Jeffries. You can call me Mr. Jeffries or Sir. Stewart will show you the ropes around here. I'm sure you'll do fine."

"Thank you, Sir."

John went back to where Stewart was waiting.

"That will be your desk," he said pointing at a desk on the other side of the aisle from his own. "But for now, you'll be sitting in this chair beside my desk. I'll be teaching you what you need to know to get started. In a week or two, we'll send you down to Long Binh for some personnel training."

"Sounds good to me."

"Essentially, what we do here is in-processing, out-processing, and file maintenance. When someone new comes in, we process their orders and update their paperwork. We record any promotions, demotions, awards, letters of recommendation, and letters of reprimand. We get most of the information from the morning reports that are sent to us from company clerks around the battalion. Ron does the morning reports and hands off the information to the other clerks around here. Make sense so far?"

"Yes, I think so."

"This is the Form 20. It is the most updated form you have in your 201 File. It's this tan color and is made of a heavier card stock. We only use pencil to update it. That way, if someone gets a promotion, we can just erase the old information and record the new rank. Same way with date of rank, DEROS, and so on."

"What's DEROS?" John asked.

"DEROS is 'Date Estimated Return Over Seas.' That's the date you're supposed to go back to the world. All of us are counting down the days."

John smiled. "An important date then. I'll remember that."

Chapter 12

Morning at the cemetery seemed to come more quickly the next day. John went over to the congregation of souls and listened in on the conversation. It turned out they were talking about him.

"John. Good morning," said Sally. "I guess your ears were burning. We were just saying what a wonderful contribution you've been making in such a short time."

"I guess it's because I didn't talk to too many people after my wife died. I just needed to catch up."

"We were wondering who you were going to visit with next."

"Well, I heard that the Smiths were interesting people. They're the ones with the obelisk, right?"

"You have a good memory, John."

"What can you tell me about them, Sally?"

"Oh, I'm not going to spoil it for you. Besides, the way you've been going, you may get a completely different opinion of them."

"Nothing ventured, nothing gained, I guess."

John left the group and made his way over to the obelisk. It was about 15 feet tall and black with silver specs in it. There was a large base made of the same material that had a carved angel and the names Charles Ellsworth Smith and Donna Beth Smith on it. He was born January 17th 1945. She was born September 3rd 1946. They had the same date of death; December 25th 1981.

"Mr. and Mrs. Smith?" John asked as he saw the couple nearby. "My name is John."

"Don't call me that!" the woman shouted. "Don't call me Mrs. Smith. My name is Donna."

"Yes, Ma'am. I didn't mean to offend you. I just saw the inscription on the stone."

"Well, that stone is a testament to this bastard here," she said pointing to a large male spirit with brown hair and brown eyes standing on the other side of the obelisk. Donna was tall and thin, with wispy blonde hair and bright blue eyes.

"Don't listen to her. She's an ungrateful bitch. Always has been."

"Ungrateful for what? Don't forget, I was born into money. You never provided anything extra," she said.

"How about a man who doted on your every whim?" he replied.

"Ha! You never doted. You just groveled. It was all about getting sex from me whenever you wanted it."

"I could have had sex anytime I wanted. But I was faithful to you."

"How do I know that? You were always sneaky and spent late hours at the office. You were probably having sex with your secretary for all I know."

"You saw my secretary. Do you honestly think I'd have an affair with her? She was a good secretary, but she was a cow. I was never attracted to her."

"I hope you don't mind my interrupting but I noticed you died on the same day. What happened?"

"Why don't you tell him, Charlie?"

"I'd be happy to. It was Christmas day. We were fighting, as usual. I was pissed. I got the witch a new Mercedes for Christmas. Guess what she got me?"

"I have no idea," said John.

"A tie! She bought me a goddamned tie, and that was it."

"It's all you deserved."

"So, I went upstairs, got my gun from the dresser, went downstairs and shot the miserable bitch. I knew I'd go to prison, and I couldn't do prison. After watching her die, I turned the gun on myself and blew my brains out," said Charles matter-of-factly.

"Typical. You assume that you had a brain. Now, I'm stuck with you in this Godforsaken place forever."

"I'm sorry you've had such an unhappy life together. Why don't you come over and talk with the group? Maybe they can cheer you up."

"They're a bunch of moron losers," said Donna.

"We don't have anything in common with that type," said Charles.

"That's the first thing you've agreed on since I met you," said John smiling.

"Why don't you go back to them, John? I think they are more your kind."

"Thank you for telling me your story. The invitation to come over is always open."

"I wouldn't hold your breath," said Donna.

John turned and went back to the congregation.

"Wow!" said John to Sally. "You said they were interesting. That's the understatement of the year."

"I've never seen a more miserable couple," Sally said.

"And they've been that way since they got here?"

"Yep. I actually thought they would have gone to hell by now."

"Maybe this is hell for them. I mean, they can't stand each other. Yet, here they are, still together."

"Good point, John. You may be right."

"Do me next! Please?"

A thin, middle-aged man with short-cropped, brown hair and hazel eyes had come between John and Sally.

"Would you interview me next?"

"John, meet Ralphie. Ralphie, John," said Sally with a smile. "I'll leave you two to talk."

"Will you talk to me, John?"

"Of course, Ralphie. Where would you like to meet?"

"Let's meet over at my tombstone. I always feel comfortable there."

The two men floated over to a larger-than-usual headstone made of a purplish stone. Ralphie held onto John's hand.

"Read the inscription, John."

In the stone, the inscription read: 'Ralph Emerson Greer, Born February 2, 1950, Died March 30, 1989, Finally at Peace.'

"My mother loved Emerson. You know the writer Ralph Waldo Emerson?"

"I've heard of him but I don't remember ever reading anything he wrote."

"I've read some but don't remember much except; 'Build a better mousetrap, and the world will beat a path to your door.' I also know he was an individualist, a poet and a lecturer."

"Sounds like an interesting man," said John. "Why does your inscription read, 'Finally at Peace?'"

"I had a very unhappy life. From the age of about 5, I liked dressing up in girls' clothes, played with dolls and identified mostly with my mother. My mother divorced my father when I was 12, and it was around this time I realized I was different from most other boys. Other boys used to call me 'queer' and picked on me incessantly. I knew I was queer but it still hurt when others called me that. By the time I was 16, I didn't hide it anymore. I got beat up several times because I approached other boys for sex but sometimes, I was able to find a kindred spirit.

As soon as I finished high school, I moved from Pittsburgh to San Francisco because I knew there was a substantial gay community there. When I arrived, it seemed as if every gay person in the country was moving to San Francisco. I loved it, and I found many friends and lovers there."

"It sounds as if you found yourself there," said John.

"I did. I had been good at art when I was in school, so I learned to paint and became quite good at it. I used to go to parties about every week and frequented the gay bars and bath houses. It was everything I dreamed of when I was back in Pittsburgh. But the flamboyant gay lifestyle eventually became a drag after about 5 years, and I wanted to find someone to settle down with. There were plenty of men who wanted a temporary companion but few who wanted a long-term commitment.

Then, I fell in love. His name was Larry and for a while, he loved me, too. He was very good-looking and he had inherited a lot of money. We lived happily together for nearly 10 years."

"What happened?"

"Larry was cheating on me. I suspected it had been going on for years. We were at our home when I finally confronted him about it. He didn't deny it and became quite indignant with me. I didn't know how to react, so I just started crying. He left me standing there crying. I was heart-broken. I didn't know where I was going to go because Larry had the apartment and all the money. Even though I was selling some of my paintings occasionally, it wasn't enough to keep up with the lifestyle I had come to know.

I called my mother and asked if I could stay with her. She said I could stay as long as I needed, so I took a bus back home.

It was shortly after I got home that I started to feel sick. I felt like I had the flu for a couple of weeks. Once I was over being sick, I didn't think anything of it until I came down with pneumonia about six months later. When I went to the doctor, he did some tests and determined I had HIV. They didn't know how to treat the disease very well at that time. And in another year, I was diagnosed with lymphoma associated with AIDs.

My mother tried to help me, even though she was having some health issues herself. She was in her 60s and had a bad hip. By this time, I was bedridden and losing weight. I was down to 120 lbs. from 180.

When Larry found out I was sick, he came to visit me. I was so happy to see him that I wept when I saw him. He was very kind and said he missed me. I decided not to spend my last days in a hospital bed and stayed at home. Larry stayed with my mom and me until the end.

My mom had purchased a couple of cemetery plots at the Garden of Peace, and that's how I got here. Mom joined me here in 1999, but she didn't stay long. I believe she's in heaven now. She was such a good person. I really miss her."

"How did she get to heaven, do you think?" asked John.

"I don't really know. One day she was here with me and the group, and the next day she was gone," said Ralphie.

"When do you think you'll be able to join her?"

"Maybe never. If God hates homosexuals, then I may stay here or go to hell and might never see her again."

"I don't think God would make you the way you are and then turn his back on you when you live that way. I don't believe God would be that cruel," said John.

"I hope you're right," said Ralphie.

"Well, Ralphie, you really did have quite a life."

"I guess I did, didn't I?"

"Yes, and it seems to me that you handled your illness with bravery."

"Thank you, John. Now I know how you got your reputation."

"What reputation is that?"

"That you are a good soul, John. You are interested in the souls you speak with, and you seem to know exactly what to say."

"But I hardly talked at all."

"Maybe that's what I needed. And what you did say was just what I needed to hear. Thank you, John."

"You're very welcome, Ralphie. It was my pleasure."

John went back to the group and listened in on a few more conversations for the rest of the afternoon. It wasn't long before the sun began to go down, and the souls moved toward their tombstones.

The sunset that evening was a brilliant array of reds, yellows, oranges and pinks, and the colors seemed more vibrant than John had ever seen.

John went back to his grave site and went into his remembering mode. Where had he left off? Ah, yes, the personnel office training in Vietnam.

Stewart helped John go through some of the regulations and showed him how to file. There was a lot to learn but John seemed to have an affinity for the work.

There were two women working in the office. One was Miss Wong who worked as a secretary and did some typing for the office. She was from Taiwan originally but she dressed more like Western women and was fluent in Chinese, Vietnamese, and English. Miss Wong was not particularly attractive, but she was very nice and worked well with the office.

The other woman was a cleaning lady. John never got her name. She always kept her head down and wore the traditional black pajamas along with the conical straw hat. She kept the office floor clean by using a short, one-handed straw fan-broom to brush the sand out the door.

A couple of weeks after John started, he got orders to go to Long Binh for a week of personnel training. Long Binh was not far from Saigon. This time, he flew by way of a C-130 cargo plane from the airport in Nha Trang. It was an interesting flight. When he got to the plane, he walked up the rear ramp with his duffel bag and sat in the webbed seating that faced toward the center of the plane. He got buckled in and put his duffel bag between his feet in preparation for the flight. A South Vietnamese soldier sat next to him. He was dressed in camouflage fatigues and carried an M-16 that made John a little nervous. They didn't speak. Both rows of seats were nearly full.

As the plane taxied, the engines were very loud. When the C-130 took off, John grabbed the webbing behind his head and held on for dear life because the rapid ascent threw him sideways. The ascent seemed to last forever. Finally, the plane leveled off but the ride didn't get much better. There seemed to be significant turbulence as the plane flew over South Vietnam. The C-130 twisted back and forth for much of the flight, and John was glad he had never experienced air sickness because this would surely have evoked it.

When they landed at Bien Hoa air base, John was very happy to have his feet back on the ground. A bus picked up the passengers and John found the ride through the city interesting. He could tell the area was much more built-up than Nha Trang, with mostly older buildings influenced by the French during their time in Vietnam along with some newer buildings. It was a relatively short ride to Long Bien from Bien Hoa. When they arrived, John was shown his quarters in a series of Quonset huts surrounded by low concrete revetments. They even had a latrine with flush toilets and sinks. John played a few games of ping-pong and did very well against the local competition.

The next day, John started his classes. The classes were held in a wooden building that looked much like the classrooms he'd been in at Ft. Knox and Ft. Gordon. The classes were simple and covered much of the information he'd already learned while in Nha Trang.

John learned about a Chinese restaurant that was close to the classroom. It was called the Loon Foon restaurant. They were given an hour to eat, so John decided to walk there for lunch. When he arrived, he saw that the restaurant was housed in an unassuming red brick building with a small sign in front. He was wearing his green jungle fatigues when he entered the restaurant and immediately felt he was dressed inappropriately for the establishment. The restaurant had a sophisticated feel with very high ceilings and colorful Chinese decorations everywhere. There were large white columns that were at least 12 feet high with ornate oriental capitals. The tables were round and had red table cloths on them. Fortunately, there were a few other GIs in the room in fatigues, so John didn't feel totally out of place.

An attractive Chinese woman in a colorful traditional dress came over, bowed and motioned for John to take a seat at a nearby table. She handed him a menu, then poured hot tea from a white ceramic teapot into a small white ceramic cup. The silverware was substantial and wrapped in a red cloth napkin. John looked over the menu and selected the sweet and sour chicken with fried rice and a cup of egg drop soup. Looking around, he felt he had been transported out of a war zone and into a beautiful place that could have been in San Francisco.

The meal was delicious. After he'd finished, John left and headed back to his classroom full and refreshed.

The rest of the trip was relatively uneventful. John completed his training, then flew back to Nha Trang a week later with as much information as he could remember and some he probably wouldn't. When he got back to Nha Trang, somehow, it felt like home.

He also found out he had been moved to another room in his barracks. This time, John was rooming with three other men from the motor pool. He got a top bunk above Fred, 'the scrounger.' Fred had the reputation of being able to get anything you needed if you had the money or the right thing to trade. Proof of that ability was the fact that theirs was the only air-conditioned room other than the colonel's in the battalion. Fred had taken care of the colonel with a window air conditioner from Okinawa, and the colonel had reciprocated with a deal to get theirs. One of the primary trading units used in these transactions were the cases of steaks Fred had access to by means of the battalion's head cook. Fred took care of the cook with parachute liners, a Jeep at his disposal and just about anything else the cook wanted, and the cook provided the steaks.

Fred had a mosquito net that draped from the bottom of John's upper bunk and went all the way around Fred's bunk and onto the floor. There were nights when John wished he'd had a mosquito net, too, but he didn't complain. He just pulled the sheet and Army blanket over his head when the biting got bad.

A few nights later, John heard a whistling sound that woke him up. He instantly jumped out of bed and onto the floor, then rolled under the bottom bunk. John was still half asleep when he heard the first explosion, then another and another. Fred tried to get out of bed but was captured by his mosquito netting when John rolled onto the netting under the bed.

"What the Hell?" Fred yelled. "What the Hell?"

The next thing John heard was the sound of the mosquito net ripping and Fred finally finding his way under the bed, shoving John over as he did so. The mortars continued to fall one after another until 25 rounds had exploded in the company area. Once the explosions stopped, Fred, John and the others grabbed their war gear and headed for the armory and the bunker. About an hour later, the all-clear sounded and everyone headed back to their rooms.

Fred inspected his ripped mosquito net.

"How the Hell did you get under the bed before me?" he asked John laughing as he spoke.

"I heard the mortars in the air," answered John.

"You can't hear mortars until they hit."

"I heard the whistle when they were coming down," John insisted.

Then John related the story of the first mortar attack and how it had scared him that he hadn't heard the entire attack.

"So, now I'm a very light sleeper."

"I guess you are. I thought I was in the middle of a goddamned nightmare," said Fred. "Explosions were going off and I was stuck in a spider's web and couldn't get out. When I tried to get under the bed, you were wrapped up in the mosquito net and couldn't scooch over."

The men all laughed, including Fred.

"I guess I don't need a mosquito net after all," he said with a smile.

John was glad that Fred took the incident so well. When he went to work, he related the incident to his office mates, and they all loved it.

The weeks turned into months with less and less excitement. John performed guard duty on the perimeter of the base a couple of times, which was a little scary. He was given an M-16 and a bandolier of ammo to take with him up to the top of the sandbagged guard post. John had a walkie-talkie and a red-lensed flashlight with him as well. The mosquitos were thick, so John pulled his sleeves down and turned his collar up. Even though it was night, the air was hot and the flak jacket just made it worse. He could hear the lizards moving in the brush in front of him. At least, he'd hoped they were lizards. There was a concertina wire fence a few yards out and bright lights trained on the area ahead but the shadows made John the most nervous. After a while, a sense of fatalism crept in as he performed this as well as other duties in Vietnam. He couldn't control what was out there in the dark. If Charlie was out there, there wasn't much he could do about it. He never fell asleep while on guard duty but eventually, he wasn't scared either.

During the week, John completed his work diligently and even enjoyed it. At lunch time, a sandwich truck stopped by, lovingly referred to as the 'roach coach.' John quit taking the malaria pill because it gave him the runs. On the weekends, the guys from the office would walk to the beach wearing their civilian shirts and shorts they'd purchased from the PX. John wore a "boonie" hat to protect his ears and face from the tropical sun. It was not uncommon for there to be steaks on grills and beer and soda in ice-filled trailers at the beach.

In his last move, John started rooming with Stewart and Mark from the office. They shared the cost of a mama san cleaning lady. By now, John's fatigues had become faded, so he didn't look like a newbie anymore. He also started a DEROS count-down calendar at the office. He didn't start it until he had less than 200 days left. Other guys who were 'short' talked about being "two-digit midgets" with less than 100 days left until they were to go home.

John also went to the movies out in the area beyond the bunker where there were old faded church pews and a plywood screen attached to telephone poles. They watched the movies *M.A.S.H.* and *How the West Was Won,* among others.

When the monsoon season came, there was nothing but rain most days. There was even a typhoon that hit not far from Nha Trang that brought terrific sustained winds and rain that blew sideways into the barracks. That night, the wool Army blanket was not enough to keep the cold and dampness away from John. Since the entire area was sandy soil, most of the water soaked into the ground with very little runoff but it had been a rough night.

A small black kitten was caught up in the rain and drifted into the arms of Sgt. Wilson from the motor pool. He plucked it from the water, took it back to his hooch, dried it and named her Mary. Sgt. Wilson was a short-timer with just weeks before DEROS. Mary was black from her head to her bent-over 2-inch tail. Other than feed her, Sgt. Wilson mostly left her to her own devices. She had plenty of sand outside to use as a litter box, and she kept herself quite clean. When he was processing out, Sgt. Wilson left Mary to Stewart and John who were glad to have her.

Mary was not a particularly affectionate cat but once she knew where the food was coming from, she began to follow John around and always showed up near the trash cans to be fed after meals. She was fearless around the dogs, even though she could easily have been torn apart by any one of them. Mary would often come to the office and curl up in John's in-box under the desk light for a nap. She quickly became the office cat. Mary was also a good mouser and lizard-catcher extraordinaire. One time, she brought in a lizard that was as long as she was. She dragged it into the middle of the office floor by the nape of its neck and after playing with it for a few moments, crunched down on its neck and proceeded to eat it from head to tail. All that was left when Mary finished was a large pile of entrails and a few bones on the plywood floor.

Chapter 13

Morning arrived, and John floated over to the group as it was forming again. John listened in on the conversation that was going on between several of the souls.

"I'm getting so tired of the nights," said one of them. "How many times can you go over your life anyway?"

"Maybe that's the point," said another. "Maybe you have to look back over the bad things you've done and face up to them."

"What makes you think I've done bad things in my life?"

"Because we've all said or done things we wish we could take back or re-do."

"Well, I think everything I did was for a good reason."

"Then I think you're going to be here for a long time."

"I know I've been here for only a short time," said John. "But it seems to me that we all have to reflect on the things we've done both good and bad. I think it's all part of the learning process. Perhaps once we've learned our lessons, we can move on."

"I've been over my life a thousand times. What more can I learn?"

"Just because we've been over the memories many times doesn't necessarily mean we've learned from them and moved on," said John. "I can think of a few moments I'd like to change. Maybe by recognizing those moments and expressing genuine regret for them or forgiveness for slights against us, then we can move on."

"Maybe so. By the way, my name is Rick. I've heard a lot about you, John."

"It's nice to meet you, Rick. Would you like to get together and talk somewhere?"

"Sure. Why not? Let's go down to the pond."

The two souls floated together toward the pond. Rick was tall, distinguished-looking, with gray hair, deep-set blue eyes and a gaunt look about him.

When the two souls got to the pond, Rick remarked at how beautiful the area was. John agreed and for a moment, the two of them just watched the ripples on the pond while the reeds and cattails swayed in the breeze.

"So, Rick. How long have you been at the Garden of Peace?"

"Since 1965. I was 65 when I died. I never married, so I was alone most of my life."

"What did you do for a living?" asked John.

"I was a real estate developer."

"Tell me about your life, Rick. Where were you born?"

"I was born in Chicago, Illinois in 1900. I was an only child, and my mother divorced my father when I was 16. He used to drink a lot and beat her, so I never blamed her for leaving us. Well, that's not entirely true. I guess I did blame her a little for not taking me with her, because he used to beat me, too. But, eventually, I got big enough to defend myself.

I left home when I was 18 and moved to Pittsburgh because that's where the jobs were at the time. I went to work in a steel mill during the war. We were making cannon parts and gears, so I was exempted from military service. I felt a little guilty for not joining up, but I felt I was doing my part for the war effort.

After the war, the steel mill let me go because the need for steel had been dramatically reduced. I had some money, so I went to college at the University of Pittsburgh. When I graduated, I had a bachelor's degree in business and lots of opportunities. I decided to take a job at one of the real estate companies. Before long, I managed the office and had the reputation of having a no-nonsense attitude and a knack for bringing in new business. In a few years, they made me a vice-president and several years later, I began building houses and eventually started developing properties. By then, I was making real money."

"You said you never married. Did you ever have a girlfriend?"

"I didn't have time for such nonsense. Yes, I had several opportunities but I never pursued them because I was so devoted to my work. Besides, I enjoyed my wealth and my solitude too much to care about such things."

"Do you have any regrets now about never marrying or having children?" asked John.

"Not really. When I wanted the companionship of a woman, I went to a house of ill-repute. That way, there were no strings. I figured that in the long run, it was cheaper than getting married."

"So, you became a wealthy bachelor. Were you happy?"

"Let's just say I was satisfied with my life. I liked my work. And, I had the companionship of my cook and housekeeper. I lived in a fine home in Oakland and had all the comforts I desired."

"It sounds as if you lived in style. Did you go to parties or belong to any clubs?"

"I did. I belonged to the Allegheny Club in downtown Pittsburgh. I used to go there almost every day. In fact, that's how I died. I choked on a piece of steak while having lunch at the club."

"How did you get to the Garden of Peace? There are many cemeteries much closer to Oakland."

"I owned this cemetery. It was just one of many investments I owned. So, I had one of the best plots reserved for myself."

"Earlier, you stated you didn't have any regrets but you mentioned a couple of things you regretted or were unhappy about."

"I did no such thing! I would have done everything the same."

"What about your mother leaving you? You said you blamed her for leaving you even though you understood. Have you forgiven her for leaving you? Have you forgiven your father for beating you?"

"My mother left for a good reason. I don't know why she didn't take me with her. Maybe it was because she couldn't afford to take me at the time. I don't know. And as for my father, why should I forgive him? I didn't do anything to deserve those beatings."

"I don't think of forgiveness as something that needs to be deserved, Rick. Forgiveness is something you do for yourself. It prevents old wounds from festering."

"Nevertheless, I can't forgive them. I mean my father."

"You also said you felt some guilt about not joining the military during the war. Has that ever nagged at you?"

"No! I served my country in the steel mill. That was hard, dirty work. I have no regrets at all. I would do it all the same way if I had it to do over again."

"I didn't mean to make you angry, Rick. I was just trying to help you see why there might be reasons why you are lingering here. I'm glad you had a good life. It sounds as if you deserved it."

"I didn't mean to flare up at you, John."

"Think nothing of it. Why don't we get back to the group? Thank you for sharing with me, Rick.

Back at the congregation of souls, there was continued discussion about how one was to pass on to the next level.

"You have to be baptized in the church. If you weren't baptized, you can't go to heaven," one man said. "It says so in the bible."

"I don't think my wife, Brenda, was ever baptized, and I believe she's in heaven now," interjected John. "There are a lot of conflicting statements in the bible. I believe we get to heaven by the grace of God. It's all up to Him. He can show mercy to anyone he wants."

"Well, I disagree. God laid down his words in the bible for all of us to follow. The bible is our roadmap to heaven."

"John," said Sally, "I'd like you to meet Reverend Murphy." The reverend was wearing a gray suit and bright yellow tie. He was heavyset and had thick, wavy brown hair that was combed back.

John extended his hand toward the man and the two of them shook hands.

"Are you still trying to save souls even here, Reverend?"

"Yes. I believe this must be the reason I'm still here. It is my mission to help others on their way to heaven."

"Have you had any luck?" asked John.

"I believe it is my effort that counts," replied the preacher.

"Would you like to go somewhere and see what you can do to help me get to heaven?"

"Certainly. Let's go over to my headstone."

The two men floated over to an area near the center of the cemetery where a modest gray granite headstone was located.

"That's my wife's headstone next to mine. Margaret has gone to heaven."

"I see you both died on the same day. What happened?" asked John.

"We were driving back from a retreat in Somerset when we were hit head-on by a truck."

"It must have been a quick death."

"It was. We were both killed instantly. There was no time to prepare. One minute we were alive and happy, the next minute we were dead."

"Do you mind telling me about your life, Reverend?"

"Not at all. I was born in Opelika, Alabama in 1955. My father was a Baptist minister there. My mother raised all seven of us children while my father took care of his flock. He was a very busy man, so I didn't see him much except at supper time and at church events. I think he was a good man, even though he was very strict with us. We received regular spankings from our father when we didn't obey our mother during the day.

I heard the call when I was 18 and went to Samford University's Beeson School of Divinity in Homewood, Alabama and followed in my father's footsteps as a Baptist minister. I met my wife Margaret at Samford and were married after I received my divinity degree. Upon graduation from Beeson, I received several offers from around the country. For a time, I was an assistant minister in Denver, Colorado. Those were lean times, but we loved the mountains and did a lot of skiing.

After we had our first child three years later, we felt it was time to lead a church of our own. I had an offer to be the minister of a small church in Murrysville, Pennsylvania, so I took the job. This was an up-and-coming community within 45 minutes of downtown Pittsburgh, and we did very well there. We eventually had four children. My oldest son followed in my footsteps and became a Baptist minister."

"You must be very proud of him."

"I am. He was the one who performed our eulogies and our funeral ceremonies."

"Did you believe in ghosts when you were alive, Reverend?"

"No. I can't say that I did. This situation is very different from what I expected. I thought I would go to heaven immediately, like my wife did."

"Do you think your sins are holding you back?" asked John.

"No. My sins were so minor I think God forgave them as soon as I prayed about them."

"Tell me about your work in Murrysville."

"Certainly. I helped grow the church there from a membership of approximately 150 to one of over 500. At the time of my death, our church had two full-time assistant ministers and a choir director. My wife and I had a house in town, I drove a nice car, and we took two or three vacations every year.

My normal duties were to give sermons each Sunday morning, Sunday evening and Wednesday evening. I performed marriages and funerals and visited the sick of the congregation."

"Do you think about your other children?"

"Of course. Fortunately, they're all grown now and on their own. We didn't leave them much because the church owned the house and car, and we didn't have much in savings but they'll all be okay. We lived a good life."

"Tell me about your wife," said John. "What did she do?"

"Margaret was a wonderful wife and mother. She helped in the church, too. She led the nursery and helped organize special events such as Christmas and Easter. We were very good together, and she was the perfect minister's wife. We sometimes had disagreements but she always accepted my directions as head of the church and our household."

"It sounds as if she was very selfless."

"She was, wasn't she?"

"Perhaps that's why she went to heaven right away," said John.

"You may be right, John. I guess all I can do is pray that I can be with her soon."

"So, what do you think I need to do to get to heaven from here?" John asked.

"I think you need to pray for the forgiveness of your sins."

"I can do that."

"You also need to show God that you can be one of his ardent followers."

"That may be a little difficult for me. I think God loves me for who I am."

"But you must let God know you love him with all of your heart. Otherwise, why would he let you into heaven?"

"It doesn't seem to have helped you so far, Reverend."

"I guess we shall see, won't we, John?"

"I guess so."

John left the reverend and met Sally as he neared the group.

"What did you think of Reverend Murphy?" she asked.

"He was very interesting. Seemed a little full of himself like he knew everything about the Bible and what we should all do to get to heaven."

"That's him all right. He's a real Bible thumper whenever conversation heads that way."

"By the way, Sally, I haven't seen James around recently. Why isn't he here?"

"James hasn't been himself recently. He's over at his grave site up near the gate. Maybe you could visit with him today."

"Sounds like a good idea. Thanks, Sally."

John floated over near the gate and spotted James hovering over his grave.

"James! How are you doing?" John asked when he arrived.

"Not so well, I'm afraid."

"What seems to be the matter?"

"At night, I've been recollecting things in my life that I can't get out of my head."

"Would you like to talk about them?"

"Okay. Well, I'll start when I was a young boy at about 10 years of age. I had an uncle who used to babysit me and my siblings. He molested all of us though none of us knew about the others until much later in life. I'm embarrassed by what he did to me."

"At age 10, what could you have done?"

"I don't know. Maybe I should have told my parents. That might have stopped him from molesting the others. I guess I was too ashamed to speak up."

"Again, you were only 10. You were probably scared of what would happen to you if you went to them. It wasn't your fault, James."

"I know you're right but it's difficult to get out of my head."

"Have you forgiven your uncle yet?"

"No."

"Maybe that's what you have to do to release yourself from that memory's grip."

"I guess I can try to do that."

"I'm not saying it'll be easy but I know it worked for me in similar circumstances."

"Thanks, John."

"Since we're talking, why don't you tell me more about your life? You're one of the first people I met here and you were so outgoing. I'm sorry I haven't really talked with you yet."

"As they say, there's no time like the present," James said. "Well, I was born in 1940 in Helena, Montana."

"You're a long way from home," said John smiling.

"Things weren't going too well for my father at the time in Helena. He was a welder, so when I was 11, we moved to Pittsburgh where there was plenty of steel work available. We eventually moved into a nice house in McKeesport."

"I've been there many times."

"After we moved to Pittsburgh, I had a good life. My mother doted on me, and my father was good to her. I graduated from McKeesport Senior High School in 1958 and from there, I went on to college at Penn State. I received my Masters of Business Administration from there also. The Vietnam War was still very active at that time but my draft number was 320, so I was never called to serve. I was against the war and participated in some marches on campus.

Not long after I graduated, I married my high school sweetheart, Beth. I got a job at Westinghouse, and we moved to Plum where we had three children. We had a good life for many years until my wife died of cancer in 1990. Beth fought hard for several years but the cancer finally got her.

My children are all grown and have families of their own. When I died of a liver failure in 2010, I had four grandchildren. I probably have more now but the kids never come to visit, so I don't know."

"It sounds as if you had a very good life, James."

"I did, didn't I?"

"Thank you for telling me about your life."

"It's about sunset, so I'd best be going."

"Yeah, me too. Thanks again," said John.

"You're very welcome."

The sun was just getting ready to set, so John went back to his grave site and went back to his personal reflections.

Chapter 14

Back in Vietnam, John had the opportunity to take an R & R, so he decided to go to Australia. He'd been reading a copy of Phillip Roth's book, *Portnoy's Complaint,* and finished it on the plane. When they arrived in Sidney, customs officials boarded the plane. One of them got on the loudspeaker and said that weapons of any kind, drugs of any kind, and pornography of any kind were strictly prohibited from being brought into Australia. He said they were going to walk down the aisle with a paper bag and passengers were to put their contraband in the bag. If they found any contraband on individuals during their search after they got off the plane, such individuals would likely go to jail for trying to smuggle contraband into the country. When the man with the bag came by, John remembered his book had some very graphic sex scenes in it. He asked the man if *Portnoy's Complaint* was considered pornography. The man just said, "If in doubt, I'd put it in the bag, mate." So, he put the book in the bag. It didn't matter since John had already read it anyway.

When they got off the plane, the servicemen were escorted down a narrow passageway at the airport. Each soldier was taken into a private room, and the door was closed. John was frisked from head to toe. He was then asked to strip down to his underwear. John complied and after turning around and checking under his arms and the bottom of his feet, the guard told him to get dressed and go down the hall. It was the most thorough inspection John had experienced. He pitied the person who ever tried to bring anything illegal into the country.

After heading down the hall, John had to pick up his luggage from customs. The customs official had John open his suitcase, and he rifled through it before declaring him good to go. From there, John went to a large area where the soldiers lined up at different stations to determine where they would go. When it was his turn, John was interviewed by a nice lady and was given several options: going aboard a boat for deep sea fishing, going to a party boat, staying in downtown Sidney, or staying on a farm with a family where he might do some horseback riding and such. John chose the farm because he was mostly looking for some peace and quiet.

He was given a ticket for a short plane trip to a small community in New South Wales called Uralla. That night, John spent the night in a hotel in downtown Sydney where he rented some dress clothes for the evening and went down to a restaurant in the hotel for dinner. He was seated at a table that was centered in the room, while the rest of the patrons were seated in booths around the sides of the room. John ordered a steak with all the trimmings and when asked what he wanted to drink, he ordered scotch on the rocks. He'd never had scotch before, and the moment he took a drink, John immediately began to choke. He coughed and choked for some time and was very embarrassed by the incident. When the steak finally came, John dug in as if he'd never had a steak before, and felt very exposed throughout the meal.

The next morning, John took a cab to the airport and was surprised to see that the cabbie was wearing Bermuda shorts. The cabbie was very friendly and conversed with John the entire way. At the airport, John found that the plane was relatively small and only carried about 20 passengers. It wasn't a long flight to Uralla and once he arrived, an attractive blonde woman in her mid-30s was waiting for him at the tiny airport.

"Hello. Are you John Sample?" she asked.

"Yes, Ma'am, I am."

"Welcome to Uralla, Australia!" she said as she shook his hand with enthusiasm. "I'm Laura Findley. I was born in America and came here when I was 17, so I speak Ausie and American. Let's get your luggage into the car, and I'll take you back to our farm."

"Thank you. It's very nice to meet you."

As Laura drove, she talked a mile-a-minute and John tried to keep up. The countryside was beautiful and there were few houses along the way. In about half an hour, they came to a yellow-sided, ranch-style house that could have been in an American subdivision. The yard was flat and looked like it was composed of a short weed-looking grass. Near the house was a traditional-looking small white barn. A black cat sat near the barn door.

Laura's husband and a nondescript, medium sized brown dog came out of the house to greet them.

"G'day! John, is it? I'm Russel Findley. Welcome to our farm!"

The two men shook hands and Russel grabbed the suitcase from the car. Russel was about 6' tall and lanky with thick, brown hair and brown eyes. He was wearing a long-sleeved shirt, short pants, and knee-high rubber boots.

"So, how are you liking Australia so far, John?"

"I think it's beautiful and the people have been very friendly. In many ways, it reminds me a lot of home back in the U.S."

They went inside the house and John was very surprised at what he saw. The entry led directly into the kitchen which looked as if it could have been from the late 1800's. There was an old wood-fired cooking stove and older-looking wood cabinets. The wood floors and cabinets were not shiny and the living room was up a step and beyond the kitchen. Russel showed John through the house and into a bedroom where he placed the luggage on the bed.

"I hope you'll be comfortable in here. We're very happy to have you visit, John."

"Thank you very much."

John noticed that Russel had been watching a cricket match on a small black-and-white television.

"I've never watched cricket before."

"It's a great game. You might find it interesting to watch a live match while you're here in Uralla," said Russel. "I know Laura has several things lined up for you to do this week."

John noticed the distinctive Australian accent as Russel spoke, and he had to listen carefully to understand everything Russel said.

"I spent a little time on a farm back in Indiana. What kind of farm do you have?"

"We have a sheep farm. The farm is 40 acres and we have nearly 200 head of sheep, 4 pigs, and 20 chickens."

"If you don't mind my asking, how much does an acre of ground go for around here?"

"I bought the 40 acres for $7.00 an acre 10 years ago. Now, it's probably worth $70.00 an acre. But we're in the outback, so things are cheaper out here than near a city or along the coast. By the way, I'm about to go into the barn and slaughter one of the sheep if you want to come along."

"No thank you. I think I'll go in and take a nap if that's all right with you."

"Perfectly all right. I'll talk to you later, mate. Nice to meet you, John."

"Likewise, Russel."

John went into the bedroom, put his suitcase on the floor, then flopped down on the soft bed.

John woke up quite some time later. It was dark outside. He went into the living room where Laura and Russel were watching TV.

"Well, good evening sleepy head," said Laura. "I'm afraid you've slept through supper, John. I was afraid to wake you. You yelled out in your sleep once like you were having a nightmare."

"I did? I don't remember it." John was embarrassed about yelling out.

"I made some stew, would you like some?"

"Yes, thank you."

Laura lit the stove and heated the stew in a small pot. John sat at the dining room table, and Laura soon brought over a steaming bowl of stew. It was tasty but John didn't recognize the flavor.

"I'll bet that's the first time you've had mutton stew."

"You're right about that. It's very good. Thank you."

"Tomorrow, I thought I'd take you around to see Uralla and the countryside. We have some friends with horses, and you can do some riding if you like."

"That sounds like fun," said John.

"I have some other things planned as well but we can talk about that later. After such a long nap, I hope you'll be able to sleep tonight. We go to bed earlier than you do probably."

"Don't worry about me. I'm sure I'll be able to sleep just fine."

The next morning, Laura fixed John a breakfast of bacon and eggs. Russel had already gone to the barn.

"I thought we'd do a little sight-seeing today and let you see a little of the territory. It looks like it's going to be a beautiful day. Perhaps you can do a little horseback-riding this afternoon, if you'd like," said Laura. "I hope you brought your camera."

"I did. And that sounds great. I look forward to it."

After Laura cleaned up the breakfast dishes, she put the dog outside and took some food out for him.

"Come along then, John. We'll get on the road and see what's out there."

Laura drove him through the small town of Uralla. It was a quaint-looking village that seemed like it could have been right out of a picture of merry old England. The streets were made of cobblestone and the shops were small brick buildings, each identified by painted signs on the windows. There was a baker, a butcher, and a chemist. She also drove by the local lawn bowling country club and let John get out to take some pictures. Behind the country club was a lawn bowling green where he could see the participants wearing white outfits. There was a low fence surrounding the club and trimmed, red rose bushes all around. The club members paid him no mind as he took pictures.

They stopped by the local cricket field and got out of the car to watch a game that was underway. Laura led John up to where the men in their white pants and sweaters were waiting for their turns at bat.

She went up to one of the men and said, "This here's John. He's an American soldier from Vietnam visiting Australia for the first time. Wondered if you could give him a little lesson in cricket while you're waiting."

"I can sure enough do that for you, Yank. My name's Trevor. It's nice to meet you." The two men shook hands. Trevor went over to his equipment bag, then brought back a ball and bat. "I understand that our ball is like your baseball," he said as he handed it to John to hold.

"You're right, except this ball is reddish brown and has two seams up the middle. It feels a lot like a baseball, though," said John.

"Right you are, mate. Now, here's our bat."

The bat was wider than a baseball bat with a rounder side and a flatter side, although it was not exactly flat. It had a longer handle that felt comfortable in John's hands. Trevor went on to explain the game.

"Thanks for the lesson, Trevor. It was nice to meet you."

John and Laura watched the match for a while, then got back into the car.

"Do you think you have cricket figured out, John?"

"Not really but it looks like fun."

They drove out into the countryside and stopped at a quaint, country church called Gostwyck Chapel that was covered with ivy. John got out and took some photos. There was also a small stone bridge nearby over a clear stream, and he took some pictures of that, too.

"I brought some sandwiches if you're hungry."

"Yes, Ma'am. Sounds good."

After lunch, Laura drove for a while and pointed out a family of kangaroos which John got some photos of as well.

After a couple of hours of driving through the countryside, Laura took John to her friend's farm. She introduced her to John and they led him to the barn where the horses were kept. The lady brought out a chestnut mare and saddled her with a black, English saddle.

"I've never ridden with an English saddle before," said John.

"Don't worry. If you can ride a Western saddle, you can ride an English saddle. Sadie's as gentle as a lamb, so she won't give you any trouble. Just keep her out of the thickets and come back in an hour or so."

"Thank you, Ma'am. I'll do that."

John stepped into the stirrups. Once he was steady in the saddle, the lady handed him the reins, then he rode off through a gate and past the barn. The saddle was comfortable but felt odd without the horn. He rode at a slow walk through the field of grasses and scrub over a slight rise. There were only a few trees along the way, and John did not recognize them. One thing John did recognize was the amazing number of rabbits he saw, and they were huge. He rode comfortably for about half an hour and then turned back. John did not see any kangaroos during his ride but it had been fun. When he got back to the barn, he saw the two women sitting on the porch.

"How was your ride, John?" asked Laura.

"It was great! You have a lovely property, Ma'am. And you were right. Your horse was very gentle. We did kick up a few huge rabbits on the way."

"Around here, we call them 'hares', John, and they're a real nuisance."

John got off the horse and gave her a good pat on the shoulder. He took the horse by the reins to her owner and thanked the lady for letting him ride.

"You're quite welcome, John. Come by anytime."

As they left, John waved.

"She seems like a very nice lady," John said.

"Yes, she is."

"I think we'll head back to our place now. How did you like the tour and the horseback ride?"

"I loved it. This is very beautiful country."

"I think so, too."

Back at the farm, Russel was just coming out of the barn.

"How was your trip today, John?"

"It was great. We went to a cricket match, went to the country club, saw the town and the countryside, and had lunch near a church. Then I got to do some horseback riding. All-in-all, it was a great day."

"Glad you enjoyed it. Why don't you get washed up for supper? We're going to have mutton chops on the barbie tonight."

John watched Laura prepare the mutton chops and wrap them in aluminum foil before taking them out to a small, free-standing grill in the side yard. She put some briquettes in the grill and placed the chops on it but didn't light the fire.

John was out watching the grill when he noticed a line of ants forming at the base of the grill. They marched steadily up the grill and into the chops. John went inside and reported this to Laura.

"Don't worry. We'll just brush them off. They disappear soon after we light the grill, anyway."

As they ate, John realized he wasn't thrilled with the taste of mutton but he politely ate all that was on his plate.

When John got up the next morning, Laura fixed him oatmeal for breakfast. Again, Russel was already out tending to the farm by the time John got up.

"How would you like to do some hunting today, John?"

"Hunting for what?" John asked.

"Hares, like you saw yesterday. I have some family that owns a farm not far from here, and they're always looking to thin out the hares."

"Sure. It sounds like fun."

Later, Laura took down a short rifle from the top of a cabinet and put it in the car. They drove out along a different route from the day before and eventually, ended up on a gravel road that led to a beautiful property on a hill with a large white older house on it.

Before getting to the house, Laura pulled the car over beside the road and the two of them got out.

"Here is where you can hunt," she said pointing out a triangle of land bordered by the road and a fence-row. She got the rifle out of the backseat of the car and handed it to John.

"There's 10 shots in the clip," she said.

John looked at the strange rifle in his hands. It looked like a typical .22 rifle from back home but there was no bolt that John could see and no way of feeding the bullet into the chamber.

"How do you get the bolt to go forward?" he asked sheepishly. It seemed odd that a soldier would be asking a woman for advice on how to fire a rifle.

"You just pull the trigger and it fires," she said. "Take a shot at that fence post and you'll see."

Sure enough, when John aimed at the post and pulled the trigger, the rifle fired and John hit his target.

"That's good, John. I'm going up to the house, and I'll be back to pick you up in an hour or so. Good luck."

"Thank you. I'll see you then."

John watched Laura drive up to the house, then surveyed the property he was going to hunt. The ground was thickly-covered with dried, knee-high grass and there were a couple of fallen trees on the ground. John stood motionless for a while before he noticed some movement in the grass near a fallen tree. The hare was only about 50 yards in front of him but all he could see were the ears. John aimed a few inches below the ears and fired. The ears went down but John wasn't sure he had hit it until he walked up on it. It lay dead at his feet, shot through the head. John took the hare back to the pick-up point and laid it down before heading back to the place where he had shot it.

John shot two more hares within the hour and waited for Laura. He sat on a stump and waited for a few minutes before the car came back.

"Wow!" she exclaimed. "Three shots and three hares. That's pretty good shooting, John."

"Thanks," he said. "Are we going to eat them?"

"No. We just give them to the dog and cat. We shoot them as often as we can to try to thin out the population but it's a losing battle."

John put the dead hares in the trunk of the car and placed the rifle on the back seat. When they got back to the farm, Laura took the hares to a spot near the barn door and dropped them to the ground. It didn't take long for the dog and cat to spot them.

The next day, Laura asked John if he knew how to roller skate.

"Absolutely, I do," replied John. "I used to live close to a roller rink and skated all the time."

"Well then, that's what we'll do today. There's a roller rink in town. It might give you a chance to meet some other people your own age," said Laura.

When they went to the roller rink, it looked old and had a hardwood floor. But John got his skates and proceeded to skate around the rink. There were quite a few people younger than he was but not many his own age. Nevertheless, John had a good time. Laura didn't skate but watched from the side. After John finished skating, Laura drove them back to the farm after a stop for ice cream.

The next day, Laura drove John to the airport and hugged him goodbye. He told her what a great time he'd had visiting with them. She wrote to him once after he got home and encouraged him to write back, but he never did. It was one of the regrets of his life.

Chapter 15

John remembered getting back to Vietnam from Australia. It seemed like he had been away from Vietnam for a long time and he was very relaxed. By then, he was feeling 'short' with 119 days and a wake-up left to go. He told everyone in the office about Australia and how great it was. John described Australia as something out of America's past, like during the early 1900's with lots of beauty, land and opportunity.

John's old girlfriend, Pamela, from Ft. Worth got his Vietnam address from John's mother and began writing to him. They wrote back and forth several times while he was there. She encouraged him to try to stop by and visit if he got the chance. The insinuation was that she might be interested in getting back together.

There were a few more mortar attacks but nothing serious. The beach was off limits because of security concerns, so there wasn't much to do on the weekends. To pass the time in the evenings, John read *The Godfather*, *The Andromeda Strain* and *Love Story*. He played a little volleyball with his office mates on the sand between the barracks and time moved on.

In November, there were reports coming down from the upper echelons that there were going to be some 'early outs.' Stewart got to go home early and since he was drafted, he got discharged from the military as soon as he got back to the states. He was planning to get married soon after he got back to the 'world.' His wedding date was scheduled for February 6th, which was John's original DEROS date. By now, Stewart had made sergeant and with mixed emotions, John wished him well as he got ready to take off. It was obvious he was very happy to go.

Even though he was still only a Spec. 4, John became one of the senior men in the office, and it wasn't long before John got orders to go home at the end of December. Now, he really felt short.

Finally, on December 26th, John packed up the belongings he hadn't sold, said goodbye to his friends, and headed for the pickup point for the convoy that would take him to Cam Ranh Bay. The convoy to Cam Ranh was one of the scariest times John had experienced while in Vietnam. The road was paved but narrow with banana trees and similar foliage on either side of the road. *Perfect for an ambush*, John thought. But the convoy arrived without incident.

When John got to Cam Ranh Bay, he stayed one night before getting on his 'freedom bird.' The plane was a Brannif International and he was surprised to find beautiful stewardesses on the flight. Everyone was quiet as they taxied down the runway and then there was a thunderous *"Yaaaaay!"* from all the soldiers as the wheels left the ground. It was an exciting moment. The flight back was much more comfortable than the flight to Vietnam on Flying Tiger airlines.

When he arrived back at Ft. Lewis, Washington, John got several briefings on what to expect from life away from Vietnam. One of the briefings was conducted by a drill sergeant who was recruiting men to become drill instructors. The main benefits of becoming a drill instructor were: immediate promotion to the next higher rank upon graduation, choice of basic training duty stations, and $50 extra per month. Since John had 14 more months to go on his enlistment, this sounded good to him. So, he signed up to go to drill sergeant school at Ft. Knox, Kentucky, which was only 2 ½ hours by car from his home in Lafayette, Indiana.

John was also able to obtain a plane ticket to Ft. Worth, Texas to surprise Pamela on his way back to Indianapolis and then Lafayette, Indiana where he would have four weeks leave before having to report to Ft. Knox.

Upon arriving in Ft. Worth, John took a cab to a hotel near the airport. When he got to the hotel, he took a shower and relaxed for a while before calling Pamela. Over the phone, she sounded very surprised to hear from him but also sounded pleased. Pamela said she would drive over and pick him up in the morning and said he could stay over with her mother and her instead of having to stay in a hotel.

When Pamela arrived, she was driving a newer blue Mercury Cougar and was wearing a fur coat.

"It's so nice to see you, John," she said. "I'm glad you made it home safely."

"It's nice to see you, too, Pamela. This is a nice car."

"It belongs to my fiancée. He goes to Abilene Christian."

John looked at her in disbelief. She showed him her engagement ring as she drove.

"Mom is really looking forward to seeing you."

"Likewise," John said still in shock.

John's first thought was to have Pamela drive him back to the hotel but for some reason, he couldn't say it. The rest of the ride was filled with small talk about John's time in Vietnam and the military.

When they arrived at her home, Pamela's mother was waiting. She welcomed John and offered him some breakfast, which he gladly accepted. She made pancakes and bacon. Pamela watched him eat and talked about attending Abilene Christian and how much she loved it.

"I'm glad you like it. I'm sure it suits you," said John.

Later that morning, John called several airlines trying to get a flight out. Unfortunately, this was December 31st and all the planes were booked solid for New Year's Day, so the first flight out to Indianapolis was January 3rd. Pamela and her mother suggested he stay with them until then. John had little option but to accept.

They planned a get-a-way excursion to Pamela's grandparents' cabin in the country on the weekend. Her grandparents were very nice but the entire time, John just wanted to get through this seemingly never-ending embarrassment. The cabin was very rustic and the property was mostly small trees and a lot of rocks with a small stream not far from the cabin. At one point, they did some shooting while they were there, and that was the only fun John had. Once they got back to the house, Pamela packed up to go back to Abilene and wished John well.

Before she left, Pamela told John that she still had feelings for him and that was why she wrote to him while he was in Vietnam but she felt a greater love for her fiancée. John wished her the best of luck at ACC and on her engagement. After she left, John stayed one more night and Pamela's mother took him to the airport very early in the morning and apologized for the way things turned out. He thanked her for her hospitality and left for the plane. John was glad the excruciating experience had finally ended and looked forward to going home.

John called home from the Dallas airport and planned for someone to meet him at the Indianapolis airport. He had orders to report to Ft. Knox at the end of January, so he had about 26 days left of his leave.

His mother was the one who met him at the airport at 9 a.m. She hugged him tight and said, "I'm so glad you made it home safe and sound, John. It's good to see you. You look thin. Are you okay?"

"I'm good, and I'm glad to be back, Mom," he replied.

John put his duffel bag and suitcase in the car and climbed in.

When they started on their way, John asked, "How is everyone?"

"Well, you know Uncle Bret died of cancer this past summer."

"I remember you telling me that in one of your letters. I was sorry to hear he had passed away.

John's mother proceeded to give him a report on her brothers and sisters most of whom were doing well.

"Paul is graduating from Jeff this year. He just went back to school after his Christmas break. He'll be glad to see you."

"How's he doing in school?"

"He's doing very well. He plans to go to Purdue in the fall," she said.

"I'm glad to hear he's doing well. As for myself, I will be going to drill sergeant school at Ft. Knox at the end of this month. I still have a year and two months left on my enlistment but since I'll be near Louisville, Kentucky, it should only be about a 2 ½ hour drive. I hope to be able to get home every couple of months. But, we'll have to see."

"It certainly is good to have you home safe. It'll be nice to have you closer to home, John."

They drove the hour drive from Indianapolis to Dayton, Indiana where they had recently moved, and his mom filled him in on all he had missed over the 11 months he had been away; who had died, who was sick, who had gone away to school and who'd had more kids. There was no way John was going to remember all she told him but for once, it was good to hear her tell it all.

When John got home, he thanked his mom for driving out to get him. He put his duffel bag and suitcase upstairs by his bed and lay down to take a nap. He fell asleep the moment his head hit the pillow.

Suddenly, John was startled by the sound of a siren like he'd known in Vietnam when mortars were landing. He rolled off the bed and tried to get under it but it was too close to the ground. It was then he realized he was home and the siren was the one that sounded every day at noon in the little town. He got back to bed and never told his mom or dad about the incident.

John's father came home that evening and seemed genuinely glad to have his son home again, and John was glad to be home. But in the same way he had when he was home before leaving for Vietnam, he quickly got bored since everyone he knew was either working, off to college or had moved away.

While he was in Vietnam, John spent many hours perusing different sports cars in magazines and sales brochures. Based on a price he could afford, he found a small sports car at a Fiat dealership in downtown Lafayette. It was a bright orange-red Fiat 850 Racer with a black-vinyl hardtop, and he bought it for a little over $3,000 right off the showroom floor. There was a 58-horsepower aluminum-block engine in the rear and a slim trunk in the front. There was a small 'jump seat' behind the front seat that was in no way designed to be seated in. At best, it could handle a suitcase and a duffel bag. The car was very sporty-looking but also very small and low to the ground. He used to say that he had to look up at people in Volkswagen Beetles. But it was also very fun to drive with its short-throw 4-speed shifter in the upper center console, and its rack-and-pinion steering made it feel almost like a go-kart when he drove it on winding roads. Just as a comparison, he remembered looking at a 1969 Corvette that was selling for $6,900 that might as well have been a million dollars as far as he was concerned. So, John was very happy to settle for the Fiat.

John received a wedding invitation from Stewart Butler, his best friend from Vietnam. He was getting married on a Saturday in Chicago which was about two and a half hours away from Lafayette. John drove up there for the wedding, and it was good to see Stewart again and to meet his wife, Julie.

When John went to Ft. Knox, it felt like old home week. He drove around the base and familiarized himself with the streets and different locations. As a basic trainee, he had not seen much of the base. He remembered the reception station, the PX, and he had seen the gold depository building once before. John drove by his old basic training unit, and it brought back a lot of memories.

Finally, John drove to the administration building and gave his orders to a Private First Class who was at the desk.

"You're early by a day," said the PFC.

"Better early than late," said John.

"That's true. You're scheduled to report to Bravo-13-4 tomorrow. Let me call over and make sure they have a spot for you."

John waited while the PFC called.

"I just spoke with the person on duty there. The unit is between basic training cycles and the staff doesn't report back until Wednesday. Since this is Sunday, you can go over there and find a bunk. You have free time until 6 a.m. Wednesday, so you might as well get situated and learn your way around the base. Just give your papers to the First Sergeant when he gets there."

"Can you give me directions to Bravo-13-4?"

"Sure. Take a right out of the parking lot, take your first right, go three blocks and take another right and you'll be there. The unit is marked on the building. Here's your paperwork. Good luck."

"Thanks," said John.

John found the red brick building that had the bold painted letters and numbers, B-13-4 and parked in front. He grabbed his suitcase and duffel bag and went into the building. The company office was just down the hall, and there was a private manning it.

"Specialist John Sample reporting for duty." It seemed odd reporting to a private.

"The sergeant will be back in a few minutes. He'll tell you where you need to go."

A few moments later, a staff sergeant drill sergeant came into the office. John stood and introduced himself.

"I'm Staff Sergeant Masters. Nice to meet you. So, you're going to hard-hat for us for a while?"

"That's my expectation, at least until I go through DI school," said John.

"It's a tough job. Are you in shape?"

"I didn't do much PT while I was in Nam, so I guess we'll have to wait and see."

"Don't worry," said the staff sergeant. "You'll get in shape pretty quickly around here. Have you had anything to eat yet?"

"Not yet. But, I'd like to stow my stuff away before I go. Can you show me where I'll be bunking?"

"No problem."

The staff sergeant showed him his room on the main floor, and John picked out one of the two empty bunks that were in the room.

"Where's the mess hall?"

"It's two buildings over. Breakfast is probably over but they should start serving lunch in about half an hour. If you want to put your gear away, I'll stop by and walk you over."

"Sounds good. Thanks," said John.

Chapter 16

Morning at the cemetery was a bright one with a beautiful, yellow sun peeking out over the trees. John headed over to the group.

"What's the talk about this morning?" asked John to no one in particular.

"The talk is about you, John. You've become quite the leader here," said Sally.

"I don't feel like a leader," said John. "I just got here. I simply talk to people and listen to their stories."

"But you don't judge them. That makes a big difference. You've talked to quite a few souls around here, and now the rest of them are lined up to talk to you."

"That's great! I love talking with everyone. It's helping me, so at the same time it might be helping them."

"Good. Next up is Summer. I'll let you two introduce yourselves."

"Good morning, Summer. I'm John."

"Your reputation precedes you, John."

Summer was a beautiful, middle-aged woman with long blonde hair and green eyes. She was tall and thin.

"Where would you like to go to talk, Summer?"

"Let's go to the big oak near my grave stone. I don't know why but that oak tree has been a comfort to me."

The two of them floated together over to the large, spreading oak. When Summer took John's hand, there was an instant connection and John could feel her pain.

"I sense that you had a lot of pain in your life, Summer. Would you care to share your story with me?"

"You sense correctly, John. Where should I begin?" asked Summer.

"The beginning is always a good place to start."

Summer laughed.

"All right then. I was born near San Francisco, California in 1965. My parents were Hippies back then, and we lived in a commune several miles away from the city. They farmed and shared a large farmhouse with several other people. It was an interesting way to grow up, but I didn't know much about the rest of the world as we had no TVs or radios in the commune. People there would sing, dance, and play their guitars for entertainment. I got to be fairly good at the guitar, actually. My father was the leader of the commune and though they never married, my parents told me they were always faithful to each other."

"You must have had quite an interesting childhood. How long were you with the commune?"

"Until I was 17. I met a boy who was traveling through and he stayed with us for a while. I fell in love with him and we left the commune together and moved to San Diego. He left me for another woman two years later. I was pregnant with his child and I didn't want anything to do with him or his child, so I had an abortion."

"I'm sorry you had such a difficult decision to make. Are you still all right with your abortion decision?"

"No. I wish I had given the baby up for adoption. I often wonder what kind of man he would have become."

"What happened afterwards?"

"I went back home for a while but the commune had changed—or I had, and it didn't hold any interest for me anymore. My parents wanted me to stay and help work the farm but I had to move on. I took what little money I had and decided to go as far as the money would take me on a bus. I got as far as Pittsburgh, and that's where I stayed.

I played my guitar in little bars and sang songs I'd written and ones I'd learned in the commune. I made enough money to live on but not much more. Then I met Terry at one of the bars I played. He was handsome and funny and we made each other laugh. We fell in love and soon, we were married. Terry and his family were very well off, so we bought a big house and had nice cars. It was quite different from commune living."

"I'll bet it was," said John laughing.

"We were very happy. Then we tried to have children. Unfortunately, I was unable to have children due to the way my abortion was done. I never told Terry about the abortion. The doctor just told him I was unable to conceive. Terry was very disappointed. We finally decided to adopt. Eventually, we adopted two children—a boy and a girl; William and Wendy."

"It sounds as if you have a very nice family," said John.

"We did. And life was good for several years. Then I found a lump in one of my breasts and it turned out to be cancer. The doctors encouraged me to have a double mastectomy, so I had it done. It was a very difficult recovery time and an even more difficult adjustment for me and my husband after the surgery.

Two years later, the cancer was back. They tried chemo and radiation but it metastasized and killed me in 2007."

"You must have endured a lot of pain during your illness."

"I did. But the hardest part was having to say goodbye to my family. My parents even came to see me before I passed."

"So, you've been here for 10 years now. How are you getting along?"

"Okay, I guess. My husband and children still come here on Memorial Day. I really miss them."

"Do you have any regrets or any idea as to why you're still here?" John asked.

"I regret having the abortion. And I regret not hugging my family more when I was alive. But otherwise, I feel like I led a good life. Since I've been here at the Garden, I've tried to pray for forgiveness."

"I don't know what else you could do. You seem like a very good soul to me. I would guess that it's just a matter of time before you go to heaven. Just keep praying."

"I hope you're right."

"I've really enjoyed hearing your story, Summer. Thank you for sharing it."

"Thank you, John. Now it's your turn. Tell me how you got here."

John summarized his life story and told her how he had died.

"You led a very interesting life, John. I appreciate your having been here for me. I hope you get to heaven soon."

"Likewise, Summer. Thank you."

John and Summer went back to the assembly of souls where he met Sally again.

"Summer is so nice," John said.

"She is, isn't she?" replied Sally. "Did you have a nice talk?"

"We did."

"Are you ready for the next one?"

"I think so," said John.

Sally took John's hand and led him over to a male soul near a bronze plate in the ground.

"John, I'd like you to meet Mort. Mort, this is John."

"It's nice to meet you, Mort," John said reaching out his hand to shake. But Mort did not reciprocate. He was a thin, older man with thinning grey hair and blue-grey eyes.

"What do you want?" asked Mort.

"John's just here to talk with you and listen to your life story," said Sally impatiently.

"What if I don't feel like talking?"

"Then maybe I can tell you a little about myself," said John.

"Go ahead. I'm listening."

"I'll leave you two alone. Have a good talk," said Sally, then she turned and left.

"Well, as Sally said, my name is John. John Sample."

"How did you die, John?"

John recounted his grocery store events and subsequent heart attack.

"Yeah. I died of a heart attack, too," said Mort. "Only my heart attack occurred when I was shoveling the damned snow off my driveway. I laid there in the snow until I died, and no one found me until the snow melted three days later."

"That's horrible! You must have lived alone."

"Obviously."

"How old were you when you died?"

"I was 76. I know, I shouldn't have been out there shoveling at my age. But until my heart gave out, I thought I had been in pretty good shape and got around very well."

"I was 69 but I wasn't in that great of shape," said John. "Do you feel up to talking about the rest of your life? I was wondering where you grew up."

"All right. I'll tell you. But I don't want you blabbing to everyone else."

"It's a deal."

"So, I was born in Pittsburgh in 1930. My parents were immigrants from England. My father was an auto mechanic and worked for a Ford dealership in West Liberty. He worked there for 30 years and died shortly after retirement at age 55. We lived in Dormont until Dad passed away, then we moved to Forest Hills. My mother worked as a maid for wealthy clients. As a teenager, I was ashamed of my mother for the kind of work she did. I didn't like the idea of her being a servant. But later, I realized she was just a hard-working woman who did what she had to do to support her family. I had a brother and a sister who were both younger than I was.

I was drafted into the Army in 1950 and went to Korea as an infantryman with the 9th Infantry, 2nd Division. I was wounded in my right arm by an exploding grenade during the Battle of Bloody Ridge and was subsequently sent home. My arm never healed right, so I had to learn how to do everything with my left hand. I never did forgive God for doing that to me."

"You were lucky to be alive," said John.

"I didn't consider being left a cripple to be 'lucky.'"

"I guess I can understand that. What did you do after you came back?" asked John.

"Mostly, I felt sorry for myself. But I got a job working in a factory that made cardboard boxes. I worked there until I was 62. I never married. I just worked, came home, ate, watched TV, and slept. It wasn't much of a life but I survived," said Mort.

"Forgive me for saying so, Mort, but it seems like you were bitter ever since you came back from Korea."

"I guess I was. I was full of self-pity, and I never got over it."

"Why didn't you ever get married? I'm sure you had chances."

"What good woman would want to be burdened by a cripple?"

"I'm sure there were plenty of women who could have loved you if you had given them the chance."

"Well, I didn't want to give them the chance to turn me down."

"So, what did you do in your retirement?" asked John.

"I did pretty much the same in retirement as I did when I worked. I watched TV, ate and slept."

"What have you been doing since your death, Mort?"

"I keep to myself. Occasionally, I go up to the congregation to see what they're gossiping about. But mostly, I'm alone."

"I'm sure the group would love to have you spend more time with them."

"I doubt it. They know I'm a cranky old man, and that's the way I expect to stay."

"Have you given any thought to forgiving God for the troubles you experienced in your life?"

"Why should I? What did He do to help me? He got me blown up is what He did. My life was miserable after that. No. He doesn't deserve my forgiveness."

"Perhaps it wasn't His fault. I think we're judged by what we do with our individual challenges. One thing I've learned is that everyone has problems. It seems to me you did fine overcoming your handicap, but you just couldn't progress socially. You didn't let others get close to you because you were ashamed of your disability."

"Maybe so. But what can I do about that now?"

"I notice that you don't have a problem with your arm now. Maybe it's time to move on and take responsibility for the actions you took after the injury. If you spent more time with the congregation, I'll bet you would come out of your shell. You appear to be a good man who just didn't know how to cope with a devastating injury. You could be here for some time. Why not spend your time here in some kind of happiness?"

"I guess I never thought about it like that."

"Why don't we go back to them now and you can try to put your best foot forward? What have you got to lose?"

"You have a point, John. Thank you for talking with a cranky old man."

"It's been my pleasure, Mort. And, you're not as cranky as you think."

When they got to the group of souls, John shook Mort's hand and told the group he and Mort had had a good talk. The souls in the congregation also shook Mort's hand and talked with him.

John backed away from the group and let Mort have his moment. It had been a good day.

Chapter 17

That evening, John went back to his grave with a sense of satisfaction. He had successfully helped a troubled soul get some healing, and he felt good about it. John prayed for quite some time. He prayed for forgiveness for the sins he had committed in his life and he prayed to go to heaven so he could be with Brenda.

John then went back to his memories. He remembered he had left off when he went to Ft. Knox to start drill instructor training.

When he got back to his room at B-13-4 after eating, another soldier had taken up residence in the room and was lying on the other bunk. The other fellow was dressed in civilian clothes and got up from the bed when John entered the room. He was very tall, maybe 6'3", and extremely thin. His hair was brown and cut shorter than John's.

"The name's Billy. Billy Anderson," he said reaching out his hand.

"John Sample. It's nice to meet you, Billy. Are you here for DI school, too?"

"Yep. I guess we're here to hard hat until we start school."

Billy had a distinctive Southern drawl.

"Where are you from, Billy?"

"Tupelo, Mississippi—the birthplace of Elvis Presley."

"I could tell you were from the South. You have just a little bit of an accent."

Billy laughed.

"So, do you," he said. "Let me guess. You're from Ohio."

"Close. I'm from Lafayette, Indiana, home of Purdue University."

"I've heard of it. Purdue, that is."

"I just got back from Vietnam. How about you?"

"Turkey. I spent two years at the Incerlik Air Base."

"How did you get attached to the Air Force?"

"They have an ammunition depot near there. That's where I was stationed."

"How did you like Turkey?"

"It was great. How did you like Vietnam?"

"I didn't have it so bad, and I survived. So, it was great, too." Billy laughed.

From that point on, Billy and John became friends and spent most of their free time together. They spent most of the first basic training cycle watching the DI's train the troops. Billy and John were both assigned to the 2nd platoon under Staff Sergeant Murphy. As it turned out, SSG Murphy was the kind of sadistic little jerk that made drill sergeants look bad. He was very short and thin and was constantly clearing his throat when he talked. He knew his drill and ceremony though. John remembered most of it from his own basic training days but he learned a lot from SSG Murphy. Away from the trainees, Murphy was still a jerk but he wasn't mean to John or Billy except that he had them do most of the physical training that required the strenuous exercise.

The senior drill instructor was Sergeant First Class Williams. He was a rather heavy set, very dark-skinned black man who had a bit of a speech impediment. SFC Williams was rather easy-going and fair but firm. He always knew what the training days' schedule was and always carried a clipboard with him. He also had a funny laugh, like a deep chuckle.

John learned how to play poker with the DIs who sat in the back of the ambulance and played cards while the trainees were in classes or on the firing line under the tutelage of specialized training Non-Commissioned Officers or NCO's. John wasn't very good at poker, but he managed to stay even most of the time.

After the first training cycle was over, John and Billy were sent to Drill Sergeant School which was located just a few blocks from their building. Mentally, it was the toughest training John had ever experienced, including his own basic training.

The Senior Drill Instructor at the school explained that each individual soldier at the school started out with 1,000 points. Each uniform infraction or 'gig' was worth a deduction of 2 points; each missed question on a ten-question test was a deduction of ten points. If a soldier was late to a formation, the first infraction was a deduction of 25 points and the second was a deduction of 50 points. If a soldier was late a third time, it was an automatic dismissal from the course. 700 points were required to pass the course. If you passed, you were automatically given a boost of one rank. However, one thing the recruiter didn't tell them was that if you failed the course, you would lose a rank. So, there was a lot of incentive to pass the course.

Every day, there were two inspection formations; one at 7 a.m. and one at 1 p.m. Each soldier had to take on a different role; one day they would be a member of the squad, the next day they might be squad leader, the next a platoon leader and finally, the company commander. During each formation, a training DI inspected each individual soldier. Following closely behind him was another training DI with a clipboard. Each uniform was inspected for "excessive threads" in button holes or patches, incorrect placement or color of insignias on caps and lapels, polish on boots, etc. Each gig was marked down on the clipboard and recorded in that soldier's record. Each mistake made during the formation was a gig. In other words, there were many opportunities to lose points.

Each day, the training was intense. There was drill and ceremony instruction, classroom-teaching instruction, and PT instruction. Each soldier was required to teach classes on different topics and was graded accordingly.

John and Billy would often take a short nap after lunch since they usually had an extra twenty minutes after they ate. They overslept once and were late to formation. They were called into the senior drill instructor's office and were each given a 25-point deduction. It happened a second time, and each of them got a 50-point deduction. There were no more naps after that.

At the end of the DI training, only 63 of the original 97 candidates passed the course. Despite the large point deductions, John ranked 7th in his class. The instructor told him that he would have been first had he not been late those two times. John and Billy were both just happy to have passed.

At his graduation ceremony, John was promoted to Sergeant E-5 and presented with his round, brown campaign hat—the mark of a drill instructor. He also got the 'This We'll Defend' drill sergeant badge and patch and his training certificate.

When they got back to their unit, John and Billy were both made assistant drill sergeants to SSG Murphy. The next cycle was typical in that it was made up almost equally of draftees and volunteers. As usual, John and Billy were often in charge of extra PT and extra individual training as required.

Some of the rules expressed in DI school were that drill sergeants were never to yell at, swear at, strike nor otherwise mistreat trainees. SSG Murphy was guilty of all these rules, but he knew how to get away with it.

At just 21 years of age, John was very young-looking for a drill sergeant, so he took the approach of trying to keep his voice low and firm without raising his voice, except during PT and calling cadence during a march. He tried not to swear but occasionally, foul words would just escape.

One difficult situation he experienced was when it was discovered rather early on that one of the trainees could not tell his left from his right and therefore, could not even do a left face or right face. This individual was taken to the barracks for some individual training. Three DIs, including John, tried working with him but he just couldn't do the simple drill and ceremony commands.

John went to the company clerk and got this trainee's 201 file where it was discovered that he had a GT score of 54, which was considered so extremely low as to be mildly retarded. After some sympathetic questioning, it was learned that he had joined the Army with his brother after being turned down by the Navy and Marines because of his low scores. They found a disreputable recruiter who managed to give the questions to the duo, and this trainee still only managed a 54, with 90-100 being deemed average. The brother was a good recruit with average scores and normal abilities. John reported these findings to the other drill sergeants, who then reported them to the senior drill sergeant, who in turn reported them to the company commander. Much to his and his brother's dismay, the trainee was released from the service on a general discharge.

On the other hand, John also found an outstanding trainee who had a much different outcome. During a situation where John had CQ duty or Charge of Quarters, this trainee was tasked with assisting John throughout the night. John's duties required him to check each training bay on the hour to make certain that the fireguards were doing their watch properly and to make sure there were no problems. In conversation, John discovered that this person was a mortician who had experience in removing corneas in preparation for transplantation. John later reported this to his superiors. Subsequently, before the end of his basic training cycle, this trainee was offered the rank of Major to teach at an Army medical facility in Texas. The only caveat was that he would be required to do a 4-year stint in the Army instead of his current 2-year enlistment. Even though he found the decision difficult, the trainee decided to take the position.

John and Billy had graduated from DI school in June and after the first cycle in August, they had a few days off. John asked Billy if he wanted to go with him to see his grandmother in Cincinnati. Billy happily accepted the invitation, so John drove the two of them in the red Fiat to his grandmother's house. John had called ahead, so his grandmother had supper waiting for them. She had made chicken-and-dumplings, and Billy loved them. Billy's Mississippi southern ways charmed John's grandmother and they got along famously.

The next morning, they had a breakfast of bacon, eggs and toast before heading back to Ft. Knox. It had been a lot of driving but they had a good time.

The next basic training cycle was unusual as it was for R.O.T.C. or Reserve Officer Training Corps trainees. These trainees had to be handled much differently, and their training only lasted six weeks instead of eight. Since these trainees were still civilians, they could quit the training at any time.

Drill and ceremony was much easier because the R.O.T.C. trainees had already received some training at their colleges and universities. The trainees still had to go through rifle training, bayonet training, hand-to-hand combat training, and limited physical training. Many of the classroom trainings were given by specialized instructors instead of the usual drill instructors. John and Billy still assisted SSG Murphy during this training but his rants, swearing and rough treatment of these trainees was greatly curtailed.

When the R.O.T.C. group completed their training, there was a special ceremony on the Ft. Knox parade grounds near the officers' homes. The Post Commander at the time was Brigadier General George S. Patton, Jr., son of the famous general Patton of WWII fame. He reviewed the troops as he rode while standing up in a special reviewing jeep.

John had another couple of friends at B-13-4. One was a DI by the name of SGT Ron Carrey. Ron had been a semi-pro golfer, and he taught John to play on the two main golf courses on the post. In the summer, they played nearly every weekend they had free.

In August, John heard about the possibility of an 'early out' for any soldier who was enrolled in a college. He applied to Purdue University for the fall semester of the following year, 1972. John was accepted into the pre-med program despite his mediocre grades and 22 credit hours, transferred from Abilene Christian. In December, John got his orders for a 6-month early out which meant he would be discharged from the Army in March.

The winter was difficult for drill sergeants. They still had to march everywhere, do PT, close combat training, bivouac, night-fire training, etc., except that it was much colder. There was not a lot to do in the off time in the winter except to play poker, so that's what John did. He got better at the game and once left the table with $97, which was the equivalent of a week's pay.

When March came around, the company commander called John into his office.

"Sergeant Sample reporting as ordered, Sir!"

"At ease, Sergeant. Take a seat."

"Thank you, Sir."

"I know you're planning to go back to college but have you considered reenlisting? You have an excellent record and you could probably make E-6 next year. For someone your age, that could put you in a position to have an excellent career in the Army."

"I've enjoyed my time in the Army, but I think it's time to move on, Sir. I thank you for your encouragement, though."

"Well, I had to ask. Good luck to you in school, Sergeant. That is all."

John stood, saluted and said, "Thank you, Sir," and once he got a return salute, left the office.

When March rolled around, the other drill sergeants gave John a little party and presented him with a small bronze statue of a drill sergeant on a pedestal which had a small plaque that read, '*Sgt. Sample, B-13-4.*' John was very touched and shook hands with everyone. Then, on March 8th, he went through out-processing and was given an honorable discharge.

John was glad to be out but he was very proud of his two and a half years of service.

After getting out of the Army, John went home and stayed with his parents and his brother for a little over a month, with little to do but watch TV.

His friend, Eric, had gotten married to his high school sweetheart, Jennifer, while he was on leave from Germany. By the time John got out of the Army in March, Eric had already been out of the military for a few months. Eric got John a job with the Cement Construction Company doing a variety of concrete work, including building pig pits, a cow pit, driveways, patios, and sidewalks. They worked in a crew of 4 to 6, and they usually got along well.

The pits were designed like large concrete basements which would eventually get a building built on it. The pigs or cows would be housed in these buildings and would walk and live on smooth concrete lintels that stretched from one side of the building to the other. There were spaces between each lintel so the waste from the animals would go down into the pit where water was mixed with the waste and then pumped out for use as fertilizer by the farmers. Most of the buildings were ventilated with large fans and vents.

It was very hard work carrying the wall forms from the flat-bed trailers to the pit sites. The pig pits required a concrete slab that was approximately 4' below ground level. Two-foot long reinforcement bars, or re-rod as it was called, were cut to size and placed around the edge of the slab. When the slab dried, they put the wall forms in place around the perimeter over the re-rod. The wall forms were attached to each other by built-in clips and metal ties. Boards were used to hold the wall forms in place in preparation of the concrete pour and then the insides of the wall forms were sprayed with oil to make removal easier.

When the concrete came, the crew helped pour the concrete into the forms from the cement truck. That, too, was hard work as they had to push and rake the concrete from a central location and then, throughout the wall. Bolts were placed in the top of the wall while the concrete was still wet. The next day, the crew came back to remove the forms from the semi-cured walls. The clips were unfastened and the forms were pulled away from the concrete and loaded back onto the flat-beds. The metal ties that protruded from the concrete were knocked off with hammers.

Wherever they were working, they would find a place to eat where the crew would go to lunch. One time, they went to a little diner and ordered lunch. The waitress who appeared to be in her 40s asked everyone if they wanted pie. John ordered a slice of cherry pie. When the waitress returned, she brought him a slice of apple pie by mistake. John pointed out the error to the waitress and her response was, "You'll eat it or wear it." Of course, the crew got a big kick out of the exchange. By the time John got home each day, he was exhausted and didn't feel much like going out, except occasionally to go over to Eric and Jennifer's house to visit.

John did this work for most of the summer but when it was time to go to Purdue, John quit and found work as an orderly at St. Elizabeth's hospital. He received two weeks of intense training alongside several young women who were going to be nurses' aides. They all learned Cardio Pulmonary Resuscitation, how to take blood pressures and temperatures, and how to do catheterizations. The students also learned how to prepare the dead. John mostly ended up doing work on the orthopedic ward working with circle beds and Stryker frames, but he also did a rotation on the urology ward.

John liked the work, and he fit in almost immediately. More than ever, he wanted to become a doctor. But when he started pre-med at Purdue, he had no idea the courses would be so difficult. During his first and last semester, as it turned out, John was assigned the following courses: algebra, pre-med biology, pre-med chemistry, political science and philosophy. He did not do well and had a difficult time with each of the courses, except philosophy in which he did manage to get an 'A.'

John found a room to rent not far from campus. There were three rented rooms in the upstairs of an older lady's home. She was very heavy and could barely get around with a cane. John mowed the grass of the home to reduce his rent. Between his low-paying job at the hospital and his G.I. Bill compensation, he was not making much money.

He still had his Fiat, but it was starting to deteriorate. One of the four spark plugs had been cross-threaded in the aluminum block engine, even though all work had been done by the dealership. It never ran very well after that. Also, the driver's window-rolling cable had broken and there was a leak in the front of the car, and it would drip on his feet when it rained hard. The car was also on its third set of tires. This had all happened in less than a year and a half after he had bought the car.

John did some looking around at used cars and found a red 1966 Thunderbird. Its interior was a luxurious black cloth with bucket seats in the front and back. It had a 390-cubic-inch engine and an automatic transmission. John loved the car and traded his Fiat in for it.

A few days later, the brakes on the Thunderbird started to get mushy and blue smoke began to pour out of the tailpipes. He took it back to the dealer but they refused to do anything about the problems. John then took the car to a friend who did work on cars and received the bad news that the car needed a new master brake cylinder and new piston rings. He got the work done but it was expensive. Over the next year, the car also needed freeze plugs, a new radiator, an electrical short correction, and a new water pump. As bad as it was, John still loved the car when it was running and not costing him a small fortune.

While he was working at St. Elizabeth hospital, John met Mandy, a nursing student, and he asked her out. She accepted and for nearly a year, they were boyfriend and girlfriend. Mandy was only 19, very thin with short, dark hair and a beautiful smile. Mandy's father was a Methodist preacher, and he and his wife lived in Oxford, Indiana.

When Mandy went back to college in Indianapolis in the fall, John visited her on weekends. Mandy's sister, Carla, also lived in Indy with her boyfriend, Craig, who was a druggie. John and Becky spent several weekends with them. Even though he had been around it in Vietnam, this was the first-time John had ever smoked pot. Craig said the pot he used was laced with hashish and was very powerful. They listened to Jethro Tull's *Thick as a Brick* album and looked at a book of Salvador Dali's artwork. John got high every time he went over to their house. Mandy, as it turned out later, had been dating someone at the college at the same time she was dating John.

In July, John quit his job at the hospital with the plan of going camping in the Rocky Mountains for a month and perhaps finding a job out West while he was there. He sold his camera, his telephoto and wide-angle lenses, filters and all the equipment for the bargain basement price of $250 to help pay for the trip, then packed his bags and left his rooming apartment for good. John planned to meet up with Mandy in Grand Junction, Colorado a little over two weeks later.

John packed up his camping equipment. He had been camping many times before and read a book about backpacking before he left, so he felt he was ready to handle whatever might come his way.

The trip to Colorado took 14 hours. Along the way, John picked up a couple of hitch-hikers. They were young and Hippie-looking, so he figured they were harmless. The young woman sat up front with John, while her boyfriend sat in the back. They talked for some time, and then John smelled the familiar odor of pot being smoked in the back seat. He was worried that if they were stopped by the police for any reason, John could get into trouble because of the pot. John told the guy he didn't appreciate the pot being smoked and he would let them off at the next gas station. He had taken them several hours closer to their destination, so John didn't feel too bad about dropping them off.

Other than nearly hitting a deer during his night driving, the trip went well, and John ended the day at a park in Sterling, Colorado where he spent the night in his sleeping bag in the back seat of the Thunderbird. The next morning, John drove three hours to Estes Park near the entrance to Rocky Mountain National Park. He had spent hours at home planning his camping trip in that park. But when he got to the park and asked about backpacking into the more rustic and less trodden areas to camp, the park ranger told him he could only camp and have a campfire in designated areas of the park. John asked if there was anywhere else he could do such camping, and the ranger recommended the Arapaho National Forest just a couple of hours south of Rocky Mountain National Park. So, John turned around and headed south. John stopped by a Sheriff's office on the way and bought a topographical map of the area. He told the Sheriff where he was headed and that he planned on being back in a week or 10 days. The Sheriff told him to be sure to check back in when he was finished. There was a general store near the Sheriff's office, so John picked up a few fishing flies, a clear casting bobber and a fishing license.

John went back to the main road, then found a rocky road near an area known as Eagle's Nest Wilderness Area and drove to a lake where there were three or four other cars parked nearby. It was a Saturday when John arrived and there were several day campers hiking the trails around the lake at the base of the mountain. He took his backpack out of the trunk and took his rolled sleeping bag and placed it on the pack. He also had his hunting knife and hatchet with him. John put on his backpack, which was about 60 lbs. and headed for the lake trail. From the topographical map, he estimated the altitude to be at approximately 8,000 ft. The trail to the top of the mountain would take him up to over 10,000 ft., so he decided to stay at the lower section for a day or so to get used to the altitude.

After hiking around the lake, John set up his tent not far from the main trail and turned-in for the night. At some point during the night, he heard animal sounds outside. He kept his hunting knife and hatchet close by just in case.

The next morning, John had some beef jerky for breakfast, then packed up his camp and headed up the mountain trail. The lower sections of the trail were mostly grassy areas on one side and Aspen trees on the other. On the way up, he passed other campers coming down the trail. At one point, he saw a grizzly bear cub standing in an Aspen grove to his right. John stopped for a moment to take in the scene and the two just stared at each other for a few seconds. Then John realized that the mother bear was probably not far away, so he cautiously continued his way up the trail.

It took approximately two hours to get up to the top. When he got there, he couldn't believe the beauty of the clear mountain lake amid an evergreen forest. John noticed two sets of campers who had set up camp on opposite sides of the lake. He set up his camp equidistant from the two on the East side. After he'd set up camp, he built a small fire in a rock fire pit he'd made a few steps from his tent. He tried to cook a freeze-dried pork chop but found it nearly impossible to boil water at that altitude. It eventually cooked, but it wasn't that good.

John went fishing after lunch and immediately caught a small brook trout. It was beautiful and very easily caught on the fly he'd purchased at the general store. He released the fish and tried again. Sure enough, he caught another one, which he also released.

John noticed that the young couple across the lake had packed up and left. The other campers were to his right about 75 yards away. They were three young men who were also fishing nearby.

"Hello!" said one of them.

"Hello!" he replied.

John reeled in his line and attached his hook to one of the eyelets before walking over to the other camp.

"Hi, I'm John."

"Phil," said the first one shaking John's hand. "That's Bobby and that's Harry over there," he said pointing to the other two. They waved from their fishing spots.

"How are you doing, John?"

"Good! This is a beautiful spot. I love it up here."

"Yeah, it's great. Hey, we're going to have a fish fry tonight. Do you want to come over later and join us?"

"Sounds great. I just let a couple go, but I'll see if I can catch something to contribute."

"Great! I'll come over and get you when we're ready to start cooking."

"I'll see you then, Phil."

John went back to his fishing spot and fished for a couple more hours and only caught a couple Brookies. Later, Phil stopped by the camp and told John they were getting ready to put the fish on the fire. John grabbed his two Brook trout and walked with Phil back to their camp. The other men had already cleaned their fish and had them on a baking pan sprayed with liquid *I Can't Believe It's Not Butter* margarine. John went down to the water, cleaned his fish and brought them back up to add with the others. Altogether, there were 15 trout with one of them bigger than all the rest. Phil pointed to the largest one.

"That's a Rainbow. I just caught him a little while ago," he said.

"Nice fish. What did you catch him on?"

"The same thing we're all probably using; a mosquito dry fly."

"Yep. Me, too."

Bobby had the baking pan over the fire and was tending to the fish while Harry was scrounging up more firewood. Phil was putting his fishing equipment away and John sat on a log not far from the fire.

"Where are you guys from?" John asked.

"Texas!" said Bobby. "The three of us just graduated from Texas Tech, and this is our last hurrah before we head our separate ways."

"That must be bittersweet," said John. "I went to Abilene Christian for a year before going into the Army."

"How did you like Texas?" asked Phil.

"I loved the people but didn't much care for Abilene. It was quite dull. I'm from Indiana, and we have real trees there."

Phil laughed.

"That's Abilene for you. I think Lubbock is nicer but it's still pretty flat and all."

"What kind of degrees did you all get?"

"We were all in Ag Business."

When the fish were nearly done, John went back to his camp and got his mess kit and multi-function knife with a fork on it. When he got back to the others, they were already passing out the fish. They had a plastic yellow lemon containing lemon juice that they added to the fish. The trout tasted great, and they all talked about college and where they were planning to go once their camping trip was over. John told them about his plans to meet up with his girlfriend in Grand Junction.

When it started to get dark, John thanked the guys for their hospitality and told them he was going to turn in. It had been a good day but it was starting to get cold. That night, John felt like he was freezing to death. His sleeping bag wasn't made for freezing temperatures and he put on his socks, pants, shirt, jacket and even a hat in the sleeping bag. It was a long night but he survived the 30-some-degree temperatures.

Fortunately, that was the coldest night he had to endure. During the day, the temperatures got into the 80s. John spent most of the time by himself but Phil came over one day and brought some pot with him. They smoked it and got a little high while they talked. The other guys spent most of their time fishing until they packed up and left on a Friday.

On Saturday, after 6 days of paradise, the Boy Scouts arrived. They were loud, obnoxious, splashed in the water while trying to build a raft and generally screwed everything up. So, John packed up his camp and hiked down the mountain. The trip down was far easier and faster than the trip up.

When John got back to his car, he loaded it up and drove back the way he came in. He decided to go camping in another part of the National Forest and found a great spot not far from a ranger's tower and close to another beautiful mountain lake. There was no one around, which was just what he was looking for. Little did he know he was going to need help.

Chapter 18

When morning arrived in the Garden of Peace, John was still remembering his trip to Colorado. He soon joined the congregation of souls to see what was going on.

"Welcome back, John," said James.

"What is everyone talking about today?" asked John.

"Sally left us last night."

"That's wonderful!" exclaimed John.

"Yes, it is. But we're all going to miss her here."

"Sure, but think of what this means. It means we can all have hope that we'll be able to go someday, too."

"You're right, of course, John. But it's tough waiting your turn."

"I guess I haven't been here long enough to experience that longing. I'm still taking it all in at this point. There are still a few people I haven't talked with yet. Do you have any suggestions?"

"Well, let me see. Have you talked with Archie yet?"

"No. Which one is Archie?"

"He's the one by himself in the south section over that way. Can you see him?"

"I think so. Is that him way over there?"

"That's him. He never comes to the congregation. I talked with him for a little while a long time ago, but I didn't have much luck with him."

"I'll see what I can do."

John drifted over to where the male soul was located. The soul was tall and thin with gray hair. When he got there, John extended his hand.

"Good morning! My name is John. Are you Archie?"

When Archie did not reach for John's hand, John dropped his.

"What do you want?"

"I haven't been here too long, and I'm just trying to meet everyone."

"Okay. I'm Archie. Now you've met me."

"I was hoping to get to know you, Archie. If you'd like, I can tell you about myself first."

"I'm not really interested in hearing about your great life. Some of us didn't have it so good."

"Then why don't you tell me about your life? Sometimes it helps us to tell our story to others."

"It won't do any good. I'm going to hell."

"How long have you been here?"

"Many years. I don't know exactly."

"If you were going to hell, why haven't you gone yet?"

"Maybe God's torturing me. How do I know?"

"Wouldn't you like for someone to give you a second opinion? Perhaps you're not a candidate for hell after all."

"Fine. I'll talk to you. Where do you want me to start?"

"When and where were you born?"

"I was born in New York City in 1937. I had no brothers or sisters."

"Were your parents from New York City originally?"

"No. They were from Germany. They left Germany when Hitler was rising in power. They weren't Jewish. They just saw the writing on the wall and came to America for a better life."

"It sounds as if they were lucky to get out when they did."

"That's true," said Archie. "It got much worse after they left."

"How did you come to the Pittsburgh area?"

"My father was a tailor by trade in Germany. When they got to New York City, my father worked in the garment district and eventually made shirts and suits for wealthy New Yorkers. I lived there and worked for my father until I was 30 when he passed away. I was a pretty good tailor but not a good businessman, and the business failed two years later. After that,

I got a job as a long-haul trucker to support my mother. I worked for several companies over the years and then got my own rig and began working for myself.

When my mother passed away in 1977, I decided to leave New York to be more centrally located. I got a lot of my work from Pittsburgh, so I moved here. I retired in 2000 and moved to Delmont where I lived until I died in 2008."

"It sounds as if you had a good life. Why do you think you're going to hell?"

"Because I murdered 21 women."

"You what?" John asked incredulously.

"When I was driving across the country, I picked up women and murdered them."

"Why would you do that?"

"I don't know. The first time was kind of an accident. I picked up a hooker at a gas station and we went to the truck. When she started to give me oral sex, I was disgusted by what she was doing and I pulled her off me. I told her to leave but she wanted to be paid. We argued and fought. When she said she would go to the police, I grabbed her by her hair and slammed her face down onto the gearshift. It knocked her out. I then took her to an isolated stretch of road where I choked her to death and dragged her body into the woods.

The killing gave me a thrill that I can't explain. But whatever it was, I had to have more. So, whenever I got the chance, I did it again and again and again. It was like an addiction."

"And you were never caught?"

"No. I don't think the police ever had a clue. The bodies were dumped in secluded places across the country in about 15 or 16 different states over 25 years."

"Well, now I have another question for you," said John.

"Why haven't I gone to hell yet?"

"Yes."

"I don't know the answer to that."

"Did you not have any empathy for those women or their families?"

"I've thought about the women over the years but I never had any regrets. I only remember them so I can relive the experiences."

"Did you ever think that you'd have to pay for your sins?"

"No. I didn't believe in God or the devil or heaven or hell."

"Do you now?" John asked.

"I think so. But if I'm so evil and if there is a hell, then I should be roasting right now. Right?"

"I don't presume to know what God has in store for us. Perhaps you're here to reflect on your misdeeds."

"I'm not sure why but I still don't care about the women I killed. At night, when I remember my life, I think about my mother and father and my childhood."

"What was your mother like?"

"I hated her. She was overbearing and used to beat me all the time for no reason when I was a child."

"Do you see a possible reason you had no empathy for those women?"

"You think I was killing my mother all those times?"

"I don't know. I'm not a psychiatrist. But I think you may not have had any respect for women because of your relationship with your mother. What happened to your mother?"

"She got Alzheimer's and slowly lost her mind. I tried to take care of her but she didn't know me anymore. I put her in a nursing home and visited occasionally, but I never forgave her for the way she treated me as a child. When she died, I had her cremated and flushed her ashes down a toilet."

"I don't know what to say about that, Archie."

"I do. It was my way of saying, 'Good riddance.'"

"Have you prayed about your situation?"

"What do you mean?" asked Archie.

"I mean, have you prayed for forgiveness?"

"No. I haven't."

"Well, it couldn't do any harm, don't you think?"

"It all just seems so hypocritical. I haven't regretted my actions, so how is praying for forgiveness make any sense?"

"Maybe you should think about regretting your actions. Think about the other lives you ruined when you murdered those women. Most of them probably had families and some of them may have had children they were trying to support. I don't condone their methods but they may have felt they had no choice."

"I never thought about the families. I just thought about the thrill of the kill. Maybe I can think about them at night. And maybe I'll try to pray."

"Like I said, it couldn't hurt."

"It was nice to meet you, John. You're the first soul I've ever told my story to. Thank you for not judging me."

"I can't say I'm not judging you, Archie. Your actions were heinous. And, I'll never be able to forget what you've done. But I don't know the mind of God or what he has planned for us. Perhaps he'll take your mental state into consideration. I don't know."

"That's fair, John."

"And don't worry. I won't share your secret with the others. In fact, it might be helpful if you joined the group occasionally and listened to the stories of others. That might help you gain some insight into the value of other lives."

"I'll do that. Thank you, John."

The two shook hands and John made his way back to the congregation where he listened to the others for the rest of the day.

Chapter 19

When evening was upon them, the congregation separated and went back to their tombstones. John went back to his gravesite and began remembering where he had left off the night before.

John was camping in the Arapaho National Forest. He had been able to drive right into a nice campsite just a hundred yards or so from a ranger tower. There was a large log near the fire pit, and he was just a few steps from the lake. There was also an outhouse a few feet away up a slight grade from the campsite. John set up his tent, then took his fishing gear over to the lake. The lake was so clear and calm he could see the fish swimming not far from shore. It wasn't long before he'd caught two small rainbow trout. He cleaned them and brought them back to his camp, made a fire in the fire pit using the abundant kindling found nearby, then prepared a delicious lunch of fresh trout.

He stayed at the campsite for two days and relished the peace and solitude. The day John packed up his camp, he put out the campfire and had some beef jerky for breakfast. When everything was ready to go, he went up to the outhouse and did his morning business. John got back to the car and felt his pocket for his car keys. They weren't there. He looked on the seat and in the ignition. Still no keys. He looked on the ground around the camp. Nothing. Finally, he thought he might have dropped them in the outhouse and looked up there for them. He even used his flashlight to look down the hole, but there was no trace of the keys.

The last place he thought they might be was in the trunk but he had no way of getting into it without the keys. John didn't know how to hotwire his car, so he walked to the ranger tower to see if he could find someone to help but no one was there. He remembered seeing a small general store and bar back up the road a couple of miles, so he started walking to see if he could get some help there. When he arrived, John was out of breath. There were three men inside, including the owner, and after hearing the story, one of the men said he knew how to hotwire a vehicle and offered to drive John back to his car.

The man drove John back to the campsite and hotwired the Thunderbird. John got directions to the nearest town that would hopefully have a locksmith. It was 25 miles away, and John was low on gas to boot. He thanked the man and offered him $10 but he told John to keep his money. It was a nerve-racking drive down to the town. Fortunately, it was almost all downhill, so he got good gas mileage. When he arrived in the town of Frisco, he found a locksmith who quickly gained entrance to the trunk, and there they were. The keys were sitting right on top of all his camping equipment. The locksmith was also able to undo the hotwiring so he could get underway. John joyfully paid the locksmith and was then on his way to a gas station. When he filled up the tank, it was the most John had ever put in the tank, so he knew he was almost on fumes.

On the way to Grand Junction, John stopped in Glenwood Springs, Colorado at the local hospital to see if he could get a job there. He filled out an employment application and had an interview with their human resources person. They seemed very eager to hire him because of his experience at St. Elizabeth hospital. Unfortunately, the pay was very low for his job description, but they also offered him additional work with the ambulance service to supplement the income. John said he would check out the cost of living in the area before making his decision. The rent for just a sleeping room would have been more than a week's pay. He determined he wouldn't have the money to make his car payment and have a decent place to live, so he turned down the offer.

John drove the rest of the way to Grand Junction and met up with Mandy at the airport. By now, he was sporting a full beard and looked quite scruffy, but Mandy didn't seem to mind. They kissed.

"I missed you," said Mandy.

"I missed you, too."

They drove to a KOA campground nearby that had a shower and a place to pitch the tent. Mandy caught John up on all the goings on at the hospital, and John told her about his adventures in the wilderness.

When they got to the campground, it all seemed rather luxurious compared to what he'd been used to the previous couple of weeks. After picking up some groceries and some wood for the fire at the office, John and Mandy went and set up their camp. They both took showers and returned to the tent. John started a fire and prepared for the night. He made peanut butter and jelly sandwiches for supper, then they turned in for the night.

The next morning, they packed up the camp and headed for the Grand Canyon. John drove for several hours, then stopped for lunch in a small town in southern Utah. They continued until they got close to the Grand Canyon and pitched the tent in the pines near the park before dark.

The next morning, they spent the day at the Grand Canyon. They both loved the scenery as they drove around the park stopping at the occasional overlook. They also went to the visitor's center and purchased a few souvenirs before heading out.

The plan was to visit John's Aunt Winifred in Iowa City on the way back. They stopped a few times on the way at small towns and another KOA campground to eat, camp and get cleaned up. After listening to her for hours on end, John was feeling less and less attached to Mandy as they went along. He wasn't sure why but it was happening, nonetheless.

When they got to Aunt Winifred's home, she greeted them warmly and invited them into the house. Winifred was a professor at the University of Iowa who taught French and Spanish. She was the aunt who had encouraged John to do his music and to complete his education. Aunt Winifred spent months in Europe and South America back in the 1960s doing missionary work. She was always a great inspiration to John.

John and Mandy had lunch with his aunt, and the three of them had a very good conversation. After lunch, they hugged his aunt, said their goodbyes and were on their way to Oxford, which was still about five hours away. That evening, they pulled onto Mandy's street. John helped Mandy unload her suitcase and sleeping bag, gave her a hug and a kiss and was on his way home to Lafayette. He had enjoyed his trip but was glad to get home to his parents' house.

When the end of August rolled around, John decided to find a job instead of going back to school. He felt he didn't have the ability to become a doctor, so he didn't see any reason in going back to school. John went to the other hospital in Lafayette, Home Hospital, and took an orthopedic technician position. After a little on-the-job training, John was doing traction set-ups, working in the emergency room, and spending most of his time on the orthopedic floor. The money was still poor there but by living at home, he could get by.

One day at work, as John got off the elevator to go to lunch, he noticed a young woman who was getting ready to enter the elevator. John had shaved his beard but kept his moustache and was wearing his scrubs. The young lady was extremely attractive and petite with long brown hair and beautiful brown eyes. She was also wearing a short leg brace. John recognized her from high school.

"You're Brenda Green, aren't you?" John asked.

She looked down at her name tag, smiled and said, "Yes, I am. Who are you?"

They moved away from the elevator to get out of the way of the others, and John introduced himself.

"I'm John Sample. We were in the same class at Jeff."

Brenda acted as if she was trying to remember him.

"Did you always used to wear jeans to school?" she asked.

"I wore them a lot."

"I think I remember seeing you in the hallways at Jeff, but I don't think we had any classes together."

"I think you're right. Have you had lunch?" John asked.

"I just finished."

"Maybe I could join you for lunch tomorrow? What time do you come down to eat?"

"I usually eat around 11. You're welcome to join me if you'd like."

"Great! I'll meet you around 11 tomorrow. It was nice to see you, Brenda."

"Nice to see you, John."

The elevator had arrived again and Brenda got on. John went for lunch but was immediately struck with the feeling of love at first sight.

The next day, John finished his rounds and was able to leave for lunch shortly after 11 a.m. When he arrived at the dining room, he looked for Brenda. He spotted her sitting with several of her friends.

"Mind if I join you?" John asked.

"No, I don't mind," Brenda replied.

John sat down next to her and started to eat.

"I'd heard you were in a car accident our senior year. I wasn't even sure you were alive."

"I almost wasn't. I was riding with my boyfriend in his car at the time. He went off the road and hit a mailbox that came through the windshield and hit me in the head."

"Oh, my God!" exclaimed John.

"The brain injury caused me to have a left-side paralysis, so I don't have much use of my left arm and hand. And, that's why I have to wear a leg brace."

"You seem like you're doing very well now. When I was in high school, I was told that you were a vegetable after the accident."

"That's nice to hear, John. What was I, broccoli or lettuce?"

John laughed.

"You're right. I'm sorry. That was kind of crude of me to say. Why don't you let me make it up to you? Would you go out to dinner with me Friday night?"

Brenda looked at John and smiled.

"Okay."

"Can I get your phone number and address? I'll pick you up at 7 if that's okay."

Brenda wrote down her phone number and address on a napkin and gave it to John.

"I'll see you then," she said.

She had finished her lunch, so she got up and left. John was impressed with himself at how easily he had been able to ask her out, and he was ecstatic she was willing to accept.

It was on Friday, October 5th, 1973 that John went to Brenda's home to pick her up. He went up on the porch to the side door by the driveway and knocked. Her mother answered the door.

"Hi. I'm John," he said.

"I'm Brenda's mother, Deloris. Brenda is still getting ready. Come in, and you can wait for her in the living room."

Brenda's mother was very short and slightly built with her gray hair up in a bun. She was polite but John had the sense she didn't trust him.

John went into the living room and sat on the couch. The house was small and sparsely decorated but very tidy. Brenda's mother sat on a chair on the opposite side of the living room.

"Can I get you anything while you're waiting?" Deloris asked.

"No, thank you."

"So, you know Brenda from the hospital?"

"Yes, Ma'am. I work as an orthopedic technician. It's a fancy title for 'orderly.' We met near the cafeteria. We also went to Jeff together."

"How long have you worked at the hospital?"

"Just a couple of weeks."

"What did you do before you worked at the hospital?"

"I was in college at Purdue. Before that, I was in the Army."

"Oh, really? My husband was in the Army right after the war."

Just then, Brenda came out of the bathroom and joined them. She looked beautiful.

"I'm sure my mother has talked your ear off," she said.

"No. We were just having a nice conversation," said John. "Are you ready to go?"

"I'm ready."

"You two have a nice time," her mother said.

"It was very nice to meet you," John said. "We won't be too late."

Brenda led the way out the door and down the porch steps to the car. John got the door for her and though she had a little difficulty getting into the car with her braced leg, she managed. He shut her door and went around the car and got in.

"Have you ever had Chinese food before?" John asked.

"You mean other than Chow Mein in a can? No, I haven't."

"Chow Mein in a can doesn't count. I think you're in for a treat," John said with a smile.

"If you say so."

They didn't talk a lot as John drove to West Lafayette. They mostly talked about work at the hospital. When they got near the Purdue campus, John parked a half a block from the Peking restaurant. The two of them walked slowly to the restaurant as John held her hand. When they entered the restaurant, they were seated in a booth and given menus.

"We can either go to the buffet and try a little of everything or I can recommend something for you."

"Why don't you recommend something?"

"Well, the Sweet and Sour Chicken is always a safe bet."

"That sounds good," said Brenda.

When the waitress came over, John ordered the Sweet and Sour Chicken, egg rolls, fried rice, water and hot tea for them.

John and Brenda continued their talk of work until their meals came.

The Chinese waitress soon brought their meals. John advised Brenda that the egg roll would likely be very hot and poured her tea for her. He also pointed out the Chinese mustard and sweet and sour sauce for dipping the egg rolls. John watched Brenda as she took a bite of the chicken, looking for a reaction.

"It's good," Brenda said. "Very different."

"I'm glad you like it. You might also want to dip your egg roll into the Sweet and Sour sauce. If you're brave, you can try the hot mustard."

As the two of them ate, John was a little disappointed that Brenda wasn't eating much. She just seemed to pick over the items on her plate, though she did try each of the foods. Brenda also took very small bites and chewed each bite very thoroughly.

"There's so much food!" she exclaimed.

"The portions are usually very large at Chinese restaurants. There will be plenty left to take home if you'd like. Otherwise, I'll be happy to take them."

John recounted his first encounter with Chinese food at the Loon Foon restaurant in Vietnam. When they were finished, he paid the check, left a tip and asked for the leftover food to be packaged for him.

John drove them back to her house and it was barely 9 p.m. when they got back. They sat in the car and talked for a short time before John got out and opened the door for Brenda.

They went to the door and John kissed her. It was a sweet first kiss and it seemed very special to John. Later, Brenda would refer to the kiss as 'a little peck.'

Dawn was breaking at the cemetery, so John floated over to the congregation to see what was going on. James came over to John.

"Good morning, John."

"Good morning! What is everyone talking about this morning?"

"We were just saying that you've met almost everyone. I think there are still a few souls you haven't met yet."

"I'm anxious to meet them."

"First, I'd like you to meet Gary. You'll find that Gary is special. He's right over here."

The two of them moved to the outside of the group where a middle-aged-looking, heavy-set man was milling about with his head down and his hands clasped together at his chest. James approached the man.

"Good morning, Gary!" said James.

The man looked up and smiled.

"Hi, James."

John noticed there was something different about Gary.

"Gary, I'd like you to meet someone. Gary, this is John. John, I'd like you to meet Gary."

John reached out to shake the man's hand but Gary kept his hands clasped at his chest.

"Gary, don't you think you should shake John's hand? That would be the polite thing to do."

"Yeah. I can shake his hand." He unclasped his hands and reached out to John.

John shook Gary's hand one time, then immediately went back to his clasped hands. John felt a deep sadness and empathy for this man.

"Good morning, Gary. I was wondering if you'd like to go somewhere and talk to me for a while."

"Okay," said Gary.

"Would you like to talk over by your grave, Gary?"

"Yeah."

Gary led the way to a small headstone not far from the shed. When they arrived, John read the inscription on the stone aloud.

"Gary Matthew Lassiter, Beloved Son and Brother, June 1, 1970 to August 8, 2016."

"That's right."

"So, you've been here for about a year then," said John.

"A long time."

John was certain now that Gary was retarded in some way.

"That's a nice headstone you have."

"Yeah. That's where I'm buried."

"Where did you live, Gary?" John asked.

"257 School Street, Murrysville, Pennsylvania, 724-555-3723."

"Did you live with your mom and dad?"

"Yeah. I lived with Mom and Dad. They come and see me sometimes."

"That's good. Did you go to work somewhere?"

"Yeah. I worked at Ferris's grocery store. I bagged groceries for the customers."

"I'll bet you did a good job."

"Yeah. I did a good job."

"What did you do at home when you weren't working?"

"I played video games after supper."

"Were you any good?"

"Yeah. I was pretty good."

"Do you know how you got here?" asked John.

"A long car brought me here."

"Did you get sick or get hurt?"

"Yeah. I got hurt on my bike."

"What happened on your bike?"

"A car hit me while I was on my bike. They tried to fix me but I was hurt too bad."

"What do you remember after that, Gary?"

"They put me in a box and my mom and dad came to see me. They cried when they put me in the ground."

"I'll bet you were a good son."

"Yeah. I was good."

"I think you'll be in heaven soon, Gary."

"Yeah. This is heaven. I don't see Jesus though."

"I think you'll be seeing him very soon."

"Yeah. I'll be seeing Jesus."

"Gary, it's been very good talking with you. I think you're a very nice man. Is there anything you'd like to talk to me about?"

"No."

"That's fine. Do you want to get back to the group now?"

"Yeah. I'll go back."

John floated with Gary back to the group of souls where James was waiting for them.

"That was a short visit," said James.

"Gary is a man of few words," said John.

"That he is," said James. "I can't figure out for the life of me why he is still here. Did you pick up anything as to why?"

"I don't understand why he is retarded in the afterlife," said John. "So far, I've seen sick people well, and the blind see here. It doesn't make any sense."

"Maybe we'll understand later."

"Maybe so."

John went back to the group and went up to James.

"Do you have someone else lined up for me?"

"Yes. I think you'll find Emily very interesting, too. She's located on the other side of the pond."

The two of them floated across the cemetery and over the pond. There, amid a variety of beautiful flowers was an elderly woman hovering above an elaborate headstone that was in the form of a life-sized angel. The lady was thin, silver-haired and had blue eyes. Her face was gaunt with a multitude of wrinkles. She wore a long dress covered with multi-colored flowers.

"Miss Emily? I don't mean to disturb you but I have someone here I'd like you to meet."

The woman looked up at them and gave a sweet smile.

"You must be John. I've heard about you, and I've seen you on the other side of the pond talking to others. It's nice to finally meet you, John."

"It's nice to meet you, too. Do I call you "Miss Emily?""

"Oh, that's what they call me because I'm so old. You can call me just Emily if you'd prefer."

"Okay, Emily. How long have you been here at the Garden of Peace?"

"I've been here for over 20 years. Add that to my 95 years, and I've been around a long time."

"Ninety-five. To what do you think you owed your long life?"

"I guess I just kept getting out of bed and breathing every day."

John laughed.

"Did you have a special diet?"

"I ate oatmeal for breakfast every morning, ate a lot of chicken and soup and drank a lot of tea."

"Well, it must have worked very well for you. You look terrific."

"You mean I look terrific for a 95-year-old."

John laughed again. "I guess so," he said.

"After I retired, I walked around my neighborhood every day, which kept me pretty fit. I also did a lot of gardening around the house."

"Can you tell me something about your life? When and where were you born?"

"I was born in 1901 in Washington, D.C. My father was a United States senator at the time."

"Wow! That's impressive."

"Well, I didn't really have much to do with it."

John laughed.

"He was considered a good man and tried to serve his constituency the best he could. We lived in Augusta, Maine most of the time."

"What did your mother do?"

"She took care of me and my three sisters and took care of our home. Before we got up in the mornings, she would write. She wrote children's books."

"Did she get her books published?"

"Oh, my, yes! She had 20 of her books published during her lifetime."

"So, it sounds as if you had a good childhood."

"I did. Augusta was a quaint little town when I was growing up. I went to school at St. Augustine under the Sisters of the Presentation of Mary. They were very strict teachers but they were fair. I found that I had a knack for writing stories like my mother. When I graduated from high school, I went to Columbia University where I studied journalism. I soon realized that I wasn't a very good journalist but I was an excellent editor.

I landed a job as a junior editor for the New York Times in 1923. It was a very exciting time. I was young and single and it was the middle of the roaring twenties. It was also a wonderful time to be a part of the largest newspaper in America."

"Did you get married?"

"Twice. The first time was when I was 28. Donald was a journalist working the Times' international desk. He was greatly admired for his reporting on Europe after the Great War. He would often travel to England, France and Germany to cover their news. I was able to go with him a few times but I mostly stayed in New York and worked at my editor's desk."

"Did you have any children?"

"Yes. We had two children; Robert and Anna. Once I had Anna, I quit my job with the Times and stayed home full time. That was just expected back then. Besides, Donald was making enough to support us, so I didn't have to work. Robert came two years later."

"What brought you to Pittsburgh?"

"Donald joined the Army in 1941 right after Pearl Harbor. He was too old to join but they gave him an exemption because of his language skills. They were put to good use because he became an OSS officer who interpreted German transmissions during the war. In 1944, he was killed in action in France shortly after D-Day."

"I'm sorry to hear that."

"Thank you. It was a very difficult time, and I missed Donald terribly. I decided to leave New York and moved back in with my parents in Augusta because I had no income, and I needed to be with my family. By then, my father had retired as a senator and they welcomed us with open arms.

My mother knew I needed something to do besides taking care of the children, so she taught me how to write children's books. I published my first book with my mother's publisher. It became a best seller and I made very good money from it. With the publication of my second book, I became confident enough to decide to move out of my parents' house.

I had sent out resumes before I finished my second book to see if I could find a regular job. As it turned out, I got a job offer from the Pittsburgh Post-Gazette for an editor's position. So, that's how I got to Pittsburgh."

"Where did you live in Pittsburgh?"

"At first, we moved into a townhouse in the Mexican War Streets area close to downtown. I hired a nanny to help me with the children and continued to write children's books on the side."

"It sounds as if you had a good life at that time."

"We did. We lived in Pittsburgh for a few years until I remarried in 1949, this time to a lawyer by the name of Herbert Johnson. He was an assistant district attorney working downtown and was very good with the children. I sold the townhouse and moved in with Herbert who lived in Churchill. A year later, when it was time for Anna to go to college, he encouraged her to go to the University of Pittsburgh where he had graduated. But she had a mind of her own and decided to go to Penn State. When Robert was ready to go to college a couple of years later, he went to Pitt. It was expensive to put them through college at the same time but we had a good income, and I had another successful book that helped a great deal.

Anna graduated with a master's degree in French literature, taking after her father in languages. Robert got his MBA in

International Business. They were both fluent in French and often spoke in that language at home when they visited."

"Did you have any grandchildren?"

"Oh, yes! We had six grandchildren and there were 5 great grandchildren. Herbert retired in 1970 and played golf as much as he could. Five years later, he got cancer of the esophagus and passed away. It was a hard way to go.

I retired in 1976 but continued to write children's books until 1990. By then, I was starting to deteriorate physically and mentally. I lived with Anna for a couple of years but they ended up having to put me in a nursing home. I lived four more years until I fell and broke my hip. That trip to the hospital was the end of me, and I died there the result of an infection."

"How did you end up here in the Garden?"

"My nursing home was in Monroeville. Herbert wanted to be cremated, so he was never interred. One day, I asked my daughter to drive me around to some of the different cemeteries. She didn't want to but she acquiesced. We looked at several but I liked the way this one was tucked away, and I loved the pond. So, here I am."

"You lived an interesting life. Do you have any regrets?"

"No. I learned a long time ago that we make our decisions based on our feelings and situations at the time. Oh, I might have changed a thing or two if I knew then what I know now, but who knows what would have resulted. One decision can change everything. Each action and decision causes an endless chain reaction."

"That's very profound. I never thought of it quite that way. Why are you still here, do you think?"

"Maybe it's because I like it here. I have friends here. I have a beautiful spot, and maybe I didn't go to church enough. Who knows?"

"Well, it sounds to me as if you deserve to get to heaven sooner rather than later. But I'm glad to hear you're contented here."

"I am."

"Would you like to come back to the group with me?"

"No, thank you. I'm still enjoying the ducks. They are endlessly entertaining. They've become like my pets."

"It was very nice talking with you, Emily."

"Likewise, John. I'm sure I will see you around from time to time."

"I'm sure of it."

John floated across the pond and headed back to the congregation.

James was waiting.

"Nice lady, isn't she?" asked James.

"Very nice. I don't understand why she hasn't gone to heaven yet. It's very confusing to me why some people haven't already gone to hell and some haven't gone to heaven."

"It is a mystery, isn't it? If I get to heaven, that will be one of my first questions."

Chapter 21

John went back to the group and listened to some of the conversations before night began to fall. He was anxious to get back to his grave site that night because he was remembering where he'd left off—his courtship with Brenda.

After their first date, John knew he was in love with Brenda. He'd already had a date lined up with Mandy and he didn't want to break it, so John drove to Indianapolis where Mandy was back in college. They had their date in the student union hall of the college and were pleasant to each other. John knew the spark was gone between them, but he didn't want to tell her that he was in love with someone else. Instead, he decided to take the coward's way out and wrote her a letter when he got back home after his date.

John and Brenda spent almost every day together in some way. They ate together in the break room at the hospital as often as they could. In the evenings, John spent time at Brenda's home where she made him hot tea and then made out on the couch after her mother had gone to bed.

During their conversations, Brenda let John know she had been seeing another man before she met John. His name was Homer and he was in his 40s. She said she was not the least bit serious about him but he had taken her to the American Legion for dinner a few times. He had been her employment counselor, and he was the one who found her a job in the insurance department at the hospital.

Things between John and Brenda seemed to be going well until about five weeks into their relationship. One Friday evening when John came over, he knew something was wrong by the way Brenda's mother acted. When Brenda was finally ready, she was not in a good mood when she came out. John had no idea why she was so upset but decided to wait until they were out of the house to discuss it. The Thunderbird was in the shop again, so John had borrowed his dad's old pickup truck for the past few dates. He helped Brenda into the truck and after he got in, asked what was wrong.

"Just drive," she said.

John drove to the Dog & Suds drive-in for something to eat. Brenda didn't talk on the way there and when they ordered, she said she didn't want anything. John went ahead and ordered for himself and then asked her again what was wrong.

"Explain this," she said gruffly as she gave him an envelope that was addressed to her. John noticed there was a stamp on the letter but it was not post-marked.

John opened the envelope, took out the typed letter and read it aloud.

"Dear Brenda,

I just wanted you to know that John is not who you think he is. He is my boyfriend and we had a little boy together. His name is Johnny, Jr., and he will be 6 months old this month."

John started to laugh. He continued to read aloud.

"I know he is very romantic and it is hard to resist his charms. He is even charming in his old truck but he is mine. I don't want you to break up our little family."

John laughed again but he could tell Brenda was not amused.

"Please let him come back to me."

The letter was not signed.

"This entire letter is a lie, Brenda. I'll bet you Homer wrote it to break us up. There is no 'little Johnny.'"

"How can I trust you?" Brenda asked sternly.

"How can I prove it's not true?"

"I don't know."

They sat there in the truck for several minutes. John's food order came from the waitress, and she placed the hanging tray on his half-opened window. He drank the root beer from the frosted mug and munched on his breaded pork tenderloin sandwich and French fries. He offered Brenda some fries but she refused. When he'd finished his root beer, he flashed his lights for the waitress and she took his tray from the window.

"Why don't we go to the Purdue student union to talk?" asked John.

"That's fine," Brenda said roughly.

John drove over to West Lafayette to the Purdue student union, parked and helped Brenda down. They walked together but did not hold hands. They climbed the stairs and walked down the wide hallway to a quiet section of the student union. When they sat down on a leather couch, John began to speak.

"I swear to you, Brenda, everything in that letter is a lie. It was written by Homer or Mandy with the intention of breaking us up."

"I just don't know how I can trust you."

With tears in his eyes, John spoke from the heart.

"Well, you've kind of forced my hand. I was planning to ask you on your birthday but I'm going to go ahead and ask you now. Will you marry me, Brenda Green?"

John could see that Brenda was shocked but her demeanor changed when she answered.

"Yes. I'll marry you, John. After that letter, I don't know why I trust you, but I do."

"I love you, Brenda."

"I love you, too, John."

They kissed a long, loving kiss and then held each other for a long time.

"I don't have much money but I think I'll have enough to buy you a ring before your birthday."

"I have a little money saved and we can buy the rings together," said Brenda.

"Do you want to see if there are any jewelry stores open tonight?" John asked.

"Okay."

They walked back to the truck hand-in-hand. John drove to downtown Lafayette and saw the lights on at Chupp's Jewelers. He parked the truck in front of the store and they went in together. Mr. Chupp was a heavy-set older man with gray hair and bushy gray eyebrows. He helped them find a set of wedding rings for her and a matching ring for him. They put the rings in layaway and thanked the jeweler for his help.

On the way back to her house, John suggested they wait to tell anyone until her birthday on November 23rd or at least until they got her engagement ring. Brenda agreed.

When her birthday came, it coincided with Thanksgiving, which they were planning to spend with her family at her sister's house in Indianapolis. By then, they had been able to purchase the rings and Brenda wore the engagement ring to the gathering.

It was a very joyous occasion when the two of them announced their engagement that day. Even her mother seemed happy.

In November, John changed jobs again. He began working for Kmart in the appliance department as an assistant manager. The pay and benefits were better than the hospital, though the hours were more varied with quite a few evenings to have to work. His boss, Theo, was in his 50s, was a jerk much of the time, and John soon realized he wasn't to be trusted.

John sold all kinds of appliances there, including TVs, stereos, washers, dryers, stoves and refrigerators, along with small appliances. Selling was the easy part. The difficult part of the job was unloading the appliances from the big trucks, stacking them in the warehouse and setting them up in the showroom.

Brenda and John selected February 23rd for their wedding date. They took care of the usual things together like the flowers, the invitations and thank-you cards, photographer, tuxes and so on. Both had been attending the Assembly of God church and spoke with the pastor who insisted he would not marry them unless he counseled them beforehand. They agreed and had two sessions with him. What they got out of it was that he advised them to combine their money into a joint account. Brenda wasn't thrilled about that but she agreed to do it.

John found a furnished one-bedroom apartment on North 21st Street near the hospital, and they moved their things in just before the wedding. There were a few steps to negotiate to get up to the front porch, and there was a side parking space beside the converted home. In front, there were quite a few steps up to the main level from the street.

When the day of the wedding came, the weather was rather mild for February in Lafayette, Indiana. John's best friend, Eric, was the best man. Brenda's sister was the matron of honor, and Brenda's brother-in-law, Jay, walked her down the aisle as her father had passed away five years earlier. The wedding was very nice but simple with about fifty people in attendance. Brenda looked radiant in her white wedding dress. The women in the wedding party wore mauve dresses and the men looked handsome in their black tuxes with frilly mauve shirts and matching black and mauve bowties.

The wedding went flawlessly except for the minor faux-pas during the ceremony in which Brenda said, "I do-do" which was kind of funny, and John chuckled over it. After the ceremony, many of the people who attended the wedding went to Brenda's aunt's home in West Lafayette for the reception where they had cake and ice cream. When the reception was over, John packed up the car with the gifts, and they left for their honeymoon to Rennselaer, Indiana which was just about 45 minutes away. They stayed in a large motel with an indoor swimming pool. They went swimming that evening with John lifting Brenda up to the surface of the water as he waded in the shallow end. That night they made love as if it had been the first time for them both.

The next day, they looked out the windows and saw several inches of snow. They drove back to Lafayette since they both had to work on Monday, and it was still snowing and blowing. When they got back to the apartment, they could not get into the parking lot on the side of the building because of the snow, so John had to park out front below the steps. He carried Brenda up the steps to the apartment, then carried all the gifts in. He was very tired and out of breath by the time he had finished. Brenda began opening the gifts and showed each one to John and told him who they were from. Most of the gifts were kitchen items, which was fine with them.

That afternoon, Brenda set about preparing their first home-cooked meal for them as a married couple. She was baking turbo fish fillets. But when they sat down to eat, John realized his fish fillet was still cold in the middle. He felt bad for Brenda but he couldn't eat it. He ate cereal instead and was in the dog house over it. Brenda was crying and locked herself in the bedroom. A little later, John went to check on her and realized the door was locked. He knocked on the door and asked if she was okay, but she didn't answer. He knocked again and he still didn't get an answer. John was getting worried and threatened to break down the door if she didn't open it. However, she still didn't answer. John put his shoulder to the door and broke the molding around the lock. Later, she told him she was just playing coy and pretended to be asleep. After that, Brenda cooked several different dishes but never tried to cook turbo fillets again. She never locked John out again either.

Married life seemed to suit them both, and they got along very well for the most part. They had their first child, John Jr., a year later. Brenda did well in childbirth though she had to be induced and almost choked John when she got her arm around his neck during one of her contractions. John went into the delivery room with her and witnessed the joyous birth of their son. Back at work, John was congratulated by everyone.

One day, Brenda was talking with one of her friends from high school, Linda Gallow, and mentioned to her that John wasn't very satisfied with his job at Kmart. Linda's husband, James Jr., was co-owner of a jewelry store in downtown Lafayette and was looking for someone to help at the store. John met with James Jr. at the jewelry store and he showed him what they did there. They were jewelry makers and had a store and shop on the second floor of a building in downtown Lafayette. John was excited by the idea of learning the jeweler's craft and told James Jr. he had his GI Bill money that he might be able to use during the training period. The two of them worked together to set up a 4-year apprenticeship program in which John would receive $5.00 per hour partly from the GI Bill and partly from the jewelry store. In January of 1975, John left Kmart to work for the Gallow jewelry store.

John had a special talent when it came to the jewelry work. Since most of the store's business came from repair work from other jewelry stores, he spent most of his time sizing rings, setting diamonds and other stones, and soldering gold and silver items. He also learned to make wax models, rubber molds, and prepared rough castings into finished pieces. While he was there, he also took a correspondence course on diamonds from the Gemological Institute of America or GIA. With that information in hand, John also did some diamond sales and jewelry design for the store.

John began looking for a house shortly after going to work for Gallow's and one day, stumbled onto a small, 3-bedroom, 1 bath bank-owned bungalow on the north side of Lafayette on the corner of North 19th and Perrine Streets. When John went to the bank and asked about the property, the manager told him the property was part of an estate and had gone up for auction that very morning but hadn't sold because the bids were below the asking price of $13,000.00. John offered the asking price if the bank would do the mortgage for him. It took some time but the bank finally agreed. John's parents made them a loan of $600.00 to help with the down payment. The house needed some work on the interior but John, his mother and his friends worked together to steam the old pink wallpaper off the walls and ceilings, repaired some plaster problems and put in new cabinets and a sink in the kitchen. There was a lot of painting and wallpapering to do, but John knew how to do it and was not afraid of the work.

When they moved in, the house was very cute for 1976. Each bedroom had a wall with wallpaper and trim and three walls of complimenting paint. The baby's bedroom was right across from the master bedroom and had a nice crib and bassinette in it. John and Brenda had not purchased a bed yet, so they slept on a mattress on the floor of the master bedroom until they could afford to buy one. The dining room had wallpaper depicting colonial scenes and there was an attractive hanging light that hung over a large antique dining room table that had been given to them by John's parents. There was also a pine wooden bench that had been stained a dark color to match the table and four chairs.

A year later, John got the bug to move again. He found a house that was a Housing and Urban Development foreclosure in a newer neighborhood in the Southside of Lafayette on Bamford Ct. It was a four bedroom, one and a half bath ranch with an attached one-car garage and a large weedy yard. It needed some work—mostly painting and papering, new flooring and some landscape work but nothing difficult. The asking price was $14,000.00. The bidding process was difficult and used sealed bids sent to HUD. John worried over how much to bid. When he was at the bank, he overheard someone talking about bidding $17,000.00, so he bid $18,550.00 and got the house. John and Brenda quickly sold the Perrine house for $19,900.00 less the cost of rewiring, which was about $1,250.00.

With the left-over equity from the Perrine house, John was able to pay his parents back, make the down payment on the new house and purchase a new red, 1975 Chevy Monza with a stick shift.

John repaired the new house, painted and papered the rooms and had new carpet installed in the master bedroom. When they moved in, the house, which was built on a slab, felt very large compared to the Perrine property. John's parents gave them an old couch and chair they had received from John's grandmother, and it helped to fill in the new living room.

One day, tragedy struck. John had gone to the YMCA with his brother, Paul, to play in a pick-up basketball game. By this time, John Jr. was just learning to walk and Brenda had been bathing him. When she finished, she had just let the water out of the tub when the phone rang in the living room. Brenda went to answer the phone and just as she picked up, she heard water running and John Jr. screaming. She went back to the bathroom as quickly as she could and found their son standing in the scalding hot water he had turned on. Brenda turned off the water, wrapped him in a towel and walked to the neighbor's house where she asked them to take her and John Jr. to the hospital. They instantly obliged and drove them both to the emergency room. Once there, she asked if someone would call the YMCA and try to reach John.

John got the call and immediately drove to the emergency room. When John arrived, the pediatric surgeon was debriding the tiny feet while John Jr. screamed. John comforted Brenda during the procedure. Finally, they completed the debriding and told the couple there were second degree burns up to their child's ankles and there was a danger of the burns advancing to third degree. They admitted John Jr. to the hospital and put him in isolation to help prevent infection. The doctor had placed salve on the child's feet and wrapped them in bandages. John Jr. was placed in a metal cage crib that had a door with a locking mechanism on the side. John's mother and father were called and they soon visited. Brenda called her mother to let her know as well.

Any visitor had to put on a gown and mask before entering the room. At first, John Jr. would not eat. But then, John's father got his grandson to suck on a Popsicle. Not long after that, John Jr. started eating regular food.

Each day, the surgeon personally changed the bandages and checked the tiny feet. The good news was there was no progression of the burns. The bad news was the child had to stay in the hospital for a week. John Jr. was very brave throughout the process even though he hated being in the caged bed. He would often hold onto the bars and try to stand but the pain was too great and he would get back down on his knees. It was torture for Brenda and John to watch him go through the pain. There was always someone with him in the hospital room whether it was one of John's parents, John or Brenda.

A couple of times, their original pediatrician stopped by and peaked into the room from the doorway. They later found out that their pediatrician had charged them for five hospital visits even though he never went into the room. They were furious with him and soon dropped him. Eventually, they found out that the kind, young and talented pediatric surgeon had died of cancer not long after treating their son.

Chapter 22

It was sunrise again in the cemetery. John had spoken with almost everyone in the Garden of Peace, so he just hung around and listened to the others until nightfall. Now, he was more concerned with his own history and looked forward to his time alone.

That night, John recalled that it had been only about a year after moving into the Bamford property that he began to get the itch to move again. This time, he found a small, two-bedroom cottage on five acres across the road from the Tippecanoe River in the Monticello area just down from the dam. It needed a little work but John, as usual, was prepared to do it. Brenda was reluctant to be so far away from any town since she didn't drive but she went along.

They sold the Bamford house for $28,800.00 which gave them almost a $10,000.00 profit in just a year. With the profit from the house, they made a substantial down payment on the river property that was priced at $26,000.00 and moved in. There was something quaint about the river property, and they quickly made friends with three of their neighbors. The property had about an acre of ground around the house that was lawn, a large garage and a small barn that housed several sheep. The rest of the acreage was in pasture. Shortly after having the sheep shorn, John sold them at auction.

It was relaxing living out in the country. John bought a riding mower to take care of the large lawn. It took longer for John to get to work and he was late a few times, especially during the winter when it snowed.

But John was still a good employee and did much of the jewelry repair work for the other stores with whom the Gallows had contracted. In fact, James Jr. had told him one Saturday morning that they were both going to be rich someday with the plans he had for the store. Unfortunately, things didn't turn out as planned. James' brother, Randy, needed a job, so the Gallows hired him and taught him the trade. Randy liked making rings through casting, though he was not great at design. However, James Jr. tolerated it.

Randy and John were sent to Dallas, Texas to a 3-day casting seminar. There, they learned the finer points of wax model-making, mold-making and casting. One evening at the hotel, Randy broke out some marijuana and offered it to John. John was reluctant but went along anyway. They both got stoned and talked the night away. John kept the part about getting stoned from his wife.

It wasn't long after the seminar that the Gallows brought in James' sister, Cindy, to work at the store. She helped with the bookkeeping, answered the telephone and waited on customers. John could see the writing on the wall. He felt he was slowly getting squeezed out.

Not long after this, John decided to buy an engraving machine to make plastic signs and do regular engraving. John had worked for the Gallows for three and a half years. Then, one day, James Jr. took him into the office and fired him. He had apparently found out about the side engraving business and felt John was competing against them. John was furious and told James what he thought about the situation. But, he was fired nonetheless.

John tried to make it with just the engraving business but it was hard to get new customers. Brenda helped with the engraving while John went out and tried to sell other jewelers and hardware stores on his services. Unfortunately, the work just wasn't there.

When they were down on their luck, John went to the bank in Monticello and told them he was currently unemployed and was unable to make the next house payment. John was pleasantly surprised by the bank manager's reaction.

"Most people don't bother to contact the bank until after they've already missed a few payments. You let us know before you missed one. That's a sign of character, so we're willing to work with you. We can stop your payments for a few months until you find work and then re-do your loan if we need to," he said.

John thanked the bank manager and said he would try to find work as quickly as possible. It wasn't long before John found a minimum wage job at $3.50 per hour at a small plastics factory in Brookston, Indiana. At first, he was a press operator which was very hot, dirty and difficult work. He was soon promoted to the shipping and receiving position. With that promotion, he became part of the management staff and sat in on the management meetings. Within a few months, John's pay went up to $5.00 per hour, and he was able to catch up on his mortgage payments without having to re-do the loan. The materials he was working with were fiberglass reinforced plastics which were used as plastic insulators in varying forms. The fiberglass dust from the factory stuck to the skin and was breathed in. When John got home, his breath smelled like plastics and he felt like he was lying on a bed of needles when he got between the sheets to go to bed every night.

Meanwhile, Brenda had her hands full with John Jr. When he was four years old, he would sometimes get away from her and start running through the fields where she could not get to him. One time, when John was building a small addition to the house, he left a ladder leaning against the roof. Brenda was outside with John Jr. and a short time later, heard him say, "Look at me, Mommy!" She looked around but couldn't find him. Finally, she looked up and saw John Jr. sitting on the roof. She tried to coax him down but he didn't know how.

Brenda went to the neighbor's house and found their 16-year-old son who volunteered to help. He went up the ladder and brought John Jr. down with no harm done.

The second year they were at the river property, John and Brenda met with a farmer who did share-cropping and offered to split the profits if he could plant corn on the four acres that were currently just in pasture. They agreed. The farmer bought the seed, plowed the field and planted the corn. He also had the field sprayed with fertilizer and weed repellant. The corn grew very well that season and after harvest time, the farmer gave the Samples a check for over $900, which was their share after splitting expenses. This was a huge amount of money for them at the time.

They share-cropped with the farmer for three more years with two years in corn and one year in soy beans. The fourth year, they left the field go fallow. The following spring, one of John's neighbors suggested buying a couple of feeder calves to raise for the summer. So, John and the neighbor went to the cattle auction and purchased two Black Angus calves that weighed approximately 600 lbs. each. The neighbor bought one of them from John, and John's dad agreed to pay for half of the other one. At the end of the summer, the cows had grown to about 900 lbs. each and it was time to send them to slaughter. The beef was split up three ways; one cow was packaged up for the neighbor and the other was split with half going to John and the other going to John's dad. John rented a large freezer from a neighbor who owned a bait shop and lived just a short distance away. The fee for the freezer was a small portion of the meat. When they got low on meat, John walked to the bait shop and picked up the meat they needed for the next week or so. John used to say they were eating steak when they could barely afford hamburger.

That winter, there was a blizzard on its way and John got caught in it while driving home after a late night at the factory. The long stretch of road was quickly getting covered by the drifting snow that was blowing across the open fields. John tried avoiding the drifts and was doing fairly well until he encountered one that stretched across the road. He tried gunning the motor to plow through it, but it pulled him into the deep end and was stuck. John knew it was unlikely to encounter another vehicle on the road, so he decided to get out and try to walk to the nearest house, which was over one hundred yards away. The temperature was hovering around zero degrees with the wind chill well below that. John had a coat but no gloves or boots. He walked through the snow to the house with the porch light on. There were moments when he didn't think he would make it and would end up frozen to death in the middle of the road. But, he made it to that little house, knocked on the door, and was greeted warmly by the woman who lived there. She brought him inside, got him a blanket and helped him phone the wrecker company that was located just across the street from the plastics factory. He gave the wrecker owner the address and directions and waited in the warm house. He then called Brenda to let her know that he was all right. The lady of the house was very kind and made him a cup of hot cocoa while he waited.

Eventually, the wrecker arrived. John thanked the lady for her help then went with the driver to pick up the car. The driver said the roads ahead were too bad, so he hooked up the car and they drove back to his shop with John's car in tow. When they got back to the shop, the tow-truck owner pulled the car into his heated garage. The driver said the best thing was to let the car thaw out until morning before trying to start it. John agreed, then called his wife again to let her know what was going on and then walked over to the factory where he slept on his office floor until morning.

John awoke the next morning and went across the street to the wrecker company and got the car started. The storm was over and the trucks had been out to clear the snow from the roads, so John drove home. It had been a harrowing experience but John had survived.

Soon, Brenda was pregnant with their second child, so John felt it was time to try to find a different job as he didn't see himself getting anywhere at the factory. John saw an ad that said a jewelry company was looking for an assistant manager, so he applied for the position. With his strong resume, he was hired almost immediately. The jewelry company was the Shane Company located on the 10th floor of a bank building in downtown Lafayette. Shane's was known for their large newspaper and TV ads featuring the company's owner traveling to Antwerp, Belgium to buy diamonds directly. Even though they had the reputation for selling second-rate diamonds, it was difficult to compete against them if customers shopped around for diamonds. The jewelry location was small, but there was a large selection of engagement rings and wedding rings on display. John was relieved to have a good job again, and the pay was the best he'd ever made.

The manager, Fred, was short with a receding hairline, a moustache and was in his mid-30s. There were two other employees at the store. Sue, who was married, did the books and helped with sales. Mattie was a blonde in her early 20s and was very attractive. She also helped with the books and with sales.

One day, Fred was on the phone with his supervisor and was seated with his back to the door. Julie, Mattie and John were behind the main counter when a young man in his early 20s with long, stringy brown hair and eyes that looked as if he was high came into the store. He was wearing a worn jean jacket, old ragged jeans that were frayed at the bottoms, and he was carrying an old, brown briefcase with electrician's tape wrapped around it.

John was immediately suspicious of the young man.

"How can I help you?" John asked in as calm a manner as he could.

"I, uh, want to see some big diamonds," he said.

John started to open the safe door but then closed it, turned back around and said, "Under the circumstances, I'm afraid I can't show you any diamonds today."

For a moment, the young man had a confused look on his face, then said, "Then, can you get these off me?"

The young man held up the briefcase and for the first time, John could see the briefcase was attached to the man's wrist by a set of handcuffs. John turned to look at the girls behind him. They were wide-eyed and had their backs to the wall. Fred was still on the phone and oblivious to the situation.

"I'm sorry," said John. "I don't have any tools here. But there's a locksmith just down the street. I'm sure he can get them off."

The young man did not reply. He just stood there for a few seconds and then walked casually out the door. John nudged Fred and said he needed to use the phone but Fred just looked at him like he was crazy.

"I'm on the phone with my supervisor!" he exclaimed.

John walked to the door and opened it to see where the man went. John saw the man get on the elevator, so he went into the hair salon across the hall and asked to use their phone. John called the police and told them what had happened. He told them he thought the man might have a bomb in the briefcase and told them where he thought the man was headed. He asked the police if they would let them know what happened, and they said they would.

John went back across the hall to the store and by this time, Fred was off the phone and the girls were filling him in on what had happened. They were very shaken up.

About two hours went by when a policeman came into the store.

"Thank you for calling us," he said. "When we caught up to the guy, we were also concerned the briefcase might have contained a bomb, so we had it x-rayed. It contained a large bag of pot and a handgun. He was arrested and is now in jail."

The policeman took their statements before leaving the store. Fred was shocked when he heard what had happened. John was commended for keeping cool under the circumstances, and his value as an employee seemed to grow from that point.

John's ability to sell diamonds was very evident but Fred used to make fun of him for his inability to remember the names of customers. Fred had an amazing talent for remembering the names of customers, what they purchased, and the approximate dates.

After just six months, the supervisor offered John the opportunity to manage a store of his own in Indianapolis. By this time, Brenda and John had had their second child; a girl named Anita. Brenda was a little reluctant to move to Indianapolis but she relented. Besides, she still had her sister living there, so family wasn't far away.

The district supervisor took John to dinner at St. Elmo's Steak House in downtown Indianapolis. It was by far the fanciest place John had ever eaten. The waiters all wore tuxedos, and the food was amazing. It was the first time John had ever had a filet mignon and shrimp cocktail. They also visited the store he would be taking over. It was on the 7th floor of the King

Cole building near the center of downtown Indianapolis. The store was bigger than the one in Lafayette and had more merchandise and more employees.

Once he was back home in Monticello, John put the river property up for sale for $39,900.00, and they quickly accepted an offer for $36,000.00. The district supervisor put John and Brenda up in a distinguished, old downtown Indianapolis hotel and the next day, he took them apartment shopping. They looked at several apartment complexes and ended up selecting a three-bedroom in the Fall Creek Apartments complex that was about 30 minutes from work. It was a very nice apartment that was just a half flight of stairs to the front door. The Shane Company provided a moving company to take care of the move.

When John took over the King Cole store, there was quite a bit of office intrigue and unexpected competition from a sister store within the Shane Company called Smith's Diamond Brokers, barely a block away. Smith's was known for 'big, bold diamonds' at very low prices. Basically, they sold larger diamonds of very poor quality, but they sold a lot of them. Smith's was also known for very strong sales tactics referred to as the 'T-O' or turn over. They would start out with one salesperson and at some point in the sales talk, would turn over the sale to another more senior salesperson. This aggressive sales tactic was strongly encouraged by the company's president, who was also the company's diamond buyer. He was a crude, cigar-smoking individual who favored the Smith's sales approach and had his office in the same building with them. John's main customers at the Shane Company were bridal couples looking for engagement and wedding rings usually of higher quality. John preferred a more honest and educated approach for these customers and liked using the microscope to compare quality of diamonds. His supervisors tolerated this approach as long as the sales results were good. And, they were.

After a year of apartment living, John and Brenda decided to buy a home on the city's Northeast side. It was a 3-bedroom brick ranch they bought for $35,000.00 with a Veterans Administration loan with no money down. By this time, John had purchased a new, 1980, yellow, Pontiac Grand Prix with wire-wheel hubcaps.

One weekend while John was working in the front yard, he was also supposed to be watching their daughter Anita, who was about 18 months old at the time. She was playing in the yard wearing just a diaper and no top. John turned away for a few moments, then looked up and discovered she was gone. He frantically called out for her but could neither hear nor see her anywhere. He began to panic and ran and told Brenda what had happened. They got some of their neighbors out to look for her. Finally, John went down the next street looking for her. There was a man carrying Anita up the street towards him. John ran to them and collected his daughter. The man said she had been walking down the middle of the street. John thanked the man profusely and returned home realizing things could have turned out much worse.

The Shane Company had plans to put a new store in a strip center near a mall on the north side of Indianapolis. The area was called Castleton and was building up very quickly. John was selected to manage that store and help supervise the build-out process of the space. A few months later, the store was finished. It was a gorgeous store with curved, rosewood wall sections, a shop, and a lot of brass fixtures. They had their grand opening, and the store did very well though not quite as well as the supervisors were expecting.

A few Saturdays later, as John and the employees were waiting to go into the store to open, there was a somewhat suspicious construction van parked at the unit next to the store. It was not unusual for construction companies to be working on Saturdays, so John went ahead and unlocked the door for the employees. The driver of the van was sitting and reading a newspaper. As the ten employees walked into the store, armed robbers pressed guns to the backs of the last employees going into the building,

"Just keep moving inside," one of the robbers said.

They had pantyhose pulled over their faces and carried handguns. John was already back in the office area when he realized what was happening. He was carrying his lunch in a small brown bag.

"You! Drop the bag and get to the safe. Everyone else—face down on the floor!"

John knew that the silent alarm would go out automatically without his turning it off. He went to the safe.

"Open it!" The robber yelled as he pointed the gun at John's head.

John opened the safe.

"Now, get down on the floor!"

John could hear the robbers emptying the safe and carrying out the large wooden boxes to the van. He believed there was a real possibility they would shoot him in the back of the head.

As they were leaving, one of the robbers said, "Now nobody gets up for five minutes. We'll be watching."

One of the male employees said the last robber had left, so John got up and called the police who were already on their way. The employees were pretty shaken up but each one gave their statement to the police when they arrived. John called his supervisor to let him know what had happened, and he came shortly thereafter. John got a call from the president of the company. He asked John why he opened the store with a suspicious-looking van parked outside.

John said, "I can't believe you're second-guessing me after what we just went through!"

A week or so later, the police got a tip that caused them to stake out a garage. When the robbers went back to the garage, they were captured and most of the merchandise was recovered. Shortly thereafter, the company hired an armed guard service to protect the store.

A few months went by and the store had a second robbery. This time, John arrived just after the robbery had occurred as he was working the second shift. The employees were very shaken because the robbers came into the store late one morning during broad daylight, stuck a gun in the ribs of the guard, and disarmed him before ordering everyone on the floor. The robbers did not get as much as the first robbery, but the employees said it was more frightening than the first one, and the robbers did not wear masks. John comforted the employees and the store was temporarily closed to take inventory and talk to the police.

Several days later, the police detectives came to the store to question the employees and show them pictures of the men they picked up from the robbery. The employees identified the men as the ones who had perpetrated the robbery. Then the detectives showed the pictures to John.

"Do you recognize either of these two men?" one of them asked as he showed him the pictures.

"I don't recognize the first one but the second one is a dead ringer for my great grandfather," said John. It can't be my great grandfather because he's been dead for many years.

"Interesting you would say that because his last name is Sample. Your last name is Sample, isn't it?"

John was incredulous. It all had to be very suspicious since John was the only one that wasn't there for the robbery.

"I guess if I were you, I'd be looking very closely at me," said John.

"We already have and we think you're clean. But I wouldn't be surprised if this guy isn't a relative of yours. They recently escaped from prison, and we think they chose this store because of its proximity to the highway. They've both been captured, and we found the jewelry in their possession."

"I'm glad you caught them and got the merchandise. I hope they're back in prison."

"They soon will be."

A few more months went by at the store and John found out he was in the running for district supervisor. It was down to John and the man who managed Smith's Diamond Brokers. When they chose the other manager for the position, John was very disappointed and upset. One of the main reasons the other man got the job was because he had a college degree. From that point on, John decided he would plan to open his own store somewhere.

For several months, John looked at small jewelry stores that were for sale but couldn't find anything appropriate. Finally, after attending a small business seminar and doing a lot of research, he chose Carmel, Indiana as the location for his store. It was a high-income location with a lot of new money located a few miles north of Indianapolis.

John financed the company by putting up $12,000.00 of his own money from his 401k and his savings, and by selling stock in a corporation. He went to several banks and found one that would finance $50,000.00 if John could raise an additional $50,000.00 on his own. He raised an additional $38,000.00 from the sale of stock to family members and set up a line of credit. In the fall of 1984, when John had raised the money, he quit his job at Shane's. He leased a retail spot in a strip center near a small Carmel mall that seemed appropriate, had a sign made and finished the interior with a theme that represented the name of the company—Camelot Jewelry Centers, Inc. The grand opening was in November though it turned out to be less than grand. There were only a few customers and several relatives who showed up.

John hired three employees to help during the beginning phase of operations. Two were former Shane Company employees and one was his niece. The merchandise John had purchased seemed too expensive for his clients' tastes, and that Christmas season was a bust. Fortunately, the repair business was taking off, and it helped support the business for the next several months.

By May of the following year, John had let the other employees go, and Brenda began to help with the books and sales. The store was finally beginning to be self-sufficient. However, in June, disaster struck.

On Thursday, June 20th, 1985, two men came into Camelot Jewelry and looked around. One was very tall and heavy-set, in his late 30s, with what appeared to be bleached blond hair. The other one looked to be in his 40s, with a medium build. He didn't talk and had brown hair that looked like a wig. They stopped to look at the gold chains. John was immediately suspicious of the two men.

"I'm looking for a gold chain for my wife," said the heavy-set man. "I was hoping to find something a bit heavier than what you have.

"Well, we don't have a lot of selection right now but we will be having a special sale on Saturday during a trunk show with a lot of gold chains to choose from," John said.

"Maybe I'll come back on Saturday then," the big man said. Then the two men left.

John was relieved nothing had happened. John always carried a panic button on his belt, and the security system was a good one.

On Friday afternoon, the chain dealer came and set up his chains in a jewelry case that faced the front window. An ad had been placed in the local paper, and signs were put up around the store advertising the chain show.

On Saturday morning, John and Brenda were running late and didn't have time to take John Jr. and Anita to Brenda's sister's home to babysit, so they took the children to the store with them. John was nine and Anita had just turned five. There was a carpeted play area in the enclosed back room where the safe and bathroom were also located.

There was an art fair taking place in the adjacent parking lot of the mall, and it was a bright, sunny day. A lady came in for a watch battery right after the store opened, so John was in the shop area working on the watch when the two men came back into the store. The watch crystal had come loose while John was replacing the battery, so he had to glue the crystal back on. Brenda went to wait on the big man while the watch customer waited.

"John! Come out here," said the big man aggressively. "I want you to show me some chains."

John got up from his jeweler's bench, told the customer that the watch crystal was still drying, and then headed over to the jewelry case.

"I want to see this one right here," the man said pointing at the case.

John unlocked the case and started to pull out the chain the man had pointed to. As John stood up, the man pulled a gun out from behind his back and hit John in the mouth with the barrel.

"All right, everyone go back to the back room," the big man said in a booming voice.

The other man also now showed a gun. He walked to the door, locked it, then forced the customer toward the back. The big man grabbed Brenda by her arm and started to move her toward the back room. Brenda elbowed him in the belly.

"Let go of me, you son-of-a-bitch!" she shouted.

"Just do as he says, Brenda," John said.

"Keep moving," he said.

"She's handicapped," John said.

"I know that!" shouted the big man.

When they got to the back of the store and opened the door, John Jr. and Anita were playing.

"Get on your knees!" the big man said to John.

The second man closed the door behind them and pulled some rope out from somewhere and began tying John up. He then took the panic button off John's belt. John had forgotten all about the panic button.

By this time, John Jr. and Anita were starting to whimper.

"It'll be okay," John said to them.

"I can't get down on the floor," said Brenda defiantly.

The second man was finishing up tying the customer's hands behind her back when the big man said, "Now, everybody into the bathroom."

It was a small bathroom, so it was a tight fit for five people. The robbers tied two doorknobs together to tie the bathroom closed.

A few moments later, the second man said, "There's a cop outside but he doesn't know what's going on." Then he said, "Okay. He's gone now."

For the next twenty minutes or so, the robbers spent their time loading up merchandise into a box.

When they were finished, the big guy asked, "Will the alarm go off if I go out the back door?"

"No," said John.

"Now, don't lie to me, John," he said.

"No. The alarm won't go off."

They heard the back door open and close. John waited a couple of minutes before getting out of his rope restraints and pushed the door open. After they got out of the bathroom, he called the police and reported the robbery. A couple of minutes later, the police arrived and took statements from John, Brenda and the customer. The police chief arrived, and John told his story again. The news people arrived and filmed the scene from outside the store.

Brenda drove the kids over to her sister's house and let her know they were shaken up. When Brenda came back to the store, they took inventory and discovered that more than 80% of the store merchandise had been taken. The chain representative lost all his merchandise. Fortunately, it was insured. The store was also insured but only covered 80% of the value of what was taken. Under the circumstances, John wasn't sure whether the store could go on even though he could continue to do jewelry repairs and custom jobs. Within two weeks, the insurance paid off, so they received a big check to pay off some of the jewelry that had been taken, and John planned to buy more merchandise at the next jewelry show.

As it turned out, the next jewelry show was scheduled in Las Vegas the next weekend, so John and Brenda left the two children with her sister and went to Vegas for three days. Fortunately, the cost of the flight and hotel was rather small. They stayed at the Stardust hotel and casino and worked eight hours per day looking at and purchasing merchandise at the show, which was located at the MGM Grand. They bought as much on credit as they could and paid for the rest.

They considered it a working vacation, so they spent some time in the evenings playing the quarter slots, eating at the buffets and going to one show featuring Paul Revere and the Raiders, a popular band from the late '60s and early '70s. Though it was hard work during the day, they had a good time in Las Vegas.

On the flight back from Vegas, they had a layover in Kansas City. The landing in Kansas City proved to be very traumatic. It had been a good flight until they touched down. When the nose of the plane came down, the entire plane started shaking and twisting, the ceiling panels came down and some of the luggage compartments opened. The pilot slowed the plane down very quickly and limped the plane off the middle of the runway. After the plane had stopped, the pilot came on the loud speaker.

"Now you all know what it's like when a plane has a flat tire. The tower has been notified and we'll be underway shortly. Sorry for the inconvenience, folks."

The flight attendants closed all the overhead compartment doors and checked everyone. One of them said it was the roughest landing they had ever experienced.

Several minutes later, a car with a yellow flashing light rolled up, and the driver got out and inspected the front of the plane. Then, a vehicle designed to taxi the plane back to the airport arrived. After a few more minutes, the pilot came back on the loud speaker.

"As it turns out, it wasn't a flat tire after all. There was a pin in the steering mechanism that came out causing the front wheel to wobble on landing. They've replaced the pin and we'll be taxiing back to the airport under our own power. We thank you for your patience."

The rest of the flight back to Indianapolis was uneventful. John and Brenda got back, picked up the kids and took them home.

Within a few days, John went to a gun store and purchased a .38 Charter Arms stainless steel revolver with an ankle holster and a Mossberg tactical pump-action shotgun.

John and Brenda evaluated the situation at the store and determined the rent was too high and the traffic too poor to continue at that location. They talked to the landlord and he told them about a space he owned not far from where they were in a strip center near a grocery store. The rent was substantially lower, so John signed a lease for the new location. They moved the safe, the sign, cases and merchandise to the new store. The new location was smaller but had a cozier feel to it.

Within a few months, the store was back on its feet again, and John got the bug to change houses again. This time, they moved up to a much larger ranch on Carson Street in Northern Indianapolis near Carmel. The house was in a much nicer neighborhood on a quiet street and featured a 2-car garage, three bedrooms, a living room, dining room and a family room addition on the back. There was also a concrete patio in the rear with nice-sized front and back yards.

Things were going so well that John also bought a new car—a new, dark blue Mercury Cougar. It seemed that things had finally turned the corner for the better.

Chapter 23

Several months had gone by when the police contacted John to let him know the robbers had been apprehended. John was shown an array of photos of possible suspects, and he was able to pick out the big guy almost immediately despite the fact that the perpetrator had grown a full beard. They also found some of the merchandise in the robber's mother's home. He had been caught in Florida trying to sell some of the merchandise to a pawn shop. The other robber had been killed during another robbery attempt. The police still had to extradite the robber to Indiana and then try him for the crime. John and Brenda were just glad to know he was in custody.

Things were going well at the store, so well in fact that they hired a man to input their inventory into their new computer system. His name was Will, and he mostly worked in the back room of the store. He had come from an insurance background, so John thought he might also be useful in helping to attract some insurance appraisal business.

One day, John was working on a custom jewelry piece when three men in suits came into the store. John came out from the shop to greet them.

"Good afternoon, gentlemen. How can I help you?"

One of the men said, "I'm looking for an engagement ring. What do you have to show me?"

John reached into the jewelry case and brought out a tray of engagement rings.

"Aren't you the people who had a robbery about a year ago?" one of the men asked.

John was immediately suspicious.

"That's right. We were robbed when we were in our first location."

"It's been so long; you probably don't remember much about it."

"Actually, I remember it like it was yesterday," said John. "You don't happen to be attorneys, do you?"

"Yes, we are. How did you know?"

"Just a good guess. I'll bet you represent the robber, don't you?"

"We represent the defendant."

"I think I'd better call and talk to the prosecutor before I talk to you."

"That's fine."

John put the tray of jewelry away and locked the case. He quickly found the prosecutor's card and called him. After a short conversation, John went back to the attorneys.

"The prosecutor's office said I don't have to talk to you," John said when he got back in front of the attorneys. "So, I'm not going to discuss the incident with you."

"Okay. That's your right. I guess we'll just see you in court then."

"I guess so."

The men left and John felt satisfied with the way he had handled the situation.

A month later, the prosecutor called John to let him know he would be required to testify in a hearing the following week. The night before he was to testify, John had flu-like symptoms with diarrhea and vomiting. John had no intention of missing the hearing, so the next morning, he pulled himself together and drove to Noblesville, the county seat where the court house was located. The prosecutor met him there and told him what to expect about the proceedings. There was no judge; just John, a female court recorder who was seated near the witness stand, the prosecutor, the defendant, and his attorneys.

John took the stand and was still feeling the effects of his illness. The defense attorney who approached him was in his 30s with a thin build and a full head of brown hair. From the stand, John could also see the defendant looking smug and much like he did during the robbery except that his hair was no longer blond but a thinning brown.

"Could you please state your name and spell it for the court recorder?"

John did so.

"Now, would you tell us a little about your background? When and where were you born?"

John answered. And from then on, the attorney focused on John's life and background. He asked about where he grew up, what schools he attended, what jobs he had held and so on. The questioning went on for three hours, and so far, all the questions had been about John. By this time, John's side began to ache and he was perspiring profusely. John glanced at the prosecutor and the prosecutor stood and asked for a ten-minute break. Everyone agreed, so John and the prosecutor went to an office and sat and talked.

"I'm not sure but I think I may be having an appendicitis attack. How much longer is this going to take?" John asked.

"Let me go and find out for you."

The prosecutor went out of the room and came back a few minutes later.

"I told them the offer I made was only good for another 20 minutes. The offer was fourteen years in prison of which he would only have to serve seven if he behaved himself. I think they're ready to go back in. I'll try to have you finished up in a few minutes."

John went back to the witness stand. This time, the defense lawyer began to attack.

"Mr. Sample, didn't you get an unusual call the night of the robbery?"

John tried to remember all the calls he'd received that night. All the calls had been family members and sympathetic friends.

"No. I don't recall any unusual calls."

"Didn't my client call you after the robbery?"

"No."

"Isn't it true that you and my client met two weeks prior to the robbery?"

"Absolutely not!" John was furious at the implication.

"Didn't the two of you have lunch at the Spaghetti Factory in downtown Indianapolis before the robbery to discuss how it was going to go down?"

John was suddenly relieved.

"I have never been to the Spaghetti Factory. And what's more, I couldn't even tell you how to get there."

The prosecutor stood and said, "I think the defense has had enough time with this witness."

The defense attorneys conferred with their client and then said they were finished.

John stepped down from the witness stand with severe pain in his abdomen. The prosecutor conferred with the defense and then came over to speak with John.

"They're going to take the deal, John. You did well on the stand. Are you okay?"

"I'm glad it's over, and now I'm going to the hospital."

John left the courthouse and drove back to the store in Carmel. When he got there, Brenda was waiting for him.

"I need you to drive me to the hospital, Brenda. We need to close up and go now."

Brenda drove him to the hospital where he was almost immediately diagnosed with appendicitis. His doctor was a middle-aged female.

"You could have been reading the symptoms out of the textbook, Mr. Sample," she said. "We'll get you into surgery as soon as we can get the surgeon in here. Just relax."

His surgery was started at a little after 10 p.m. that night. Everything went well, and he woke up in pain shortly after the surgery. Brenda was there in the room when he woke up. They gave him morphine injections, and there were times when John couldn't distinguish between hallucinations, dreams and reality. After a couple of days, John went home to recover, and it wasn't long before he was anxious to get back to work.

Things were going well at the store again. John and Brenda had breakfast out at the Country Kitchen in Carmel every morning before work, and their relationship was as strong as it had ever been. John saw talents of Brenda's he'd never seen before they worked together and Brenda saw some of John's talents for the first time. Brenda got to know the customers better than John ever would have. When customers came in, she would know their names and the names of their children and would ask about them by name. Brenda also handled the books. John handled the jewelry repairs, the custom jewelry, and most of the sales.

When John saw an opening in one of the retail spaces across the parking lot, he decided to move the store again. The space was brighter and more visible than their current location, so it seemed like a good idea at the time.

Once they moved everything including the safe, John set about decorating the store. There was a glass-enclosed office where John could show diamonds and work with vendors. There was also a location for the shop. It wasn't long before John added a new employee to the store. Her name was Sandra, and she was a jewelry repair person. She was heavy-set, in her 30s and was good at her job. By this time, Will was spending more time on the sales floor in addition to his computer work.

One of John's best jewelry repair customers, Mr. Thomas, was a jewelry store owner from Anderson, Indiana. During one of his visits, he mentioned he was considering retiring. He said he owned the strip center the store was in and wondered whether John would be interested in taking over the space. John drove the 40 minutes to Anderson to visit the store. It was beautiful. Mr. Thomas showed John around. It was handsomely decorated and had a fireplace, crown molding, and large, attractive cases and shelves. There was even a basement with rows of wood shelving that housed clocks—the gifts for the retirees of one of the local car manufacturers. John was extremely impressed with the store and the apparent business it did.

When he went back to the Carmel store, he immediately went about trying to figure out a way he could make a second store work. Will was eager to manage the second store and Sandra was interested in going to the Anderson location because it was closer to where she lived. John went to the bank to see about a loan to cover the cost of merchandise, and they said they would provide up to $75,000.00 for that purpose. With that in mind, John went ahead and signed the lease for the second store in

Anderson. Unfortunately, within a week of signing the lease, the bank called and said they would be unable to provide any additional funds. John was devastated. He felt he needed to go forward with the opening of the second store because of the lease, so he split the merchandise in half and moved half of it to the Anderson location.

He asked the female employee at the Anderson location, Clara, to stay on. So, now he had three employees at Anderson, plus Brenda and himself at Carmel. It was a struggle to say the least, and now both stores looked naked with the lack of merchandise.

Within two months, Will quit to go back into the insurance business. John also found out that Mr. Thomas was continuing to sell jewelry out of his home. Even though John had not had the foresight to get a "non-compete" clause built into the lease, he thought it was pretty dirty dealing on Mr. Thomas' part.

Now, John was going back and forth between the two stores, trying to manage both. He was getting very depressed and felt he wasn't doing a good job at either one of the stores. Clara was doing a good job handling the clocks but there was little other jewelry business going on at the Anderson location.

John was using his credit cards more and more to handle basic expenses and had accumulated over $30,000.00 in credit card debt. In a final move in 1990, John decided to file bankruptcy. He found an attorney in Carmel who would do it, though that attorney ended up bringing in another attorney to handle it.

There was a lot of research and paperwork for John and Brenda to deal with. He let Clara and Sandra go and brought the merchandise back from the Anderson location. John found out he would be able to keep the house, but everything else would have to be liquidated to pay off the bank loan. That meant the car would eventually have to go and so, too, the boat, the merchandise, the computer and the shop equipment.

John hired a jewelry store liquidation firm to do a going-out-of-business sale. That firm brought in a lot of cheap jewelry to help stock the cases and bring in more sales. When they had their sale, it was very successful. After everything was liquidated, John was within $7,000.00 of paying off the bank. The credit card companies and the other creditors would get nothing.

John got some poor advice from one of his jewelry repair clients who told him to make sure he paid off the government Small Business Administration loan first, so that's what he did. With only $3,000.00 left in the bank, John went to the bank and offered them that amount to cancel the remaining $7,000.00 debt. The bank refused because they were not covered by the SBA insurance since John had paid them off first, so it was understandable. The bank debt was then covered under the bankruptcy as well.

When it was nearly all over, John went to look for a new job and quickly found an assistant manager's position with Service Merchandise, a jewelry and hard lines chain based in Nashville, Tennessee. They had three locations in Indianapolis, and John started training immediately in the West Side location. Before long, they gave him the manager's job in Kokomo, Indiana which was about 45 minutes away from home.

John found a used silver Subaru to use for transportation. It got good gas mileage and was a nice vehicle for getting back and forth to work. John got along well with the employees, and it was a well-run store. They met their sales goals and always had the merchandise displayed properly, especially when the supervisors visited.

When the Gulf War with Iraq started in January, 1991, someone brought in a small portable TV so the employees could watch the war as it unfolded on CNN.

This was also the time John experienced his first severe manic episode. He began to think he could be an author. In addition to his day job, he started and completed several writing projects, including several short stories, a novella and a novel. John wrote every evening and sometimes even through the night to complete the novel in just a few months. He went many nights with very little sleep.

John tried several publishers but failed to get the novel published. He later tried a writer's agent but she wasn't interested in the novel. She did, however, find some faint interest in the novella he wrote she felt he could rewrite as a novel. John was extremely disappointed to say the least. He fell into a deep depression that made it very difficult for him to do his work.

John bought a red Dodge Daytona for Brenda who was now working at a Sam's Club in Carmel.

In 1992, John was offered the opportunity to move to Monroeville, Pennsylvania to open a new Service Merchandise store and jewelry department. This was a quick decision by the company since the manager they had originally selected planned to move from another Pittsburgh location backed out at the last minute. The money was good and John was ready for a change, so after talking with Brenda, he agreed to the move.

John went to Monroeville and stayed in a short-term lease apartment at the company's expense until Brenda could get the house sold. When the house sold, John started looking for a new house in the Monroeville area, but this proved to be very difficult because of the bankruptcy. With his poor credit, John had to look for a house that could be financed by the owner. In a few weeks, John found such a property. It was an attractive split-level, 3-bedroom, 2-bath home with a 2-car garage and nice landscaping on a corner lot located in Monroeville. The sellers were a young couple who had also financed the house through the owner a few years earlier.

John agreed to purchase the home. The plan was for the sellers to have the owner refinance the buyers while the sellers took the equity in the home and moved on. John signed the sales agreement with the sellers' real estate agent and assumed he had purchased a new home.

With the house in Indianapolis sold, Brenda prepared to move to Monroeville. Service Merchandise was paying for the move, so professional movers were to take care of the packing and the moving van. Brenda had secured a transfer with Wal-Mart to a new store they were opening about 45 minutes north of Monroeville. She was to be a jewelry department manager.

John went to the property closing expecting everything to go as smoothly as his other closings had gone. Nothing could have been further from the truth.

The closing was to take place in a large conference room in the sellers' real estate agent's company in Monroeville. John arrived at the closing and sat at the conference room table. The seller's wife was there along with the real estate agent. They explained that the owner was flying in from Florida and that the seller had gone to the airport to pick him up and bring him to the closing. It took over an hour for the seller and the owner to arrive.

When the owner arrived, he seemed out of sorts. When they all sat down at the table, the owner made it known he did not agree with the terms of the sale. He was supposed to pay the real estate commission of $7,700.00 but felt it was unfair and said he wasn't paying it. He asked for a meeting with the real estate company and the agent. In the meantime, the seller suggested they order food in because of the time it was taking, so he ordered sandwiches from a local sandwich shop, then went to pick them up. By the time they all had eaten, John had been at the closing for four hours and was getting frustrated.

The owner emerged from the meeting with the agents, and the agent stated they had reached an agreement on the sales commission amount. Then the owner stated he had a problem with the sellers' position, so they went behind closed doors and renegotiated their agreement.

When they emerged, they were still squabbling, so John finally stood up and announced he would pull his offer if they didn't resolve their disputes within the following 30 minutes. The seller and owner appeared to end their disagreement a short time later. The owner and John agreed to meet in a couple of weeks to work out the details of the payments and sign a land contract between them. The owner made a check out for $25,000.00 to the sellers and the deal was done. The seller stated he would leave a key under the door mat the day John and Brenda were to take possession two weeks later. In all, the closing had taken nearly six hours.

Brenda packed up the kids and drove out to meet up with John in Monroeville. The moving van was scheduled to be there on a Friday afternoon. Brenda had never seen the house, so John and the family went from the motel to the house to look at it.

When they got there, John checked under the mat, but there was no key. He tried the front door, and it was locked as was the back door and the garage doors. They looked in through the windows and could see the house was empty. John went to the neighbor's house and called the real estate agent. The agent lived close by, so she came over to the house to meet John and Brenda. Still no key was found.

John talked with the movers who said they would stay overnight at a motel, but if they couldn't get into the house by noon Saturday, they would have to put the contents in storage. That would have cost about $1,000.00 per month. They went back to the motel.

John got the number of the sellers and called them.

"This is John Sample, and we've looked all over but can't find the key to the house."

"I'm sorry, John, but my attorneys say I can't let you into the house," said the seller. "The owner cancelled payment on the check after the closing."

"You've got to be shitting me!" yelled John. "My family is here in a motel, the movers are at the house, and they're going to have to put everything in storage if we can't get moved in by noon tomorrow."

"I'm very sorry."

"You must not have been sorry enough to give me a heads-up to let me know something was wrong!"

John was furious as he hung up the phone. He then looked in the phonebook for a local attorney. He found one and called him. After he explained the situation to him, the attorney said, "Whatever you do, get in that house."

John drove to the police station with his sales agreement from the closing in hand.

"I need to get into my house and the seller is refusing to let me have the key. Here is my sales agreement. You can see that I own the house. The house is empty and I just want your blessing to get a locksmith to let me in."

After some discussion with his supervisor, the police officer he'd been speaking with agreed. John asked if a police officer could be there when the locksmith was doing the work. He called the locksmith and had him meet John and the police at the house. The locksmith was there within an hour, opened the front door, and changed the locks on the front and back doors. The electricity and water were still on, and John found the remote for the garage on the kitchen counter.

The next morning, John met the movers at the house. They unloaded the truck and moved the contents inside. Fortunately, Brenda and the kids liked the house, and they all worked together to get moved in. That crisis was averted, and John was satisfied with his responses to it.

Within a few days, John had the utilities turned over to his name and let the real estate agent know what he had done. She then revealed to him that the owner had asked for a ride home immediately after the closing. On the way, he asked the agent to drop by his bank so he could cover the check he'd written. Unbeknownst to her, he had gone into the bank and cancelled payment on his check to the seller and to the real estate company. She didn't know what had happened until a week later when the check didn't clear.

The owner called and wanted to meet at the house to go over the payment schedule. John agreed. When the owner came over, he insisted on a bi-weekly payment. John's instinct was to distrust the owner, so he looked the document over very carefully before signing it. Later, John found out that the sellers were in the process of suing the owner and the Samples.

By this time, the Monroeville Service Merchandise store had had its grand opening, and it was very successful. Initially, the jewelry department employed about 50 people of whom about 20 were kept on afterwards. It was a big department, and John handled it well with the assistance of a very able assistant manager named Kim.

The store manager was also very capable and ran a very tight ship. John and the manager did not always see eye-to-eye but they remained on amicable terms for the most part. John was also on good terms with the jewelry department's original district manager who was later replaced. The second district manager seemed hypercritical of John and the department, though John's department operated efficiently and showed a good profit.

John began to feel the effects of the bankruptcy, the failure of his novel, the house situation, the lawsuit by the sellers and the pressures at work. He began to fall into a deep depression which made it very difficult for him to do his work. John also went into fits of anger while driving and nearly got into a fight from road rage.

One day, John's depression turned to serious thoughts of suicide. He was supposed to work the evening shift at work, so he was home during the middle of the day. The kids were at school and Brenda was working. John got his pistol, made sure it was loaded, then sat on the side of the bed with the gun in his hand. He was crying. John wanted to end it all to relieve the pressure and sense of worthlessness he felt. Then he thought of how his kids would find his body and the horrible ways it might affect them. It would also have been another tragedy in Brenda's life, and it was she who would have to deal with the aftermath of his suicide, the lawsuit, the house situation and trying to support a family on her own.

John remembered a card Brenda had brought home from work. It was the number for a hotline. He found the card and called the number. He sat on the bed and talked with the person on the other end of the line and determined he didn't want to kill himself after all; he just wanted the depression to go away. After John got off the phone, he put the gun away and went to work. He talked to Brenda that night and told her what had happened. The next day, John went to his doctor with Brenda and was admitted to the 7th floor of the Forbes Regional Hospital in Monroeville. This was the mental ward of the hospital. Since it was a voluntary admission, John felt comfortable going in. They took his belt and shoestrings before Brenda left.

Within a couple of days, John met with the psychiatrist and he determined John likely had bipolar disorder, considering his extreme mood swings. After the diagnosis, it all seemed to make sense; the extreme manic episodes he experienced while writing and the extreme depressive episode he'd recently experienced. The psychiatrist started John out on Lithium, which he did not tolerate well. A couple of days later, the doctor switched him to a different medication, Wellbutrin, which seemed to work better.

There wasn't much to do during the hospital stay except to observe other patients, watch TV, eat, and attend groups. The groups were interesting but few and far between. It wasn't long before John felt he was the only sane person in the place.

There was also a small gym on the ward. One day, while John was feeling particularly guilty about staying in the hospital, he went to the gym with one of the nurses. He was punching the heavy bag with anger when he got it swinging, then punched it very hard. John felt his wrist pop, and he had to stop. They took him to get an x-ray and found he had broken a bone in his wrist. There wasn't any surgery required; they simply wrapped his wrist and sent him back to the ward.

Toward the end of John's stay, John mentioned to Brenda he liked being in the hospital because he had no worries or responsibilities. This infuriated Brenda as she was handling everything on her own. John apologized and asked for forgiveness before Brenda calmed down and forgave him.

The combination of medications made John feel groggy but he didn't feel anxious or suicidal anymore. He mostly felt numb. They released John from the hospital just in time for John to attend his son's high school graduation. He felt nervous and confused but was very glad to attend.

It was another week before John felt good enough to go back to work. He still didn't feel 100%, and it wasn't long before John suspected there was a concerted effort to get him out of his management position.

The lawsuit continued, so John decided to take a different tack. He quit making payments on the house and put the money in a savings account instead. He told the owner and seller that if he couldn't sell the house, then he would simply rent. John did this for approximately six months when he finally reached an agreement with the owner stating he would pay a realistic rent on the property and pay that amount in a lump sum to catch up.

John later sat before a judge between the seller's attorney and the owner's attorney. After hearing John's account of the situation and seeing his documentation, all parties agreed to let

John out of his contract and drop their lawsuit against the Samples.

By 1994, John and Brenda's credit had improved sufficiently to look for another house. They found a brick, 2-story, 1 ½ bath home in Monroeville that was for sale. There was a family room off the living room that John felt would make a nice master bedroom, and he planned to make the half-bath on the main floor into a full bath with a shower. That way, John and Brenda could spend most of the time on one floor, thereby minimizing the steps required. There was also an old in-ground swimming pool in the backyard.

The seller of that house had kept retired greyhounds as pets. When they went through the house the first time, John and Brenda thought it was odd that the owner had the windows open and the air conditioner running at the same time. He also had air fresheners strategically placed throughout the house. The house needed some work though John didn't realize just how much until after they moved in. They had planned to remove the carpeting and refinish the hardwood floors anyway, but John had not realized how much damage the dogs had done to the floors. John and John Jr. pulled up the carpets which reeked horribly of dog urine. The wood floors had dark stains on them, some of which were so deep that boards had to be replaced.

John hired a contractor who was the relative of someone with whom Brenda worked. His name was Elwood and he seemed like someone who knew what he was doing. The agreement was that he would have the floors refinished within two weeks and the bathroom shower in place a week later. There was no written contract, however, and it took an additional two weeks to get the work done. In fact, Elwood did not even finish the stairs or complete the finish work on the living room floor. Because of that, John held back half of the money until the work was done. It never was finished, so John held back the money until Elwood took him to court. The judge in the case said that since there was no written contract, he had to rule in favor of the contractor. John paid Elwood off over a period of four months.

A few months later, the district supervisor gave John an option; he would need to take over the Greensburg location or be fired. This would have been a substantial cut in pay for John since it was a smaller department, and the additional miles driving would have cost him a lot more. John asked to work part-time as a sales person until he could find other work. He was given a sales position at another location. He hated the sales position there because there was another full-time sales person who was given priority over him, and his sales suffered as a result.

During this time, John investigated real estate sales and interviewed with three different companies. What he found was that all three of the companies wanted him. Since real estate sales pay was based totally on commission, there was very little risk on their part. They all offered to pay for the cost of real estate school. If John passed the real estate exam and got his real estate license, the real estate companies would reimburse him.

In 1995, John selected Prudential Preferred Realty in Monroeville because he was most impressed with the broker in that office, Terry Alcinda. He went on to real estate school and did very well, passing the real estate exam the first time. John was more enthused about seeing the different houses than he was about working with the clients. He took the job very seriously and sold his first house within a month. John's boss told him to try to remember what he did to sell the first house and keep doing it. But the expenses were high with advertising and gas, so John literally had no income to report on his taxes the first year. He leased a white Plymouth Neon and put a lot of miles on it.

On his first listing appointment, John was early, so he waited in a driveway on a busy street not far from the house he was supposed to list. When he was ready to leave for the appointment, the traffic was heavy and he had to make a left turn. Finally, a large truck stopped and motioned for him to go. John hadn't looked left for a while when he started to pull out into traffic. Just as he did, *WHAM!* He was hit nearly head-on by a car from the left. His air-bag deployed and he was quite shaken from the jolt. There seemed to be smoke coming into the front seat, so John unbuckled his seatbelt and quickly got out of the car. When the police arrived, John described the incident to the officer. John walked to his appointment. He explained why he was late and started to go through his listing sales pitch. John started to feel ill and decided he'd better go to the hospital to get checked out. The sellers were very sympathetic and drove him to the hospital where he was given a clean bill of health. A few days later, John went back to the sellers and got the listing. John got the car repaired with the insurance company footing the bill.

About this time, John learned about a Veterans Health Administration event at a nearby Veterans of Foreign Wars lodge. He and John Jr. went to the event, and John got processed into the VHA system, got blood tests and found out he was eligible for medical benefits.

John gradually got better at the real estate business. His boss left the company and started his own RE/MAX office in Plum. It wasn't long before John's former boss, Terry, started recruiting John to come to work for him. The expenses were higher, but the commission was better, so John decided to switch to RE/MAX. It was a little like starting over.

Sales were good and John did better there. As a side income, John started doing Broker Price Opinions on abandoned and foreclosed houses for mortgage companies. He also got several listings as a result. The houses he listed for sale were often in very poor condition and in bad neighborhoods. It wasn't long before this part of the business was taking up more time than his regular sales.

Though he was making a living, John was growing tired of the foreclosure business. It seemed as if his signs were open invitations for burglars to break into those houses and steal the copper out of them.

On September 11, 2001, John was scheduled to see a dermatologist for a couple of spots on his back. He was upstairs working on the computer when his daughter told him to come downstairs to watch the news. John watched as the first tower burned, then saw the second tower struck by the plane. From then on, he was glued to the TV until it was time to go to his doctor's appointment.

When the doctor examined John's back, he found two basal cell carcinomas and removed them with a scraping procedure.

The doctor also found one on the side of John's nose. This one required a special surgery called a Mohs procedure and would be very expensive. When John told the doctor he qualified for VA medical benefits, the doctor recommended he have the procedure done there.

John went to the VA medical center near downtown Pittsburgh and saw a dermatologist who also recommended the Mohs procedure. John was sent to an outside dermatologist who specialized in Mohs surgeries. The surgeon removed the basal cell and left a pretty substantial hole in the side of John's nose in the process. After some plastic surgery, it was nearly impossible to tell where the original surgery had been done.

From then on, John got all his medical treatment at the VA. He started going to a VA psychiatrist every three months at the Highland Drive location where they got his medications changed and adjusted. John's moods stabilized more than ever.

John's love of real estate seemed to subside with each passing day until in 2006, when he began to volunteer at the VA and discovered he enjoyed working with Veterans.

Brenda and John also began to attend group counseling sessions with another couple. They found the counseling useful and the facilitator of the group, a nun by the name of Avis, was very helpful. She was also impressed with John and his ability to speak about his bipolar experience. Avis contacted someone in the VA about John, and the next thing he knew, he was taking peer-to-peer classes with several mental health specialists. The peer-to-peer program was designed to teach Veterans with mental illnesses to share their experiences with other Veterans who had similar mental health issues. John began to volunteer his time to facilitate mental health groups at the hospital's psychiatric wards. After his first group, his mentor, Alicia, told him he had a gift.

Within a month after starting his peer-to-peer work, Alice told John about a new position in the VA. The position was called Peer Support, and it was a full-time position that paid a little over $26,000.00 per year. Though the pay was not spectacular, John determined it would be a positive change from the real estate business. It seemed like a noble profession to serve Veterans with mental illnesses. He also thought it would be good to get a steady pay check with several job benefits like life insurance, health and dental benefits, several paid holidays and vacation and sick pay.

So, in early 2007, John applied for the position through an online site and waited several weeks before he was given an in-person interview. It was April before he was notified he had been hired with his first day set for May.

Right after he started at the VA, John's brother called him to inform him that their mother had passed away from a massive stroke. John did not have any vacation or care-and-bereavement days accumulated but he was given unpaid leave to go to his mother's funeral in Lafayette, Indiana.

Since his mother was cremated, they had a simple memorial service for her at her church. John and Brenda attended the service and met with Paul and their mother's other relatives during and after the ceremony. John had not been close with his mother for years, though he did speak with his parents a few times a year.

Paul and their father had taken care of the cremation arrangements and the memorial service. Their mother had been very fond of birds of all kinds, so Paul found a cremains container that was also a metal bird bath that she was placed in. The bird bath was placed in a portion of Paul's garden near outdoor bird feeders. It was a fitting resting place for her.

When John got back to work, he met with his supervisor about the job. He was to become a part of the Mental Health Intensive Case Management team, also referred to as MHICM. Because it was a new position, John was the first VA Peer Support Technician in the Pittsburgh area, and he had to start from scratch developing the job parameters. The job entailed driving to the residences of mentally ill Veterans and visiting with them. He also was to facilitate groups at the Highland Drive VA facility, which housed the mental illness wards. There was a ward for mood disorders, one for schizophrenia-like illnesses, and a long-term care ward for the most severe cases.

John was eventually given an office with a desk and computer. During a typical day, John did research into mental illnesses and other Peer Support programs around the world. He printed some of the resource materials for use with his groups and set up files. There were also several committees on which John served, so he often attended meetings. John soon went through a two-week peer support training in Pittsburgh, along with twenty other individuals.

Just a few months after starting, John received news that his father had also passed away from pneumonia while he was in the hospital. He, too, was cremated and John and Brenda went to the memorial service. This time, he spoke at the memorial service.

He related an incident when he was in high school. John's '57 Chevy had a turn signal blinker that quit working, so John and his father went to the junkyard to find a flasher part. John's father was looking at a different car while John looked under the dash of a doorless '56 Chevy. After he reached under the dash and retrieved the flasher, two bumblebees flew out from under the dash and into the cab. One went out of the car but the other one stayed behind. John was wearing cut-off jeans and a white T-shirt, so when the bumble bee landed on his jeans on his thigh, he wasn't worried, assuming the bee could not sting him through his jeans. An instant later, he realized he had assumed incorrectly because the bee stung him hard. John's reaction was to hit the bee with his hand but that just made the bee mad, and it stung him twice more before he could get out of the car.

John was yelling, "Son of a b....! Son of a b....! Son of a b....!" without remembering that his father was nearby. Now if John had said, "Son of a bee!" that might have been more appropriate. But he had said the dirty word in his father's presence.

As John ran away from the car, the bee stung him on the back.

"Son of a b....!"

"Stop, and I'll get him!" John's dad said.

As soon as John stopped, the bee stung him again two more times.

"Son of a b....!"

John's dad was finally able to swat the bee to the ground and stepped on it.

John was bent over in pain from the stings to his leg and back. He only then realized he had cussed in front of his father. John went to his dad's car and sat in the passenger's seat, while his father paid for the flasher.

When his father got in the car, John was concerned about what would be said about his swearing but the pain was still so intense he didn't care.

On the way back home, John's dad said, "I didn't know you knew French, John."

John tried to laugh but he was in too much pain. When they got home and explained what had happened with the bumble bee, John's mother mixed up a paste made of baking soda and gently rubbed it into the holes the bee had made on his thigh and back. The salve helped, but it was still very painful. John never knew whether his father ever told his mother about the swearing.

Chapter 24

Sunlight was breaking through the trees again in the Garden of Peace, so John moved over to the group. James came up to him and shook his hand.

"I have someone I'd like you to meet, John."

James led the way over to a woman who appeared to be in her 50s. She was thin with short brown hair and hazel eyes.

"John, this is Patty. Patty, this is John."

The two shook hands.

"It's very nice to meet you, John. You have quite a reputation around here. I think we're going to start calling you 'the soul whisperer.'"

"That's very nice of you to say."

"Well, you seem to have worked a few miracles."

"Would you like to go somewhere and talk, Patty?"

"Absolutely! Why don't we go down to the pond? That's my favorite place."

"Sure. That seems to be the favorite place of a lot of the folks around here."

The two of them floated over near the pond.

"Let me hold your hand, John."

They held hands, and the tingling sensation was back again.

"Why don't I start?" said Patty.

"That would be great."

"I was born in 1960 in the city of Guelph, Ontario. My father was the owner of several residential apartment buildings and made a good living there. My mother was a stay-at-home mom who looked after me and my two siblings. I was the youngest.

When I was ten, my father sold his buildings and we moved to Pittsburgh. Father made quite a bit of money on the sale and bought land to develop in Pittsburgh's eastern suburbs. He bought a nice house in Murrysville, and I lived there until I went to college at Penn State.

When I went to college, I majored in biology. My plan was to become a researcher but fate had other plans for me. I met Henry while I was away at school. He was a business major, and when I brought him home for the holidays, Henry and my father immediately hit it off. After he graduated, Henry went to work for my father on his residential developments. I never graduated. Instead, I got married, got pregnant, and we had the first of our four children.

We all had a very happy life together until I was diagnosed with breast cancer in 2010. Then things got tough. The double mastectomy, chemo and radiation took a toll on me, both physically and mentally. All the efforts were in vain as the cancer had already metastasized. I lasted a year after my treatments. It was very difficult to leave my family, and I still miss them so much."

"I'm so sorry. Do they come to visit?"

"Yes. My husband still comes to visit on my birthday and my children have come with him a few times."

"I'm sure they miss you very much, too. It still sounds as if you had a wonderful life up until you got cancer."

"I did. But enough of my sad story. It's your turn, John. Tell me about your story."

John related his general life story. He was getting good at keeping his history pithy. When he finished, Patty remarked on his interesting life.

"You lived in so many places and had so many different jobs!" she declared. "That must have kept things interesting."

"There were very few dull moments, that's for sure."

"Well, I really appreciate getting to know you, John. Are you ready to get back to the group?"

"Yes, I'm ready. It was very nice to get to know you, too, Patty."

The two of them went back to the congregation of souls and joined in the discussion. The talk centered on the question of when they would get to heaven and why it took so long for some of them to get there.

James approached John.

"I think you have one more soul to meet here, John."

"Who is that?"

"I don't think you've met Jack yet, have you?"

"I don't think so. Where is he?"

"He usually stays near his gravesite on the other side of the pond. I think he's just shy. I met him quite a while ago and he didn't seem odd or anything like that, but I don't know why he doesn't come to the group. Would you like me to go with you to introduce you?"

"I don't think that's necessary, James. I'll just introduce myself and see what happens."

"Good luck, John."

"Thanks."

John wandered over to the pond and hovered over it for a moment as he watched the ducks swimming around. He noticed a solitary figure on the other side, then floated over to him. The man appeared to be in his 30s, with long blondish hair and brown eyes.

"Are you Jack?"

"That's me. Who are you?"

"I'm John."

John reached out and shook Jack's hand.

"I thought I would come over and introduce myself. I think I've met everyone else in the cemetery. I noticed you kind of keep to yourself over here, Jack."

"I like being by myself."

"I can respect that. Do you mind if I ask you a little about yourself?"

"No. I don't mind. What would you like to know?"

"Well, just to start, where were you born?"

"I was born in Pittsburgh in the Mount Lebanon area in 1981. My parents moved to Delmont shortly after I was born."

"Where did you go to school?"

"I went to Franklin Regional."

"Did you go to college?"

"I went to Westmoreland County Community College and studied web publishing."

"That's interesting. What did you do after college?"

"I couldn't get a job in my field, so I started my own web publishing company. It took me a couple of years but I finally got it off the ground and did pretty well. I was able to do my work from home or wherever I could use a laptop. It was a nice way to make a living."

"Did you ever get married?"

"No. I had a girlfriend, though. Her name is Sophie. She's beautiful and I loved her very much. We were planning to get married but death had other plans for me."

"What happened?"

"I was riding my motorcycle on my way to Murrysville when a car turned in front of me. I hit the car and flew over it. I was not wearing a helmet at the time, and I sustained fatal injuries at the time of the crash."

"I'm sorry to hear that. How old were you when you died?"

"I was 35."

"It's unfortunate that you passed away so young. Do you get visitors here at the cemetery?"

"My parents still come to visit occasionally. Sophie visited a couple of times but the last time she was here, she told me she had met someone else and was planning to be married. I haven't seen her since. I guess I'm happy for her. But it still hurts."

"I can certainly understand that. Thank you for sharing with me, Jack. I hope the memories weren't that difficult to go over."

"No. I appreciate the opportunity to talk with someone."

"Maybe you'd like to come over to the group. Almost everyone in the cemetery comes together there. We'd all like to see you there. It can be a lot more interesting than staying by oneself."

"Maybe I will."

"Do you want to come over now?"

"I don't think so, but thanks for the invite. Maybe tomorrow."

"Also, if you want to learn more about me, I'm obviously available at any time."

"Thank you, John. It was nice talking with you."

The two souls shook hands once more before John went back to see James.

"How did it go?" asked James.

"It went well. Jack seems like a sad but nice fellow. I think it's possible he might come to the group soon. I hope so, anyway."

"All you can do is try," said James.

John and James went back to the group and joined in the conversation until nightfall.

Chapter 25

That night, John went back to his tombstone and remembered where he had left off the night before.

John got back to work a few days after his father's memorial service and quickly developed a client list of twelve Veterans he personally visited once a week or every other week. Sometimes, he simply visited them in their residences but most of the time, he picked them up and took them to breakfast or lunch or took them shopping for groceries or other necessities. The Veterans appeared to appreciate these visits. Most of them were Vietnam-era Veterans, though there were a few younger ones. John also drove his Veterans to the hospitals for their appointments when necessary.

He attended a myriad of meetings and facilitated his groups on the wards. John also attended seminars and trainings around the country. He went to training in Chicago with his supervisor and mentor and it wasn't long before John was asked to speak at some seminars. He spoke at a Penn State seminar, a Washington, D.C. seminar, and at several local seminars.

The job was very fulfilling. With vacation time and federal holidays, John had plenty of time off. The worst part of the job was having to remove snow from the government cars in the winter.

Eventually, the decision was made by higher-ups to close the Highland Drive VA facility. A mental health wing was added to the Oakland area VA in Pittsburgh, which was built to serve the mentally ill Veterans. The H.J. Heinz VA in Pittsburgh's Aspinwall area was to be the center from which his team was to work. He no longer had an office, but they gave him a laptop computer. Essentially, the MHICM team worked from home and used their government cars as their offices.

The years at the VA went by quickly. Before long, it seemed, he had turned 66 and decided to retire after working for the VA for nearly 10 years. His VA pension would only be a few hundred dollars each month, but combined with his and his wife's social security, they would be able to get by with nearly the same lifestyle as when he worked. With their savings, they paid off the mortgage on the house, which reduced their monthly bills substantially.

The MHICM team had a retirement party for John and many nice words were said about him. He said goodbye to his Veterans when he saw them for the last time and said his farewells to his many colleagues.

Once he was retired, John stayed home with Brenda. Other than doctor appointments, a few lunches out, and weekly trips to the grocery store, they mostly stayed home. Their days generally consisted of listening to talk radio, playing games on their tablet and computer, planning meals and watching TV until 10 or 11 p.m.

Then, on Sunday afternoon, May 20th, 2015, just five months after he had retired, tragedy struck. John was watching TV while Brenda was playing games on the computer upstairs. John heard the thud as Brenda's body hit the floor. He immediately sprang out of his easy chair and went up the stairs as quickly as he could. There in the office lay Brenda unconscious on the floor.

Though it was not uncommon for Brenda to fall due to poor balance and her left-side paralysis, this was different. There was blood coming out of her ears and nose, and John could not feel a pulse.

"Brenda! Wake up!" he yelled.

John called 9-1-1 and told them his address and the condition Brenda was in. He left the phone line open while he attempted CPR.

"Brenda! Please, wake up!"

After several minutes of CPR, there was still no pulse. The ambulance arrived and John had to stop CPR while he went downstairs to unlock the front door for them. The EMTs followed John upstairs and almost immediately tried to shock her to get her heart started. When they could not get a pulse, they took Brenda down to the ambulance. One of the EMTs stated they were taking her to the Forbes Regional hospital emergency room, so John got Brenda's purse, got in his car and went to the hospital.

As John drove to the hospital, he was not very optimistic. Even if they could get her heart started, her brain had been without oxygen for some time. Brenda had always said if something like this happened to her, she did not want to be revived. After her car accident, she did not want to go through that ordeal again.

When John arrived at the hospital emergency room, the doctor was waiting for him.

"Mr. Sample?"

"Yes?"

"I'm afraid your wife has passed away. It appears that she had a massive stroke and she probably died almost instantly. I'm very sorry."

John was at a loss for words; he couldn't think straight.

"Can I see her?" John asked.

"Of course. I'll take you to her. She's right behind this curtain over here. I'll have someone come see you in a few moments," said the doctor.

Brenda was there on the hospital bed. She looked so small and helpless. John cried silent tears as he stood beside her stroking her cold hand and looking at her face and lips. He remembered when he had first met Brenda and how beautiful she looked. Time had added lines, but she was still the beautiful girl he had met outside the elevator so many years before.

"You're okay now. You won't be falling and you won't need your cane anymore. I love you, Brenda."

A female hospital staff member came to the curtains.

"Mr. Sample? May I come in?"

"Yes."

"I'm very sorry to hear about your wife, Mr. Sample. Do you feel up to answering some questions?"

"Yes."

The hospital staffer proceeded to ask about insurance information, so John got out Brenda's purse and found her driver's license and Medicare card.

"Do you have a funeral home in mind?"

"The Atkins Funeral Home in Monroeville is the only one I'm familiar with."

"I have their number, Mr. Sample. I can contact them for you if you'd like. They will pick her up here."

"Yes. Thank you. I have to call my children and my brother."

"I just have a few more questions for you," she said and finished up payment information before getting copies of Brenda's license and Medicare card.

John stood beside Brenda's body and talked to her for a few more minutes while he waited.

When the staffer came back, she handed the cards back to John and he put them back in Brenda's purse.

"Is there anything else I can do for you Mr. Sample?"

"No. Thank you."

"The funeral home representatives will probably be here within an hour or so. Here's their number. Perhaps you should call your family. Do you need a private place from which to call?"

"No, thank you. I'll just call from my car."

"Again, you have my condolences, Mr. Sample."

"Thank you."

John turned to his wife.

"Goodbye, Brenda. I'll see you at the funeral home."

John took his wife's purse to his car, then sat in the driver's seat and cried for a while until he mustered the courage to call his son and daughter.

"I'm sorry to have to tell you this but your mom passed away this afternoon," he had told each of them over the phone. Each one had expressed shock and cried as he explained what had happened to their mother. He told them he was on his way home and then to the funeral home and would let them know about arrangements later that evening.

John Jr. said that he would catch the next flight out to Pittsburgh. Anita said that she would meet him at the house, then go to the funeral home with him to help with the arrangements.

John called his brother, Paul, to let him know. They spoke for a while, then John said he had to go to the funeral home. John said he would let him know when he knew the service details. Paul said he would notify the other family members in Lafayette and gave his condolences before hanging up.

John called the Atkins funeral home. The lady on the phone said two of their staff were already on their way to the hospital. She explained it would probably be best if John were to go home, retrieve some documents, and wait for his daughter before going to the funeral home. He followed her suggestion and drove home.

Everything was a blur. The entire day kept replaying over in his head as he drove home. How he ended up at the house he didn't know, because he didn't remember the drive over.

John went up to the office and found Brenda's birth certificate. They had never bought life insurance for Brenda but John had enough in savings to cover the cost of a funeral, though he wasn't sure how much the hospital and ambulance were going to cost after Medicare.

Anita arrived a few minutes after John got home. She hugged her father and cried on his shoulder.

"I'm so sorry, Daddy," she said through her tears.

"Your mom was the love of my life," he replied choking back tears of his own.

They sat down at the dining room table. John related more details of the day then Anita asked if he had eaten yet. He hadn't eaten, but he didn't feel hungry. They decided to get some fast food near the funeral home. Before they left the house, John found two pictures of Brenda, one in her 30s and the other in her 60s.

Anita drove. They went to McDonald's for a quick meal before going to the funeral home, which was just around the corner. They talked about Brenda and her great spirit and how she could be tough yet gentle, too.

When they got to the funeral home, they were greeted warmly at the door by a pleasant, middle-aged gentleman who was dressed in a gray suit and lavender tie. He introduced himself as Sean and showed them into the office where they sat and talked about Brenda and what they thought she would have wanted in terms of a funeral.

"I think she would have wanted a very simple funeral. Brenda was extremely frugal," said John.

"I agree," said Anita smiling and nodding.

Sean showed them several packages on a menu of services. John selected the second least expensive package.

"Do you know what you'd like in a headstone?"

Sean showed them a binder of different headstones with the accompanying prices.

"Again, I think she would have liked something simple," said John.

"This one looks nice," John said pointing at a slant, gray granite headstone. It had the name, dates of birth and death, an engraved single rose, and the words, "Beloved wife, mother and grandmother."

Anita agreed with the choice.

They went over the details of death notices for the Pittsburgh Post-Gazette, plus the Lafayette, Indiana Journal and Courier.

"Have you thought of a cemetery yet?" Sean asked.

"No. Do you have any suggestions?" asked John.

"Here is a list of cemeteries that might work for you."

John and Anita looked over the list.

"This 'Garden of Peace' looks interesting, and it's not too far away," said Anita. John agreed.

"Perhaps you can go out to the cemetery tomorrow and look at the various spaces available. I can call the caretaker for you now and set up a time for you to meet. I'll give you directions before you leave today," said Sean. He called, and they set up a time of 11 a.m. the next morning.

Sean said it was time to pick out a casket, so he led them to a room full of caskets and showed them around. John and Anita chose a gray metal casket that looked very nice.

They went over some final details, including the dates of the visitation and funeral, what the service would be like and the selection of thank-you notes for after the funeral. Sean had been very thorough and helpful and gave them a copy of the charges and the dates and times of the viewings and services. By the time they left the funeral home, John and Anita felt they had covered everything and were exhausted from the process.

When they got back to the house, Anita went in and stayed with John for a while to make sure her dad was doing okay.

"I've got to get back home now," she said. "But I'll be back tomorrow morning by 10 to help you pick out an outfit for Mom. Then we can take it to the funeral home before we go to the cemetery. Are you going to be all right to stay here tonight? You can always come stay with us tonight if you want."

"No, thank you. I'm sure I'll be fine. I'll see you tomorrow morning. Thank you for helping me today. I'm not sure I could have done it without you."

"You're welcome, Dad. Love you."

Anita hugged her father longer than she had ever hugged him before.

John stood at the door and waved goodbye as his daughter backed out of the driveway. When he closed the door, he looked around and realized he was now truly alone.

He wandered aimlessly through the house, picturing Brenda in every room doing her daily rituals; cleaning the house, fixing meals, doing the dishes, playing games on the tablet and computer, and watching TV. He was missing Brenda already, and he knew it would get much worse before it got better.

John sat in the recliner and stared blankly into space. He remembered he should call Brenda's sister and his best friend to let them know. He found the number for Brenda's sister and called her. Brenda and her sister had never been close but she said how sorry she was to hear the news and said she would plan to attend the funeral.

He called Eric and they spoke for several minutes. Eric said he and his wife, Sheila, planned to attend the funeral as well. When the call was over, John turned on the TV. It was set to the news, so he watched it for a while. The next thing he knew, he woke up in the dark and found the TV still on and a different news commentator was talking. It was after 10 p.m., so John turned off the TV, then got up and got ready for bed.

"Good night, Brenda. I miss you," he said to her picture on the fireplace mantle.

The next morning, John got up and went to start the coffee and realized Brenda had not made the coffee the day before like she usually did. He tried to remember how she made it, except now he would be making coffee for just one. John decided to forego the coffee and had a glass of orange juice instead, along with his usual cereal and banana he usually shared with Brenda. He turned the radio on to the usual talk station just to hear some noise.

After breakfast, John took a long shower and then shaved. As he stared into the mirror, he once again, thought of himself as alone. John got dressed, unlocked the front door and then decided to sit in the recliner until his daughter came over.

At 10:05, Anita knocked and then came in. John had fallen asleep but woke up when she opened the door.

"Good morning, Dad."

"Good morning, Anita."

"I think we should pick out something for Mom to wear."

They went into their closet and picked out an outfit. It was one he bought for Brenda for an anniversary or birthday gift. Anita took it and folded it over her arm.

"We can drop this off at the funeral home on our way to the cemetery. Are you ready to go?" she asked.

"I'm ready. Do you want me to drive?"

"Why don't I drive? I already have the GPS set for the cemetery."

"That's fine."

John and his daughter stopped at the funeral home, then found the cemetery with no problems. They were happy to find the cemetery well cared for and recently mowed. The pink rose bushes were in bloom out near the gate opening, and the ornate iron letters over the entrance spelling out *"Garden of Peace"* somehow gave the cemetery a sense of prestige.

There was another vehicle on the road inside the cemetery and as they drove up, a man got out and closed his door. Anita pulled in behind him and the two of them got out of the car and walked over to the man.

John walked up and offered his hand. The man was tall and thin with graying hair and blue eyes. They shook hands.

"Hi. I'm John Sample, and this is my daughter, Anita."

"Good morning. My name is Charlie Lewis. I'm very sorry for your loss."

"Thank you."

"Would you care to join me in my car? The cemetery road goes in a loop around the pond. It would be much easier and quicker than walking."

"That's fine," said John.

The two of them got in Charlie's car, and he drove them through the cemetery pointing out the various locations of available plots. As they went around the pond, Charlie pointed out the ducks and said the pond was the focal point of the cemetery and the plots overlooking it were more expensive.

"I will need two plots, one for my wife and one for me. Can we go back around to the other side? I think that area looked attractive."

"Certainly."

As they got back to a small shaded area west of the pond, John told Charlie to stop.

"This location looks interesting. Do you have adjoining plots in this area?"

"Yes. There are a couple of lots located right over there. Let's get out and take a look."

John and Anita got out of the car and walked over to a small, grassy knoll.

"There are two plots together here," he said pointing at the ground not far from the road, "and two more right over there."

"How much are the ones closest to the road?" asked John.

"They would be $3,600.00 for the pair. That includes the cost of opening and closing the graves for two and perpetual care. We also require a concrete burial vault at this cemetery."

"What do you think, Anita?"

"This looks like a nice spot."

"I think so, too. I'll take these two then."

"Fine," said Charlie. "I'll make the arrangements with your funeral home. Do you have any questions?"

John looked at Anita, and she shook her head.

"No. I think we're okay," said John.

Charlie took them back to Anita's car.

"If you have questions, please feel free to call me," Charlie said as he handed John his business card.

"Thank you very much," said John as he shook Charlie's hand.

John and his daughter got back in her car and drove back to John's house.

"I think that was a nice cemetery," said Anita.

"I agree. And the gravesites were nice, too," added John.

When they got back, John got out of the car and Anita followed him to the porch.

"I have to get back home," said Anita. "Do you want me to fix you some lunch before I go?"

"No, thanks. I'll just fix a sandwich. I'll be fine. Thanks for taking me to the cemetery."

"You're welcome. Love you, Dad." She gave her father a hug.

"I love you, too. I'll see you at the funeral home tomorrow."

Anita went to her car and waved before backing out of the driveway. John waved back, then went into the house and fixed himself a ham sandwich, then grabbed some chips to put on his plate. He sat down at the table and listened to himself eat.

After lunch, John went to the recliner and took a nap. A couple of hours later, the phone rang. It was the funeral home.

"We just wanted to remind you that the viewing for your wife starts at 3 p.m. tomorrow. You might want to show up about 15 minutes beforehand because there could be some people arriving early."

"Thank you. I'll plan to be there at 2:45."

"You're welcome. We'll see you tomorrow."

The day of the viewing, John got up, had breakfast, then took a shower and shaved. He couldn't get over how quiet the house was. Even though he had never talked much, Brenda had always been chatting about something; what her plans for cleaning were, what they were going to have for lunch or supper, or what bills she was going to pay that day. John had not always been a good listener, and now he regretted that fact. He wished he could talk to her now. John had not been alone like this for over 45 years. He missed Brenda's voice and her smile.

John turned off the radio, sat in the recliner and set his phone alarm for 1:45 p.m. He watched a little of the news before falling asleep. When he woke up, it was 11:30, so he grabbed some leftover meatloaf and mashed potatoes and warmed them up in the microwave for lunch. After lunch, John went back to the recliner and promptly fell asleep again. The alarm woke him up. He got into his suit and picked out a conservative tie. At 2:30, he left to go to the funeral home for the afternoon viewing. When he got there, Sean was there to greet him at the door.

"Hello, Mr. Sample."

"Good afternoon."

"Your wife is ready for viewing if you'd care to follow me."

Sean ushered John into the chapel, then up to the casket. There were already several colorful flower arrangements around the gray metal casket.

"Take as much time as you need."

John immediately noticed how radiant his wife looked. He was not used to seeing her with so much makeup on. She looked so very small, he thought. Seeing her in her outfit brought back a flood of memories. Brenda wore it to the captain's ball on their first cruise to the Bahamas and more recently, at their son's wedding. One could not tell she had had a left side paralysis from her accident many years before. There was no cane. John pictured Brenda walking normally now in heaven, even running.

"I love you and miss you, Brenda," was all he said.

Anita arrived with her husband and John's two grandsons. John Jr. came in at about the same time. John tried to comfort them all.

"She's in a better place now," said John. "Brenda doesn't have to worry about falling anymore."

John's brother, Paul, and Brenda's sister, Laura, arrived a short time later. Each commented on how nice Brenda looked.

Soon, people began to come through the receiving line. Neighbors, friends of Brenda's from church and from when she worked at Wal-Mart, and people that John had worked with in real estate and from the VA came through. John was embarrassed a few times when he couldn't remember names, but he got through it. Just before the end of the afternoon viewing, John's friends, Eric and Sheila, arrived.

Eric and Sheila went up to the casket with John.

"You know, Brenda was the one I always liked best," said Eric.

"I know. She loved you, too."

They talked for a short while, then John Jr. and Anita went up to them.

"It's almost 5:30, so we're all going to go to dinner over at King's restaurant. Eric, you and Sheila are welcome to come with us. We insist," said Anita.

At dinner, John was rather quiet as the others talked about Brenda and their recollections of her. He was tired and wasn't sure if he could make it through another two hours of viewings. But, he did.

By 9 p.m., the number of mourners had thinned out. Family and friends who were planning to go to the funeral the next day went home or to their respective hotels, and John drove home. When he got home, he hung up his suit, got into his night clothes and took his medication. He was exhausted and fell asleep the moment his head touched the pillow.

The next morning at 5:30, John got up, ate a bowl of cereal, then took a shower and shaved. The funeral was at 10 a.m., so John set an alarm on his phone for 8:30 a.m. and went to his recliner. The alarm woke him up. He brushed his teeth, then got dressed and picked out a different tie. He was ready to leave by 9:00.

John drove to the funeral home and met John Jr. and his kids there. It wasn't long before people started filing in. John and the family went up to the casket. Anita and John Jr. cried, and John hugged them. The grandkids didn't seem to know what to think. When they all got to their seats, John saw that the room had filled up. He was happy with the turnout.

A few more people went up to the casket before the funeral began. Brenda's church minister went up to the lectern after the last mourners went to their chairs.

"We've come here this morning to pay our last respects to Brenda Green Sample," he said. "She was a loving wife, mother and grandmother. Brenda was a hard worker despite a partial paralysis she had endured since she was in a car accident when she was 18 years old. She and John fell in love in 1973 and had been in love ever since.

I knew Brenda for several years since she began going to the Monroeville Christian Church. She gained the respect and love of many of our church members over those years. Brenda will surely be missed.

But death is not the end. Brenda is now in the loving arms of her savior, Jesus Christ, and she no longer needs her cane or leg brace."

The minister spoke for several more minutes, but John did not hear him. His thoughts were on Brenda and how he would miss her.

When the minister finished, the funeral director took his place at the lectern.

"For those of you planning to go to the cemetery, please turn your headlights on so our attendants can place funeral flags on your vehicles. The funeral procession will be leaving for the Garden of Peace cemetery within the next 15 or 20 minutes. On behalf of the family, thank you all for coming."

As the mourners filed out of the funeral home, John spent a few more moments with Brenda before going with Anita and John Jr. to the limousine.

"That was a very nice service, Dad," said Anita once they were in the limo.

"Yes, it was," he replied. "I was glad to see so many people there."

John Jr. nodded in agreement. He was still having a hard time keeping his composure.

The three of them made small talk on the way to the cemetery, mostly about the family members and friends who attended the funeral. The ride to the cemetery didn't seem to take very long. When they arrived, six of the men acted as pall bearers and carried the casket to the gravesite. John and the family then made their way to the chairs at the gravesite.

Anita commented on how nice a day it was as they sat under the shade of the green canvas funeral tent.

After a few minutes, the minister came and stood at the head of the casket and spoke once again.

John did not hear much of what was said until the minister said, "Ashes to ashes, dust to dust."

When it was over, the minister came over to the family and offered his condolences, and John thanked him for his kind words over Brenda.

"You should come to one of our services, John. I know Brenda always hoped you would. The church would welcome you, and now is an especially important time for you to be with others."

"Maybe I will, Pastor."

Soon, the mourners made their way back to their cars.

John stood, leaned over, and touched the casket and said, "Goodbye, Brenda. I love you."

Chapter 26

Now, two years after Brenda had passed, it was John's turn to be dead. John went back to the assembly of souls and announced to James he had caught up with his life story.

"What do I do now?"

"Well, now you get to know all of us even better and start over on your own life. You've only been here a couple of months. You'll soon get used to the routine, John."

"I think I'll start praying for the next stage."

James laughed.

James remarked that Archie had left the cemetery during the night.

"That doesn't sound good," said John.

"Why? What do you know about Archie?" asked James.

"Since he's gone, I suppose it won't hurt to tell now. Archie killed a lot of women in his lifetime."

"Really?"

"Yes. He told me he murdered 21 women while he was a long-haul trucker."

"It sounds as if he was as good a candidate for hell as anyone could be," said James.

"Does anyone know what hell is like?" asked John.

Reverend Murphy spoke up.

"I believe hell is a lake of fire with the devil torturing hell's occupants for eternity," he said.

"You seem to kind of enjoy that possibility, Reverend," said John. "Do you think someone who was a liar deserves the same fate as Adolph Hitler?"

"There is no distinction in the bible," said the reverend. "Hell is hell."

"Whatever it's like, I don't want to find out," said James.

"And, Reverend, do you believe you will receive the same fate in heaven as Mother Teresa?" asked John.

"Yes, I do. Heaven is heaven for everyone who goes there."

"Somehow, that doesn't fit my sense of divine justice," said John.

"I'm just going by what the bible says."

"What does the bible say about where we are now, Reverend?"

"I don't remember reading anything about this," he said.

"Interesting that this purgatory isn't mentioned in the bible," said John.

"I'm sure it must be part of God's plan for us," said the reverend.

"I'm sure it is," said John.

John listened to the conversations that day from the group. He did not appreciate the gossipy tone they took.

That night, John went back to his grave and prayed with more feeling than ever before.

"Dear Lord, please forgive my many sins. I'm sorry for my many transgressions against You and others. I pray You will let me go into the Kingdom of Heaven, so I may be with Brenda again. Thy will be done. Amen."

The moment he finished his prayer, a bright light opened before him. Brenda stepped out from the light with a wide smile. John reached out for her and grasped both her hands. She was beautiful and looked like she did when they first met. There was neither a wrinkle nor scar anywhere, and Brenda was no longer handicapped.

"I've come for you, John. Are you ready?"

"Yes. I'm ready. I've missed you so much."

"I've missed you, too, John. Come with me," she said. "You're free from this place now."

John rose into the light with Brenda. The light was brighter than any light he had ever seen on Earth. When they got farther into the light, he soon became adjusted to it, and he could see others from his life. There were his mother and father waiting to greet him. They, too, looked as they did when they were in their twenties. They didn't look like spirits but like flesh and blood.

"We're so glad to see you, Son," his father said.

"We missed you, John," said his mother.

John had forgotten how beautiful his mother was before age and diabetes had taken their toll.

"I missed you, too."

Nearby, behind his parents, were his friends from high school, Larry and Jessie, who greeted him.

"It's good to see you, John."

"It's good to see you, too. It's been a long time."

Both sets of John's grandparents and aunts and uncles were there smiling at him. And, coming toward him, was a beaming Jesus. When He arrived, He put His arm around John and an unbelievable feeling of warmth, love and forgiveness surrounded him.

John knew he was finally home. And heaven was definitely worth the wait.

The End

40401685R00168

Made in the USA
Lexington, KY
29 May 2019